My Favorite Tune

THIA FINN

My Favorite Tune
Thia Finn

Disclaimer: The material in this novella contains graphic language and sexual content and is intended for mature audiences ages 18 and older.
There is content within this book that may set off triggers, please check the end of book for help.

ISBN: 978-1734419245

Editing by Swish Design & Editing
Proofreading by Swish Design & Editing
Book design by Swish Design & Editing
Cover model by Chris
Photography by Wander Aguiar
Cover design by Designs By Dana
Cover Image Copyright 2023
All Rights Reserved

DEDICATION

This book is dedicated to my two favorite Aussies, Kaylene Osborn and Kimberly Osborn. Without their love and encouragement, this book would never have been completed. I will forever be indebted to them for standing by me through the hard days.

CHAPTER 1

BARDOT

Is this my lucky day?

How many times have I sat in the cockpit of a sailboat readying it for an easy day excursion? Today feels like something definitely different.

Two tatted-up guys caught my attention while walking toward the boat with all the swagger expected from bad boys who resemble these two. From the minute they stepped on the floating dock—I knew it, I just knew it—they were cocky smart-asses intended to board my boat with expectations of me taking care of their *every* need.

Ha, were they ever wrong!

Skippering the boat is my job.

That's it.

I worked with a crew of one that saw to the guests.

For over a year now, Gilley and I have worked

together, taking sailing charters out of Kemah, Texas' South Front Yacht Club. We jokingly bet when the guests arrived, they would assume Gilley was the captain and I the hostess. Surprise beamed over their red faces when they discovered the female captained the vessel. Gilley hosted with a weathered look that bespoke the amount of time he had done this type of work.

First off, the idea of cooking made me want to laugh in their faces. If they only knew how little I understood the use of a kitchen. Scrambling eggs and sprinkling cheddar cheese on top was the limit to my culinary skills. But that doesn't matter since I poured picante sauce on everything, so it all tasted the same. And that's even if it happens to land on a plate since straight from the pot works for me too.

Put me behind the wheel of a huge sailboat or the tiller of a smaller sailing craft, and I'm in my element. Before I barely acquired sea legs, my dad had me out on our boat helping him ready the craft for sailing out of the harbor and to the open waters. Wearing the salt spray on my face provided my perfect wake-up call.

Smooth, shiny, stainless steel thawed my hands as I wrapped my fingers around the wheel while Dad balanced me on his knee in the cockpit on any brisk day. The wind ruffled my dark curls, and if a strong gust blew hard enough, I felt like it sucked the air from my lungs until I forced myself to inhale, ending the slight fear of oxygen deprivation.

With my forever-present life jacket strapped around me, I learned to skipper a boat long before the DMV allowed me to drive a car. Texas law declared I had to be thirteen before I could get a certificate to drive a boat, so Dad sat beside me while I gripped the wheel, seeming twice my size.

Those priceless days lingered and were burned in my memories.

Now, the wind in my hair and the sun on my face calmed the restless nerves in my body.

I stood on the deck, unhooking bungee cords from the mainsail as the mid-morning sun warmed my shoulders, preparing to remove the sail cover. The rumble from Harleys had initially caught my attention when I worked on lines at the front of the boat. That should have been my first indication of the day ahead.

"Well, well... what do we have here, Wix, my friend?" the blond of the two posed to his friend.

His clichéd phrase matched his look—destroyed black jeans, worn black T-shirt, silver rings covering tattooed fingers.

Who were these guys? And a better question. *How did I get stuck with them for an afternoon?*

I blew out the breath I held, trying not to greet them with a smirk of my own. After all, they paid a premium to be on this rig.

"Good morning. Welcome aboard the *Miss Midnight.*" My tone was light and easy as always, even though it was the absolute last thing I felt.

Tremors from somewhere deep down rose to the surface. A first for me.

"Why thank you, *Miss Midnight*," the blond replied. "We've wanted to give this a try for months." Long legs launched him onto the boat and around the perimeter before I could tell him to remove the streak-causing heavy black boots.

"Stop!" My voice carried over the constant ping, ping, ping of the shrouds clanging against the mast, a sound that normally calmed me. Today, nothing may.

"Take off those biker boots before they scuff the fiberglass." The order escaped before I considered rephrasing it as a request.

Shouting orders at these two made me feel like an ungrateful bitch, and we hadn't even left the dock. *Great way to set the tone for the afternoon, Bardot.*

He dropped to the top of the boat above the galley area, unzipped and removed his heavy boots, setting them aside, then faced his friend who remained reluctantly standing on the dock. "Better follow Miss Midnight's rules. She bites." The comment ended with a wide grin. I'd give him one thing—his face could never be a hardship to look at. Not that that information would ever leave my lips.

Before the dark-haired one sat on the dock box following suit with his friend, one side of his mouth crept up briefly. He stood straight and stiff and looked at me like he expected his next set of orders before moving. *It's not the damn military, dude.* "Climb

4

aboard, please."

A curt nod came as he looked around for the best place to board. Automatically, my hand pointed to the opening in the line that ran the circumference of the boat, hopefully keeping newbies like him from going for a swim anytime today.

Taking a giant step off the dock, he jumped over and continued moving until he landed in the cockpit, where I stood watching.

Our bodies collided with his enthusiastic leap, making me wonder if going out today was his idea. Maybe it sounded good at the time but now, not so much, especially if the way he screwed up his face as we crashed into each other's personal space.

With a giant step back, I looked up from the chest I stood eye level with. And up. And up. I never realized while he waited on the dock how tall he stood.

My glance became more like a stare with the tight pull of material across his defined pecs. Forcing my eyes away finally, a chore I'd never faced before, I glanced back to the deepest grays staring at me. Stormy-with-a-chance-of-rain orbs deeply probed my own as though he searched my soul.

"Sorry," he barely whispered, like he rarely said it or fear settled inside him.

Perfect lips hardly moved as he spoke. A quick swipe of his tongue over the smoothness of his bottom one followed the one-word apology. The plumpness was perfectly made for biting.

I looked down, breaking eye contact, the look being too much to take in so closely.

Where did that errant thought come from? Back away, Bardot. Back away.

"No problem. Lots of people come aboard and go straight to the cockpit." I glanced around for his friend. "Most don't get on like he did either," the sarcasm in my voice was hard to miss.

"Great to know. I hate to be the only dumb shit who fell into a boat before spending four hours on it." He ended with a slight lift of his lips, almost in a smile but not quite.

It gave me enough to see dazzling white teeth. *Did people like him spend a lot of time at the dentist?* Something to ponder later when I didn't have to worry about the trip ahead.

"Yes, so..." I looked around at the chores left before we sailed. The remainder of the line I held now lay at my feet, so I went back to work with the sheets or 'ropes' in layman's terms. The two certain misfits for a boat found a place behind the wheel and watched me work.

"Ms. Midnight, you got a name?" As soon as he said it, I realized my mistake in not introducing myself when he jumped aboard.

"Oh, right, sorry. I'm Bardot Bohen." I stuck my hand out to shake theirs. "Forgive me for not starting with my name. I usually do." I glanced down at his socked feet and back to his face. "I, uh... sorry about barking orders at you. I just didn't want you to scuff the boat. Black is hard to get off the surface."

"No problem, Bardot. I get it. Kick-ass name, by the way." The smirk he gave reminded me of comments I had heard all my life. He probably thought I was a stripper in my other job as if I had time for another one.

"Thanks." I smiled in return, hoping to move past my earlier order faux pas.

"Your parents must have had a great sense of humor." His friend elbowed him as soon as the words left his mouth, then wiggled his eyebrows. *Were these two stuck in middle school?* If I had to guess, I'd go with yes.

"I'm sorry my friend is such a douche. He failed to learn manners at any point in his miserable life," the more reluctant of the two said while giving his buddy a death glare.

"That's okay. I've heard worse." I turned my eyes to the shithead staring at me. "And yes, they did have a great sense of humor, but that was my mother's maiden name. And no, she wasn't related to Brigitte that I know of."

"Don't care where it came from, it's still a cool name. Bet you've never met another Bardot in your life." A look of genuine sincerity crossed the dark-haired one's face as he ended the statement, making me feel bad again for thinking the worst of him.

"No, not even as a last name." I stepped down the

ladder to the galley, where Gilley prepared a light snack for our guests before they made another remark.

From the counter, Gilley turned and looked at me. "Okay?"

"Sure. The afternoon should be interesting." I dug in one of the holds for life jackets. Looking back over my shoulder at him, I tipped my head, letting him know everything would turn out fine.

The two of us knew each other well enough from our charters together that words were hardly necessary at times. He'd shoot me a look, and I knew exactly what he was saying or thinking. We both had the ability from spending so much time together.

Stepping back on deck, I handed the guys the preservers. "First things first. Safety. I'm assuming you're both acquainted with life jackets." They nodded. "You're not required to wear them, but if you feel unsure, don't hesitate to put it on. But, if I say put it on, do it. Please don't question me because I'll probably be too busy with the boat to answer." Again, nods.

"Also, the deck is slippery when it gets wet except where it's roughed up for traction." I pointed to the side deck where a long stretch of fiberglass had grippers built in. "You might want to take your socks off too. One, you'll be slipping for sure, and two, it's hot. Any questions?"

I searched their faces for confirmation when the

jokester asked, "Yeah, don't you want to know our names, or do you already from... well, you know?"

My eyes fluttered a few times before I wiped my hand down my face. *You dumbass. You never gave them a chance to tell me. Must be a day of stupid mistakes.*

"Oh my God. Yes, please tell me your names. I'm so sorry for my lack of good manners as a captain and a basically good human." The longer I spoke, the more I felt the red rising from my chest and making its way to my scalp. I never did this kind of thing with guests, but these two had me flustered more than I ever remembered with any of my other guests.

"Not a fucking problem, Ms. Midnight." He continued with a nickname. "I'm Arch Fallon." His hand shot out to grab mine as I offered. He shook it like he meant business. I appreciated the enthusiasm. Some men barely took my hand, thinking they might break my bones or hurt me. If I handled a forty-two-foot sailboat, I could handle a strong handshake.

When I dropped his hand, I looked at the quieter of the two. "Hello," I offered since he didn't start with his name.

"Hi, I'm Wix Stoker." He took my hand, and where Arch grasped it tightly, Wix's grip engulfed mine. His hand and long fingers encompassed mine like a warm glove. The heat drifted further up my arm the longer he held it captive. The intoxicating feeling needed to end, but I didn't want it to. His touch reminded me how good it felt to hold hands with a man and be regarded as worthy of the gesture.

He let go far too soon, and I stepped back away from him with my mind curling around the impression he left.

Damn, what had just happened?

I looked between them both and smiled. Words escaped me.

"Here ya go, guys. Snacks before we set sail," Gilley announced, stepping out of the hatch.

Thank God.

Arch jumped up and took the tray from Gilley. "These look great, and I'm starving. We didn't get breakfast before we came. Slept too long to stop off."

"I'm Gilley, the chef and your host for the day. We'll have nibbles and drinks for now, then later I'll serve a meal. She usually anchors at the oyster reef not too far offshore, so you'll be able to enjoy it."

"Sounds good to me. What about you, Wix?" Arch questioned.

Wix and I stood looking at each other. Arch's words pulled me from my stupor when I realized work still needed to be done to set sail.

"I better get busy. Enjoy your snacks. Knowing Gilley as I do, I'm sure they're delicious." I turned and made my way down into the head below deck. I had to get my act together and fast. Getting underway needed my attention. Thinking about some hot guy on my boat did not.

CHAPTER 2

WIX

What the fuck did I think when I said yes to this? The idea of being out on the ocean in a boat I had no clue how to operate scared the shit out of me. Boats needed big motors, not big sails. Yes, a motor existed on this huge tub to move in and out of the harbor, but what about escaping a storm in the open water? Could we outrun it? Hell no.

Fucking Arch lived to dream up ideas taking us from our comfort zones. I prayed this adventure didn't top the all-time dumbest list. Water and I didn't exactly work well together.

The vessel cruised easily out of the harbor, passing under a tall bridge while another boat met us coming in. I worried the mast wouldn't clear the structures holding up the bridge, but I kept an eye on the captain. This chick remained calm the entire time, so I tried to be cool and not about to piss myself, which I was.

Arch asked a million questions and ate the munchies provided by the ominous-looking dude who served them. Gilley kept a close eye on the girl, and I kept a close eye on him.

He wasn't someone I'd want to meet in a dark alley. The constant scowl on his lips would have been labeled as a resting bitch face—RBF—if he was female, and his size made me wonder how he fit down below in the galley, much less cooked. Honestly, how much space was there down the short set of steps?

After crunching on a stalk of celery filled with something creamy, Arch looked over at me. "Dude, you gotta fucking try this. I don't know what shit's filling the groove, but the flavor." He ended his comment by kissing his fingertips against his lips and swinging wide like he's some food connoisseur of all things celery. I doubted he remembered the last bite of a green stalk that passed his lips. Watching him, I couldn't decide who he was trying to impress—the chick or himself.

"Pass," I replied. "Not hungry."

"Right." He glanced up at Bardot and back at me. "You gonna be seasick? That'd be a bitch, huh? I bet people hurl on her boat all the time."

This caught the captain's attention. She paid no notice to us, given her concentration on easing through the channel. She made the moves look simple but kept a close eye on what happened all around us.

"Are you feeling okay?" she asked softly before our eyes met again. Unlike the first time today, several feet separated us, but it didn't stop me from realizing her emerald eyes held flashes of gold in them. The sun's morning brightness made me wonder if her lightly tinted sunglasses played tricks with the color.

"He likes to exaggerate. I'm fine." I knew *I'm fine* sounded lame since the words usually meant the opposite, but it was all I had, given my wariness of the impending voyage. *Was I nervous?* Hell yeah. *Was I sick?* I hoped not.

Standing to look over the front of the sleek sailboat, I watched as the channel stretched out before us before dumping into the bay. Restaurants and clubs lined only on one side with seafood markets along the other. A huge lighted, arched sign declaring the area 'The Boardwalk' was posted up from a large structure designed to gain attention.

This area looked like a great place to hang out. A huge rollercoaster captured the background space with a Ferris wheel and other fast-moving rides in its shadow.

The smell of fried sundries outdid the aromas of seafood and grilled meats. Funnel cakes conjured memories of the carnivals I attended as a child. *Mmm... that sweet, sugary dough.* I could almost taste it.

Our previous trips to the Houston area failed to point out this place. I wondered why. Were we so jaded to our surroundings from long days of travel that enjoying anything along the way never happened? It made me consider what else we missed while moving along the highway on the tour bus.

Our band usually played several cities in Texas while on tour, but we rarely chanced anything besides the usual—arrive, wake up, do promotions, sound check, play, leave—normal tour stops.

This time we wrote in a contractual clause to spend an extra day around major cities or areas that looked interesting. The days needed to be preplanned, but who cared? Our concerts filled arenas with screaming fans, and that's all it took to make our label happy.

We had our tour manager, Jones, working before we scheduled dates this time. He located all types of interests from our suggested list. Sometimes all four of us went, and other times, like today, only a couple of us. If it only sounded cool to one of us, he went on his own. Like helicoptering through the Grand Canyon. *Not no, but hell no.* If I'm seeing that deep crevice splitting the planet, it'll be from hiking to the bottom. *Zipping in and out of a canyon with two blades slicing the air around me?* No fucking way. Trotter and Kenzo held the titles for adrenaline junkies in the band, not me.

I held the title of most laid back. That's one reason I played bass. I simply floated along as the underscore of the rhythm, hooking it to the drums. I'm the link the band depended on as a backbone. Some people felt bass might be unnecessary, but I'd fight to my grave showing them they're dead wrong.

Gilley kicked my foot on his way back down and raised an eyebrow, checking if I was truly okay. I nodded in return.

"Want a beer?" he asked before ducking his head.

"Sure. That'd be great." My answer came out a little louder since the wind had kicked up some the closer we came to the mouth of the channel.

"I'll take one, too," Arch yelled across the cockpit.

"Any kind in particular?"

"Corona for me," we barked in unison. It was our go-to beer on the bus, especially in the southwest. Texas stood close enough.

He handed up two dressed cans. A little salt and lime are always a bonus.

As the boat made its way out from the mouth of the channel, the captain began working with the sails. I guessed that meant she was going to turn off our power. *Great.* I felt the hairs on the back of my neck rise. *Here we go. Please let this work.*

"Would one of you stand here and hold the wheel in place, please?"

Arch jumped at the chance. "Jack Sparrow to the rescue." He moved in, crowding her between him and the big steering wheel. She flipped them both around the opposite way and left him standing in her place.

"Put both hands on the wheel, Mr. Sparrow. The waves and wakes from the other vessels around us cause the boat to move in different directions."

"Aye, aye, Captain." The dumbass saluted her.

She eyed him for a split second and grinned. "Just keep it between the channel markers. Otherwise, we'll run aground. This'll only take a second."

She stepped up to the level above us, looked down at me, and then back at Arch. Was that a signal to keep an eye on him? I really needed to get these silent orders down before one of us ended up in the water.

The huge white sail inched up the tall mast as she turned the handle on some kind of pulley. The movement went smoothly as athletic arms easily rotated the stainless steel equipment. She finished her task and jumped back down into the cockpit with us.

I watched her movements, impressed by the simplicity, as she worked around this huge boat. The woman stood about five-foot-five with nice curves. I wasn't good at guessing weight because it never concerned me. People were what they were. Who cared?

But she wasn't stick-thin like some women who appeared at the after-parties, which was another good difference. Personally, I hated seeing and feeling pointed bones. Give me a woman with softness and curves to run my hands up and down and squeeze.

The thing was, Bardot looked fit. Her arms had muscles but not like a body builder's. Hers were toned and smooth. Her tanned legs were shapely and perfect, extending from her shorts. Her dark skin seemed made for the sun, and I knew her French genes provided some of the tint from hanging out around the water all summer in Texas. *What could i say?* Nothing but perfection.

She took back over from Arch, but not before she busted me for staring. Hey, I'm a man, and when my dick took notice, it gave a small twitch while my eyes drifted up from her bare feet. Sue me for looking.

It'd been a minute since I'd had a woman on the bus. Hence, no sex. Dragging randoms back wasn't my style. I preferred some small talk before doing the deed. Some bands who opened for us enjoyed down-and-dirty action in the green room or their dressing rooms. I knew they wanted watchers or simply enjoyed degrading their willing partners, whether it be male or female.

Our band outgrew all things public a while back. Enough of that happened on its own, but don't get me wrong, we all loved sex. When that's all it became for me, I realized it was time to give up indiscriminate hookups with women there to claim bragging rights.

We departed on this tour with Trotter and Kenzo leaving serious girlfriend issues behind. Watching these two sad and lonely or constantly messaging after a show reminded me why I decided not to get involved. I figured that could come later when we didn't tour constantly.

Their situation was one or the other, always the

extreme. The guys found themselves attached too often, and someone left on tour in crisis mode. Not me, not anymore. I grew adamant the more I watched them.

"You lost there, dude?" Arch landed beside me on the bench. "Or just enjoying the scenery?"

My eyes scanned the horizon over the edge of the boat. "Fucking sweet out here, isn't it?"

Arch's head whipped around to stare at me before he cut his eyes over to Bardot. "Yeah, if you want to go with that." His lips formed the quirky look I'd witnessed so many times.

A minute passed as I watched our captain twist a pulley on the other side, causing the front sail to rise. A choreographed dance scene played out as we witnessed her going about making the boat glide perfectly through the small choppy waves. The wind provided the music, and she moved to the sound—a fine art I'd never thought about before.

Once the sails met her expectations and the boat sailed with purpose through the slightly blue water, Bardot clipped the wheel in place and backed away to gaze into the distance. A definite intensity came with her. Did she approach everything in life this way?

"Are you getting more used to it now?" Arch continued. "I knew you only came with because I wanted to. Appreciate it."

"Yeah, it's not so bad. Thinking about it scared the shit out of me, but I knew you'd have more fun with some of us along for the ride."

"Damn right, it's better. We could throw a great party on a boat like this." He stood and swung around one of the wires suspended halfway up the mast. "What do you think, Ms. Midnight?"

She turned to him. "About what?"

"Throwing a small party on a boat like this. Our friends would love it... blue sky, blue water, hot chicks, and plenty of champagne flowing. I think it's a great plan."

"That would be a big no from me. First, this boat is too small for more than maybe six to eight people to move about safely. Add alcohol with the sun and too many guests, and it's all the makings of a disaster on the water."

I watched her spit out her diatribe, killing Arch's idea of fun. She certainly took things too seriously which made me wonder why.

"Killjoy," Arch replied, pretending to walk a tight rope around to the front of the boat. Nothing scared him about being on the water.

"Sorry," Bardot muttered to herself, but I heard.

"Are you always overly cautious about having fun?" The question slipped out before I realized it had.

She slid in beside me, close enough to be heard but careful not to touch in any way. Always careful.

"In answer to your question, yes. I'm always cautious when it comes to water. Accidents happen in the blink of an eye anywhere but especially on water."

Her face never wavered from the seriousness spread across it.

I knew there had to be a story, but I'd wait. Maybe she'd share, maybe she wouldn't. Guess it depended on how painful the memories were.

"I've seen stupid mishaps too often out here not to be leery of every situation, Wix. You'd be surprised at the dumb shit people do."

My forehead wrinkled as my eyebrows rose. This woman didn't have a clue what we did in real life. I liked it. She wouldn't be out to impress us or treat us any differently than her regular clients.

I watched her check the sails. Ever vigilant. "So, tell me some stories."

Her eyes cut back to mine. The emerald green with gold streaks lit up, mesmerizing me.

"Oh, you know. Twenty-somethings and alcohol find trouble wherever they meet up."

"You're saying then that drinking and young people shouldn't be bed partners then, ever?"

Her head tipped to one side as she pulled her white ball cap down further over her eyes. "I didn't say that, but it's probably true."

"What about in their own home? Is that a bad place to drink?" My line of questioning caused small red blotches to form above the edge of her cotton tank. It was never my intention to embarrass her.

"People can do whatever they want in their home. I don't care where they drink as long as it won't hurt other people in the process."

It sounded like her story unfolded more as we talked.

Arch perched on the front of the boat in a seat of sorts, and he looked like he was waiting for Kate Winslet to join him. He caught our attention when he started his rendition of that song from Titanic.

" "My heart will go on"..." Thank God the wind carried his made-up words away from us. I knew he sang as well as any of us in the band, but his ability to remember lyrics sucked. We constantly gave him hell about singing the wrong words. Sometimes we took his mic away, which pissed him off royally. Lots of drummers sang in bands, but he didn't need to be one of them.

When I thought we were finally spared from his assault, he jumped up and faced the water, bellowing, " "Near, far, wherever you are, I believe that the heart does go on," " while throwing his arms wide and leaning into the railing around the chair.

The two of us busted out laughing. "Well, that's a first," I squeezed out between laughter.

"For me too. Did he drink before he got on the boat? He appeared sober," Bardot added.

"He doesn't need a reason to sing. Everything inspires him," I replied.

Gilley poked his head up through the opening, looking around for Arch. "He does know Celine Dion's ears are bleeding, right?" The three of us eased into another round of laughter that didn't stop our entertainer. If anything, it egged him on.

CHAPTER 3

BARDOT

As far as passengers go, these two provided more fun than usual. Only having two of them to work around, Gilley and I took it easier than with a larger group. I enjoyed charters like this. It allowed me to spend some time with the guests if they wanted or work on the boat if they didn't.

The boat always required maintenance. Salt water made sure of it. I didn't clean, but I did shine the areas needing it or worked down below when Gilley felt the need for sunshine.

Arch and Wix let it be known which they preferred above board from the beginning. As I worked on stainless polish, they moved closer to watch. Part of me believed if I asked, they would help.

"You always work when you have guests?" Arch wondered aloud as he leaned into my sunlight, crowding me against a stay.

"No, I try to give my guests space to enjoy themselves." I smiled and cut my eyes up at him. "Some people want to be left alone to enjoy the ride or their friends."

He looked over at Wix. "Him? I see him all the time. Like way too much time."

This caught my attention. Were they a couple? With the looks I caught from them, my first inclination was no, but who knew or cared these days? Why else would they spend so much time together, though? I considered this as I smeared the polish on the winch not in use, all while keeping an eye on our tack.

"Is this something you do every day?" Arch questioned as he grabbed another beer from Gilley through the hatch that looked down into the galley.

He began to sound like a three-year-old with questions, but I was fine with it. At least he wanted to learn something about the boat and my job.

"Not every day but four to five times a week, depending on the time of year and the weather." I watched the polish dry quickly in the breeze drifting down the deck. "This kind of weather in Texas lasts almost as long as Florida and Southern Cali, so we work a long season."

"That's good, though, right?" Arch took the soft cloth from me when I started rubbing off the polish.

"Sure, if you like to pay your bills on time." I gave a quick laugh while he made the winch shine.

"Yeah, there's that too," Wix added. "We've seen our cash flow come and go, right, Arch?"

What did these two do that they were together too often and watched their income rise and fall? I wanted to ask, but it was none of my business, so I moved to the next piece needing attention. I snickered to myself when they followed me. Arch was 'all hands on deck' for working, whereas Wix only watched with interest.

"I'm going to be tacking here shortly, so we need to put this away after this one."

"And what does that mean exactly?" Wix's voice sounded unsure. The guy hadn't started enjoying the trip yet. He needed to relax more often.

"The boat will turn back toward the shore while also moving further down the channel. Like a zigzag. Have you never seen a sailboat before?"

"Yes, I've seen a sailboat." His words sounded like I had offended him. "I never paid much attention to how they operated."

I nodded my head. "All you have to do is sit still and duck your head when the boom, that big metal bar heads across this area." I pointed to the offending metal.

"No problem. I'm not going anywhere," he replied as he watched me gather the halyards I'd loosened.

The tack went smoothly as the wind was perfect for moving the boat over to the other side using the jib or front sail. I wound the winch handle around and around until the mainsail became taut, and we smoothed out going the opposite way just off the wind.

My passengers viewed the whole maneuver without a comment. This usually happened at least on the first tack. People who were unsure kept a close eye, some even ready to bail if need be.

"Wow, Captain. Good job," Arch called to me as he stood on the downwind side and climbed to the area above the galley again.

I turned to Wix, and his face looked like he was going to abandon ship or puke. I couldn't decide which.

"You okay, Wix?" *Why did I keep asking him*? He nodded but didn't reply.

I worried when he couldn't manage to form words. The boat listed over as it usually did on the downwind side—the side where he sat glued with terror on his face.

"Can I move now?" he finally breathed and asked.

"Sure. You want to join Arch?"

"No!" he yelled. "I don't want to fall in the water backward." The fear was real, so I stuck my hand out and took his, pulling him up and transferring him to the opposite bench, where he felt safer if the color of his face was an indicator.

"Thanks," he barely squeaked out. "Can I get a beer now, please?"

"Maybe you should have a big fucking shot of whisky?" Arch bellowed as he removed his shirt and lay back on the deck.

Holy shit. I knew these guys looked good, but damn, how was I supposed to work with his low-slung jeans barely covering the top of the thin happy trail under his navel? All that skin had been worked into an array of muscles forming divots up his abdomen and stomach.

Hormones, hold the door. I'm ready to climb on.

Wix failed to miss the hard gulp down my throat as I looked at the fine specimen of the male human anatomy. He cleared his throat, jerking me from my stupidity attack. His eyes hovered over my face.

I knew better than to gawk at passengers, and I'd seen more skin from barely-there bathing suits. This display took my dreams to a whole new level. Can my vibrator handle the action this memory will conjure?

"Yes, I think we need to have the snacks refilled. Gilley," I yelled down to the galley. Wix's laughter behind me told me what I dreaded.

"Don't worry, Bardot. All the women love him. Just ask him. He'd be damn glad to tell you more stories about females admiring him than you'll ever want to fucking know."

I turned with a tray of hors d'oeuvres, thrusting them into his hands. His laughter broke out even louder, capturing Arch's attention, which was the last thing I needed. With my back turned to them, trying to prevent the two from seeing the red splotches forming, I set up a small table in the center of the cockpit.

Arch fixed the tray in the indentation, intending to hold it in place with the boat's ever-changing angles. Gilley passed up bottles of cold water, and I handed them out. We never wanted to be accused of getting the passengers intoxicated, especially after I'd spoken so strongly against it while on the water.

When I perched on the back of the bench opposite Wix, my face felt like its normal shade. Thank God.

Arch rolled over and looked down at the two of us from above. "This is an awesome fucking spot to lay. The sun feels great."

"Gilley, will you please hand Arch a beach towel and sunscreen through the top? He's going to burn like a lobster if you don't," I asked.

"I've never burned a goddam day in my life," Arch proclaimed.

"And where exactly did you grow up?" I thought he'd say some place in California.

"Kansas City." He grinned as he said it, never turning his face away from the beaming sun.

"They have a lot of sandy beaches and salt water in Kansas City?" My questions were pointless, but at least I tried.

He popped his glasses up and gave me an evil eye, so I continued, "I'm just saying that burns happen faster on the water like this and can be more severe than anywhere else."

Wix jumped in, "That's the last damn thing we need is you glowing like a neon light on stage, dude. Put the fucking sunscreen on thick."

My ears perked up. *Stage?* These guys are *on stage?* Are they celebrities, and I didn't even know it? Maybe they're not that well known. Maybe I'm a damn idiot for not vetting them before they came aboard.

"No, we wouldn't want that, would we?" I followed up on Wix's protest.

"So you've finally realized who we are?" Arch rolled over, accepting the items from Gilley's hands sticking through the opening. "I thought you'd been anti-music or something."

"Or maybe she just doesn't like rock music." Wix shot me a look I couldn't decipher.

"I like all kinds of music. We play lots of different music depending on what our clients ask for. I can't afford to be picky about it."

"And when you're alone, what do you listen to?" Wix continued.

"I turn the radio on, and whatever's playing is what I listen to. Like I said, I can't be picky. We have CDs of all types on board, and I try to keep it current with the newer stuff."

He backed me into a corner on this topic. The last thing I had time for was learning artists and songs. I often hummed along to the music I heard but had no clue who played it and didn't really care. Catchy tunes came and went.

"Let's hear your playlist, Bardot," Arch added to Wix's attempt to force me with a list.

"Playlist? Uh... I don't have a playlist." I knew people made them, but I didn't have time for that and never tried to learn how.

"Then where does the music come from?" Arch continued. They both stared at me, waiting for an answer.

"We have a streaming subscription we use and also a satellite radio subscription."

"Good to know. We hate when people steal our damn music by ripping it from platforms. So many shitheads out there are willing to steal what we work fucking hard to produce." Wix's voice grew louder and grew angrier with each word. His passion for pirating was apparent.

"Yeah, I'm sorry that happens. I've read a lot about it on social media. It happens to authors as well, I understand. But we pay for the rights to use it on the boat," I sympathized with them.

"I'm still waiting..." Arch wouldn't let it go.

"Uh... let's see. I like to listen to rock music, but I'm not good with artists. I never get to see videos and stuff, so I only know lyrics to the songs I hear and enjoy."

"So, sing us some lyrics," Wix encouraged me.

"What? No way." These two band members want to embarrass me to death by asking me to sing. Hell no. Ain't happening.

"I'll sing you one she likes," Gilley called from below. "This damn song must have been on replay in her brain for weeks. Got so sick of how little of the shit she knew, I looked the lyrics up and sent them to her phone."

"Great," Wix continued with a huge smile plastered across his perfect face. "Let's hear it."

> You said goodbye
> in the dark
> Took with you
> what was left of my heart.
> Tossed it around
> Left me to wonder
> If the pieces would land
> Pulling me under.

I admitted that Gilley did a pretty good job crooning out the lyrics to one of my favorites from a few months ago, even if he did get sick of it. As he sang, I thought about the band's name who sang it. Not bothering to look up the YouTube video of it, I had no idea who they were or what they looked like. These two probably covered it at some point because it played nonstop for weeks on Alt-Nation radio.

I sang it, hummed it, and whistled it for those weeks and several afterward. The tune was catchy, and once Gilley sent the words, easy to remember. Who wouldn't sing it? I bet the girls fawned over the original band at every venue.

"I'm damn good, huh?" Gilley asked them who had yet to say a word.

"Dude, you did a great job." Arch passed on to him, causing Gilley to beam a huge smile.

"See, little girl... I told you a long time ago I missed my calling by not going to Nashville or trying out on *American Idol*."

My laughter rang across the water. Gilley told me these things after every one of his master performances below deck. The sound carried out the various windows and skylights and allowed the entire dock at the harbor to hear him. When they clapped, it spurred him on, so I didn't encourage it.

"Little girl?" Wix's eyebrow did that thing again, but this time only on one side. He used the expression for all types of emotions.

"Yeah, he calls me that when he wants to make a point with me."

"Back to the song, little girl," Arch butted in.

"What about it? I love it. The tune gets in my head sometimes, and I can't get rid of it all day."

"Several days," Gilley adds.

I shot him my best mean face. "Maybe for a while," I added. "I'm a creature of habit... what can I say? Once I get something on my mind, I can't let the damn thing go."

"Great to know you like fucking good music and even better bands." Arch's smirk unfolded on his lips.

What was up with him?

"I take it you two are in a band?" I stated, not wanting to question them about it. People shared what they wanted. Prompting came without help, and their information added to an endless supply of useless knowledge.

In this case, I did want to know more. My love for music caused me to never turn down learning about the industry. Just because I never had time to sit around watching YouTube videos didn't mean I was completely clueless about songs.

"You could say that," Arch continued, looking over at Wix. "We play a lot of that music."

"I think it's great to cover awesome songs. I bet the guys who wrote it enjoy the royalties from it too. Isn't that how it works? Other bands cover their music and then pay money to the songwriters or whoever owns the rights?" Never considering this before, I wondered, "Do y'all remember who sings this song?"

CHAPTER 4

WIX

The longer this conversation continued, the harder it was to hold back cackling like a bevy of beauties drunk in a bar. Arch knew he was setting this woman up for an embarrassing situation. Damn if I could stop it from happening, though. Her enthusiasm created a cute innocence.

"Hell yeah, that's exactly how it works. Bands pay for the rights to use others' songs. It's only fair since the songwriters spend days, months even, writing and perfecting a song for publishing."

We held this same opinion—probably every band did too. Anytime someone poured their soul into writing, whether it was music, books, or whatever, they expected to be paid for others to get their hands on it. Too bad piracy happened all the time to musicians and authors.

"What bands do you cover the most?" Bardot continued.

I wondered how long we were going to play with her.

"Oh, you know, we love to perform all the songs from Copper Crowns," Arch deadpanned, staring straight at her. My forehead wrinkled as my eyebrows touched my hairline.

It all tumbled downhill from there when Arch started laughing, making me laugh, and then we both cried tears from his comments.

Once we recovered and saw our dark-haired beauty staring at us, soberness hit us at lightning speed. At first, she smiled, and then it drifted from her face as she watched our tears running down. A frown morphed into anger in a heartbeat. By the time we stopped laughing, her glare said it all. She was pissed.

Bardot stood and marched below deck. Maybe she was tired of watching us laugh, or maybe she finally caught on to the running joke we carried a little too far. When she returned to the deck, she took hold of the ship's wheel and tacked the boat without any warning.

"What the fuck," Arch yelled as the huge boom flipped sides. He instantly dropped flat on the deck to keep from making a surprise visit to the water.

"Oh, is there a problem?" she asked with a naïve flair to her words. "I thought you understood by now what happened when I turned the wheel into the wind. I mean, after all, we've tacked several times now, and it didn't seem to be a thing anymore."

Under her breath, I heard, "Serves you right." This girl wasn't a pushover. She held her own with the best of the pranksters, Arch included. I claimed innocence in the hoax, but maybe I was guilty by association. Either way, she made a point to not engage in any further conversation until we stopped for our meal.

Ah... the old silent treatment. I bore invisible scars from it for years.

"I'm going to anchor the boat off the reef shortly. The area around Red Fish Island is sandy, so you can wade or even swim if you're brave enough." The words were clipped and short as though spoken from memory.

She turned and looked directly at me. "We'll be on the downwind side where those other boats anchored, so it's protected from the waves, but that doesn't mean the water shouldn't be respected. Ships pass not too far away and pull a strong current if they're loaded down."

"This spot right here's good enough for me." I pointed to my bench. Swimming in unknown water held no interest for me, especially when it wasn't crystal clear like in the Caribbean. Who knew what lurked beneath?

"Awe, man. I wanted to get in and cool off. It's hot on that deck." Arch motioned to his sunbathing spot while our silent treatment punishment played out.

"You'll be fine if you're an okay swimmer. People swim here all the time. It's deep enough for the boat to anchor but still good for getting wet."

Arch stood looking at Bardot. "Hey, listen, Captain, we're sorry to lead you on before. It was just too funny to listen to what you had to say about the band and our music," he confessed, looking guilty for pranking her.

"Yeah, we meant no harm," I quickly added.

Bardot nodded at us both but went back to doing the necessary tasks. Gilley stepped up to help her get the anchor set in the sandy bottom. He returned below to prep the lunch, leaving the three of us in the cockpit looking at the surrounding water. Other boats bobbed in the calm waters with swimmers playing or lounging on rafts tied off to their vessels.

She finally broke the silence with slow, straightforward speech. "So, you guys are in Copper Crowns?" Her eyes stayed glued to the brownish water after she asked the simple question.

"Yes. I'm bass guitar, and Arch is the drummer." The joke needed to be put to bed, so I responded point-blank. I felt bad for the discomfort we caused her.

Arch followed it up with drumming out a beat on the wall of fiberglass between his legs. "See, Ms. Midnight, we are who we say we are and were just fucking around stringing you along. All done in fun."

"Fun for you two, not so much for me." Her eyes

refused to meet either of ours which only made me feel worse.

We sat in silence until Gilley called out, "I'm about ready to serve. Hope y'all are hungry."

Wonderful aromas wafted from the galley while Bardot erected a full table down the middle of the cockpit. It hemmed us in but provided space to eat. Gilley produced a crab salad, the best I'd ever eaten. I thought there was no way I could eat while on the bucking boat, but the reef provided calm enough water.

The chilled crab meat tasted fresh with the perfect amount of interesting add-ins and greens under the white, flaky meat. We barely had time to sit back and take a drink before a plate of grilled shrimp, new potatoes, and perfectly cooked asparagus appeared in front of us. Damn, I felt like I sat in a five-star restaurant from the taste and presentation of the meal. Gilley needed to be a chef in a city like New Orleans.

"Dude, this food is the best shit I've eaten in ages," Arch told the big man as Gilley stood up from the ladder going below. "Why are you cooking on a damn boat and not owning your own place? Your talents need to be shared."

Gilley moved with a slow grace to the leeward side of the boat, perching on the top of the bench. "Been there, done that. Don't want to go back." He downed a bottle of cold water and allowed the bottom to drip and run down the skin of his neck into his sweat-soaked T-shirt.

"You used to own a restaurant? I bet it did a kick-ass business with you cooking. Packed all the time, too," Arch asked. "I know I'd have been there weekly if it all tasted as good as this."

"Me too. It's been a long time since we've had a meal worth talking about. You rock in the kitchen, dude." I joined in on the praises. "We eat so much shit on the road that having a delicious meal is rare." Trying not to talk with my mouth full proved difficult since I shoveled it in.

"What you boys doing on this boat anyway, seeing as you're with some big band?" The tone he used said he knew we were joking, but I still felt the need to try to smooth things over, and apparently Arch did too.

"Oh, dude, we were just giving Ms. Midnight here a hard time." He harmlessly nudged her foot. "We apologized for acting like dickwads." Arch's sheepish grin expressed.

"Heard that too. Doesn't answer my question, though." He kept his eyes pinned on one or the other of us. I felt like we were being interrogated but knew he was giving us shit in defense of his captain. He was protective of her, even though I knew she could hold her own.

I finally spoke up, "We had a concert a couple of nights ago at a venue north of Houston. The band arranged to do things while in the bigger cities so we could see some of the country."

"That a problem, usually?" Gilley asked.

"Yeah, it's always a damn problem. We ride, play, sleep, and start over. Day after day. Gets fucking old real quick." Arch's monotone voice drove home the point.

"This time, we made the label add a few days between shows. We planned to spend time seeing things this go-round. Arch and I thought maybe coming down to the Texas coast to see the sights would be different. I didn't even know they had a place like this. Or an island like the one we're close to."

"You mean Galveston?" Bardot finally joined in. I snuck in looks at her as Arch and I spoke to Gilley. She paid attention to the conversation while she scanned the area around us. Always the vigilant captain.

Arch replied, "That's it, Galveston. I'd heard of it but didn't know Kemah was on the way down there. This place is wicked cool. Big enough for fun but not so big it can get stupid crazy with too damn many people."

"You haven't seen it on a Saturday. Place gets stupid, all right. People come down and walk around drinking in the sun all day, and by the time the bands start playing at night, it takes wild to a new level. Police haul off drunks by the truckload," Gilley filled us in.

"Bands play here too?" Bardot's words sounded

like she wondered aloud while looking at the taller buildings on the island only a short distance across the water. "Never really thought about it. There are places to hang out on Galveston, but I haven't been to any. We dock there sometimes when clients rent out a weekend on the boat."

"That's a damn good way to arrive on an island," Arch gloated. "Show up on my fucking luxury boat, step off with a few hot babes draped around me, paparazzi snapping pics for *TMZ*. The fucking life we've been waiting for."

I watched Bardot as Arch finished his make-believe world announcement. Nothing he said impressed her. Shocked maybe. Disgusted possibly. Impressed, no fucking way. That life didn't register on her radar.

Her values stood out from the female groupies who followed the band. They wanted bragging rights of fucking a rock star. They opened their legs on demand, which made me want to hurl.

The band joked about living it up all the time. It was shit we liked to make fun of while we swanked over our pretend riches. Boujee never suited our ideas of living the life. We were what we were and vowed not to let fame and fortune make us pretentious pricks.

Going out on tour to open for megabands, we spent too much damn time like this. Real musicians carried our fucking vision—played good music, cared about their band, and drew the line at being douchebags to everyone. Those traits stood out. If one of us tried to slip into that zone, the rest damn sure stepped up to point it out. Arch always walked a fine line between fame and fortune, but he was a good guy at heart. It just took someone to peel back the layers to find him.

"Maybe we should find venues on the next tour that takes us to the coast more," I mentioned to Arch. "Playing over the water and shit like that."

"That'd be da bomb, right? We could wear board shorts and go shirtless because it'd be hot as hell."

"Guess that leaves out doing tours in winter," I managed to say this straight-faced before I laughed, enticing the others to join me.

Sharing laughs with new friends helped the afternoon to be even better than I thought it would.

CHAPTER 5

BARDOT

Dark sunglasses allowed me a perfect view of the two. After the joke ended, and I sulked enough at being the butt of it, I began to listen to the easiness shared between them. Did the other band members possess the same closeness?

Gilley and I had an easy friendship, but we never spent time away from the boat together. I knew he'd been the chef in his own restaurant before applying. Even if I didn't, his to-die-for dishes said everything I needed to know. He never explained, and I never asked. If he wanted me to know, he'd tell me.

After we finished this meal, Gilley torched the crème brûlée in the ramekins and placed it before the guests. He served this often, and I loved it, but I worked out hard to indulge every time he did.

"Aren't you going to try this?" our guests asked

simultaneously and laughed at each other.

"I know it's the best, but I'm going to pass today. I don't do that too often because... yeah, it's that good."

"I don't even like sweets much, but this is perfect for out here on the water. Bet too many can't say they've had cold pudding on a boat," Arch commented between bites.

"Pudding?" Gilley replied with a sneer. "Boy, that's about as close to pudding as I am from being Native American." Not much riled this big guy but comparing his dishes to something bland like an off-the-shelf pudding got him every time.

"Sorry, dude. I don't know what else to call it, but believe me, this shit is damn good. I could eat two or three more."

Gilley held eye contact with Arch for a bit, causing the rocker to shrink in his ego a bit. Finally, Gilley's laugh that lit up his entire face and spread across the calmer waters broke the tension.

"You're way too damn easy, boy. They both start the same with crème, but that's about it. I'd explain, but since you're not about to cook it, why bother."

"That's for damn sure. He can barely boil water without burning it," Wix told us with a smile of his own. "He's burned a pot or two trying."

Our chef looked at me, laughter making his eyes bright. "Sounds like your captain here. Girl has no business even owning a kitchen much less using it."

"Hey, I can do other things. I'm the one called

captain for a reason." I wanted to puff out my chest and act all high and mighty, but I didn't want to draw attention to my breasts. They both stared at me when they thought I wasn't looking.

I felt it every time their eyes rested on me, especially Wix. The quieter of the two observed everything about the boat and me. Stormy eyes noticed each move I made. Little hairs on the back of my neck kept me aware. I'd never noticed this reaction from a guy before. Was I supposed to like it? Did he have this effect on all women he kept a close eye on? I wasn't sure I enjoyed the scrutiny.

"What are you thinking so hard over there about, Bardot?" Arch pulled me from my wayward thoughts. If I turned to him, I knew he'd see how red my face was, and the sun had nothing to do with its shade.

I grabbed my hat hanging down my back from a cord around my neck and pulled it low before turning. He'd make some comment, I knew it.

Thinking quickly, I replied, "Just that dark cloud." I nodded toward a harmless gray cloud north of us. With the southerly winds, nothing would come from it.

"What?" Wix stood and turned around so fast, I feared he'd fall over the side. "Think it's coming this way?"

Arch and I both grabbed at him. "Calm down, dude. You're spinning faster than a fucking seventy-eight-speed turntable. You'll find your ass in the water," I told Wix.

For the first time today, Wix had ventured to sit on the upper area of the boat while Arch and Gilley argued over desserts, so when he stood, it put him on a small ledge.

"You can swim, right?"

I looked up his body from where my hands gripped his calves. Those tiny hairs on the back of my neck saluted him.

He dropped his eyes on me. I didn't know how I felt about our positions until a tight flutter happened in my core. The storminess directed at me felt too much. Too strong. Too deep.

"Yeah, I can swim. Doesn't mean I fucking want to."

I dropped my hands and took a step back. Wix stepped down on the bench, still standing above me with me on the cockpit floor. Turbulent eyes bored into me, laser-like, until a sound from Arch pulled me out of the head space where I drifted.

"He can swim, but he doesn't like to." His explanation was simply put, so I left it alone but knew there was more to this story. Too bad I'd never know the reason. After today, I'd never see these two again without attending a concert, so there's nothing here to dwell on.

"Well, that's good. It's totally up to him about swimming. I can't remember the last time I jumped in the water." I turned to the table and started taking it down. The two behind me spoke in low voices that didn't sound like they were arguing.

"I think I'm going to jump in and get wet." Arch pulled off the T-shirt he had put on when we sat down to eat.

Oh. My. God. Why, why, why did they have to climb on my boat? I avoided men for the most part, but with his body up close and personal, I took a double take. How did he drink and keep his abs looking so lickable?

Flexing them, Arch laughed. "Like what you see, Ms Midnight?"

He went back to the unearned nickname. Isn't that what friends did? He wasn't my friend and never would be.

And now he'd busted me again, looking all googly-eyed at his hot body. Maybe I did need to find a hookup somewhere. It had been a long time since I was with a man.

I actually couldn't remember how long. It only happened when I spent much time away from the boat, like during severe winter storms. They rarely occurred in our area, so most of the time, I was safe and didn't feel the need to go looking for trouble.

"No need to be embarrassed." Arch winked at me, making it worse. "Happens all the time. Makes me feel great about the time I spend in shitty hotel gyms when we're on tour."

"Yeah, if he can't find a gym, he drives the rest of us fucking crazy with his 'bus-er-cise,'" Wix added.

"Takes up all the damn room on the floor doing sit-ups and shit. Sorry bastard takes great pride in making the rest of us feel like losers for not joining too."

"Hey, I always ask for someone to go with me. If I can't find a spotter, then lifting is almost a no-go." His arms flex into muscle-man territory. "Can't get this tone without lifting."

"Stop showing the fuck off, Arch. She doesn't want to see that shit. Some women find it repulsive, you know."

Wix gives me a side-eye hoping for a response. I try to remain neutral since I'm in no position to comment after my obvious gawking at Arch's perfectly-formed body.

"So, you do find it sexy?" Arch asked as he posed with his pecs looking bigger than my breasts on a good day. Dammit. I blew out an upward breath, moving the wayward hair off my forehead.

"I'd prefer not to comment. I can see it causes a rift between y'all."

"Naw, not so much. We'd prefer to have riffs between us, but you know, that's a different story. I'd be happy to explore any crevices on *your* body you had in mind." With that, Arch wiggled those eyebrows again, dropped his pants, and jumped in the water but not before he treated me to a show in his tight boxer briefs.

Not much was left to my imagination of what he

held behind those dark jeans he wore.

I waited for him to surface, watching over the side. The water's depth allowed for jumping and diving, but when a guest bailed off the side, I hesitated until their heads broke the surface. To me, unknown waters were for gliding over, not so great for jumping in.

"Wow, feels fucking awesome. You two should give it a try. Cools you right off."

"Pass," I yelled down to him. "You want a float or something to hang onto?"

"Hell no. I want to swim, not lay still above the water." With powerful strokes, he quickly circled the boat a couple of times.

The rocker's muscular back decorated with tattoos caught my attention as well as the new boat of beautiful people anchored beside us. Scantily clad women flocked to watch him glide through the water.

Moving to the back of the boat, I threw out a rope for him to hang onto, trying not to stare at the females ogling him. I knew people tended to tire in the sun even while in the water. Arch drank several beers before lunch, so he could overdo the exercise without realizing it.

Several minutes passed without sound from the water, and Wix and I looked over the edge. There, Arch floated on his back, giving the women a perfect view of himself.

Gilley stepped up and joined us watching him when we saw him take a mouthful of water. "Man, you couldn't make me put that water in my mouth. Who knows what the fuck's in it? He's probably going to glow for a few days after this."

Wix laughed until he heard Gilley's glowing comment. "Dude, stop putting that shit in your mouth. It's contaminated."

"It'll be fine."

"This isn't Crater Lake, you dumbshit," Wix added.

"Right," I backed the two men up. "You realize this water flows into and out of the Houston Ship Channel. Remember me saying to watch out for ships' wakes?"

"Are y'all hell-bent on ruining my relaxation? I'll get the fuck out."

"Great idea. Swim to the back, and I'll drop the ladder for you." I dropped the aluminum ladder before handing him a beach towel as he rose from the water in grand fashion. Our boat had slipped around so the back now faced the other one.

Unlike the taunting women, the last thing I wanted to see was the water sliding down his body. I practically ran to the front of the boat to start working on raising the anchor. Where these guys were concerned, I needed to keep my thoughts in check.

When I turned back to the cockpit to start the motor, Arch wore his jeans but no shirt. At least I wouldn't have to see him in wet underwear. God only knows what that would do to my hormones.

"We'll be under sail shortly. Feel free to stretch out on the deck or the bow." I pointed to the front of the boat. "There's a great view of the harbor from the area in front of the mast."

"We need to get to know our neighbors before we go. They seem like a friendly bunch. What do you think, Wix?" He shot his bandmate a questioning look followed by his telltale smirk. "I'm sure they'd be happy to join us over here for a little fun."

Wix raised his shoulder, signaling a don't-care attitude. Nothing pointed out who was the manwhore and who was more selective in their conquests than all of Arch's suggestive comments.

His hotness was lost on me the minute I made this decision about them. While a one-and-done suited me perfectly, I didn't want someone who'd settle for any willing female.

"Dude, here's an opportunity to meet some chicks away from the venue. Maybe they'll be clueless too," Arch pointed out.

"Doubt it. We couldn't get that lucky twice." Wix aimed a look at me over his sunglasses. I tried to keep from glaring at him but failed.

The other boat drifted closer as the winds rotated us in different directions since I stopped trying to raise the anchor when Arch requested more time.

A brazen girl wearing a few well-placed strings leaned almost too far over the side and yelled, "Y'all want to join us over here for a drink? We've got an awesome bartender." The precarious position allowed for her fake tits to all but fall out of the tiny triangles.

Our two guests turned and looked at me.

I couldn't keep them from going—they're grown men.

"You're welcome to go over if you want to. You have about an hour before we need to head to the yacht club."

"Why were we leaving then?" Wix wondered.

"I wanted to sail more so you two got the true power this boat possesses in a strong wind." I watched their faces trying to decide what they wanted to do more. "If you'd rather spend that time over there, it's okay too."

Guests visited other boats here at the tiny island all the time. Sometimes friends rented several boats so they had plenty of room while sailing. Some loved to raft up and boat hop.

"How will we get over there?" Wix turned to me and asked.

"You can swim, or we can let the boats drift together and tie off until you get on theirs. It's fairly easy to step from one to the other." I wanted to say jump across but figured he'd consider that too scary.

"Yeah, let's do it, dude. Some freaks have to be aboard it," Arch encouraged Wix. "We'll stay until Ms. Midnight tells us to come home like good little sailors." His look told me it might be harder than simply telling them to come back. Blowing the air horn sounded more like it. Dude must be horny twenty-four-seven.

"Okay, let's do it." For the first time, I heard some enthusiasm from the brooding rocker.

I guess his idea of a good time included chasing nearly naked females.

CHAPTER
6

WIX

Honestly, I swear a fucking day rarely passed that Arch didn't hook up with some random.

Being a drummer in a band suited his lifestyle perfectly. I thought the saying was 'a girl in every port,' but with him, it was more like a girl or two or three in every city.

"We should have come more prepared." Arch stood ready to board the other boat while I waited on deck for our captain to get us closer. *Much closer.*

Thanks to Bardot, the vessel maneuvered perfectly after she started the motor to pull alongside the other boat. Her movements appeared swift and efficient, not like she was out for a Sunday afternoon of fun. Did she ever take out a boat for fun after doing this every day?

Copper Crowns played their instruments daily for fun whenever the mood struck. Sometimes it was to replay a particular part of a song stuck in our heads. Sometimes a melody came to one of us, and we had to get it down before moving on.

The only time I hated it came while I was asleep at night. Snippets of a song would wake me, and there was no way I would go back to sleep with it on replay in my head.

When music became my life, a pencil and paper stayed with me at all times. These days, I hummed or sang the tune into my phone. Waking up to my rough voice, I laughed, but enough sparked my memory so I could create a new melody. New music was constantly on my mind.

The boats knocked together, and I realized six women watched me as I zoned out. Glancing back over my shoulder, Bardot stared, waiting for me to help keep the two from hitting hard enough to do damage. I kneeled before the females only inches away now. My delayed Spidey senses gave me a bad feeling about what was about to happen.

"Oh my God, it's Wix Stoker."

"Wix, Wix? Look this way. I want the first picture," someone yelled.

"Is it really the bad boys of Copper Crowns?" Came another high-pitched squeal.

And on and on the cries came from the girls. Dammit all to hell. We weren't even over there yet, and they were all screaming.

Mistake, mayday, mistake, my brain shouted.

Let the mobbing begin.

"Ladies, ladies," Arch bellowed. "There's plenty of time for all that. Let us get over there first."

He hit me on the back. "Don't want our Wix Man taking a dive into the water."

"I'll save him," one yelled.

"No, I will. I'm a better swimmer," another commented.

"No need to fight, ladies. Step back and let them board." This time Bardot roared, causing them all to look up at her. From the looks on their tanned faces, the female captain surprised the anxious group.

I turned to see Bardot kneeling and holding the rail of the other boat. She made sure all I had to do was take one step across. As I looked down into the murky water, a cold chill ran across my back before I grabbed the thin wire running around the boat.

"You can do it, Wix," Captain quietly offered. "It's only one step, and you're home free."

My head tipped in a brief nod because I knew she was right. Just one step and I'd be over and then make my way to the lowest level, free from danger. Eyeing the water again, I closed them shut tight for a second before standing and practically leaping to the cockpit floor.

Glancing back at Bardot, I watched her shove the girls' boat hard enough to unhook the two. Gilley took up the extra slack in the anchor line to keep them apart. My lifeline to freedom was now separated.

Deep down, I had a feeling this wouldn't end well for me.

As usual, I should have gone with my gut as the next hour of my life felt like pure hell. Sweaty female bodies undulated around, trying to capture my attention while Arch chose a few to take down below almost before I stepped aboard. Damn good thing cold beer flowed freely because I needed a few to make this shit bearable.

I sat on the top deck and watched them dance and play. Using the term dancing was a euphemism for emulating sex. The only thing in the way was a thin string of material that honestly left little to the imagination.

I couldn't help but wonder why the hell some people felt the need to show everything that way. Personally, I like a little left to discover for myself.

When one almost sitting on me got up, another took her place. They constantly introduced themselves and proceeded to rub uncovered skin all over my arms, chest, thighs, or whatever they got their hands on.

The babble came nonstop from thickly coated shiny lips. My face probably had a glow to it from all the fucking gloss the braver ones smeared on me. Their attempts at capturing my attention grew bolder the longer I sat with them, making me wonder if the more daring girls were about to whip out my deflated cock and try to have sex or suck me off right here on deck.

And my hair. That shit was so tangled from the wind and would be thinner from all the damn fingers running through it. This situation was fucked-up in so many ways, and I wanted this over with.

Arch stepped back out, leaving his prey behind, probably trying to get clothes back on. And by clothes, think thin swatches of color. When he looked at me, I raised my eyebrow in question.

The smile on his face told me enough as he made his way over. He wrapped his hand around the waist of the woman sitting next to me.

I say woman but wondered if she'd even had her eighteenth birthday yet. These days it was impossible to tell. The label constantly warned us when we were on our own to check IDs because we didn't need a conviction for sex with a minor. Jailbait became a term we often heard from day one with those guys. Lawyers met with us as much as possible to keep us warned of new tricks and repeat old ones.

When we were backstage, the women were all vetted before entering. Underage was a no-go. Females today made themselves look twenty-five at sixteen. Most of us could spend a few minutes talking to them and knew they were too young.

Arch rarely took the time to talk to his conquests, so he caused a lot of problems for the band early on. After some close calls, he checked IDs since he didn't trust his own judgment where females were concerned.

He pulled this one close and whispered in her ear. After a giggle, he switched places with the girl and let her go to get him a fresh beer. Anything to please him. Wonder what he promised her?

"Dude, we have the pick of the litter around here, and your ass is glued to the boat."

"Not interested, and they're not dogs, so don't call them a litter. It's degrading. Have you learned nothing about sexual harassment after the last time?"

His hand rubbed down his face as a sweet smile returned in front of it, a longneck dangling between her pink-tipped fingers. "Here ya go, Arch. Extra cold in this longneck can." A longing look was plastered across her face.

Taking the frosty can from her, he knocked it back and swallowed half before stopping. "What the fuck? What's this?" he sputtered.

"It's uh, uh... it's a Coors Light in the aluminum can. That's all they would let us bring aboard. We saved money by bringing our own alcohol, but it wouldn't matter. Their boat, their rules, and no glass is one of them. Sorry."

I felt bad for her. She acted like it was the end of the world while she spoke. "It's fine. He's a spoiled shit. Thinks he can only drink those hipster beers or Coronas. We've had a fuck ton of Coors Light."

The brunette beamed at my words. Earlier when she sat next to me, I paid her no attention, but now I saw a beautiful woman standing and looking at me.

Her face appeared young, but her body said not. Long dark hair fell in waves around her shoulders with sunglasses blocking my view of her eyes.

"What's your name, doll?" Arch asked as though he cared, which I knew was farcical.

"Avril, and yes, my mom was a huge Avril Levine fan when I was born, so I got stuck with it." She placed her hand out to formally shake, but Arch grabbed it, flipping it over to kiss her wrist. It became his signature move telling us he wanted to fuck the chick it was attached to. Such a douche.

He glanced at me and opened his eyes wide, questioning if I wanted a shot first. I didn't want to, but I also didn't want to see him debase her, so I stuck out my hand as if I waited for my turn to shake it, kiss it, or pull her to me.

Arch dropped her hand immediately, not wanting to be the cockblocker. "All yours," he said before standing and walking away with his half bottle in hand. I suppose it wasn't as disgusting as he made it out to be.

"Would you like to sit back down?" Avril looked around to where Arch disappeared and saw him chatting up another of the girls.

"Sure." She continued looking at him for a brief minute. "Is he always such an asshole?"

I laughed hard. This girl had pegged him instantly. "Yes, he kinda is, especially under these circumstances. Lots of shiny new toys waiting to be picked up, and he can't help himself since he enjoys new objects." That sounded low, even to me, but it was the truth. He objectified women most of the time.

"He can have them. I don't know how I got stuck out here with my sister's friends. She invited me last minute, and I was bored. A Saturday with nothing to do makes me itchy."

"Itchy, huh?" This was a first for me.

"Yeah, you know, itching to do something fun."

"Oh, okay." I felt 'itchy' on the bus all the time unless we were jamming or writing new music. "I'll have to remember that." We smiled at each other. This girl was a beauty, but something didn't seem right about her being here.

"So, you've done this before?" I tried to come up with a conversation that didn't seem totally lame.

"Oh yeah, all the time. I live here in a house on the lake. We go sailing a lot, but today her friends rented a boat, so they had time to play without Daddy doing the work. He's kinda a bummer out here on the water, all strict about meeting up with people."

"Yeah, I don't think our captain was so happy with us jumping ship. Gave us a time limit. We paid for a four-hour trip, so she probably wants to keep us on time."

"Curfew, huh? I hate those." As soon as she said it, it gave her age away. What eighteen-year-old had a curfew these days?

"So you're not over eighteen, huh?"

"You caught that slip-up, did ya?" She giggled a sweet sound, leveling bourbon-brown eyes at me over her glasses.

This girl was destined to give some poor unsuspecting dude a hard time. Young, beautiful, and full of ideas about life.

"Yeah, sorry. Our label stays on us about age limits. How old are you?"

Her eyes dropped to the water over the side. "I'm seventeen. My sister tells me all the time to watch what I say because being seventeen is a no-go for men." She huffed and looked back at me. "She's like, 'Avril, just keep your mouth shut. You don't look seventeen, but as soon as you start talking, you're doomed.' "

"You need to be honest. Men can only do so much. You've got plenty of time to find a man who loves you at whatever age."

"Okay, Dad." She laughed. "You sound just like him."

My laughter sounded more like a bark that went on forever. "No one has ever told me I mimicked their dad before. Too funny." We both continued with the pleasant feeling laughter created.

"Sorry. I didn't mean it that way, but he tells us stuff like that all the time. 'Wait for the one who treats you like a princess' and 'you've gotta kiss a lot of frogs before you find a prince' which is my least favorite. He knows I hate frogs." Her cute nose wrinkled up for a brief second.

We enjoyed talking during the time we had left. I noticed the others giving Avril classic what-the-hell looks for monopolizing me. They randomly broke into our conversation but quickly figured out I was happy to sit and chat her up for now.

A loud whistling sound distracted me, and I saw our captain summoning us home.

I glanced at my companion. "Well, hell, think she wants us to return?"

"I'd say about thirty minutes ago. She's been trying to get your attention, windmilling her arms all around."

"What? Why didn't you tell me?" I stood ready to go.

"Because your manwhore friend is down below with 'friends.' " The sweetheart used her fingers to make quotes which made me smile again. "One of them being my sister. *Slut.*"

This time I laughed out loud. She definitely had a great personality that would keep a guy on his toes for her upcoming college years following spring graduation. Not me, though.

I took her hand and pulled her to standing. "Let's take a selfie. You know you want to."

Her perfect smile lit up her eyes with fun and mischief. Perfectly white teeth were second to her young crease-free lips, pink and natural. *Her poor dad* is all I could think.

"Thanks for being so nice to me," Avril whispered when we hugged goodbye. Her sister's friends' eyes darted toward us, green with envy since she captured all my time. Glad they weren't killer blow darts. Both of us would be dead now.

It was all okay, though, because being the pussy lover that he was, Arch did his best to entertain the rest of the women in an hour. He got off on seeing happy faces at the end of an evening, if he saw faces at all.

Bardot pulled anchor and moved over to retrieve us. This time I didn't look down but took a giant step to her boat, landing easily.

A sailboat wasn't as bad as I thought it would be.

CHAPTER 7

BARDOT

Constant laughter surfing across the water's surface kept me on edge. Did I laugh so much when I was that age? At twenty-five, I didn't have much on these girls, but still, I'd been an adult a long time. Forever, it seemed. The noise sounded as fake as the breasts looked on a few of them.

Stop, Bardot. Why did I care what the guys did? They're guests and entitled to do whatever they want for the time they paid for.

"You keep looking that way, and them boys'll think you're jealous of the young things they're playing around with." Gilley leaned out of the stairwell.

"As if I care what they're doing. They're grown-ass men and can do what they want as long as we get paid." Even to me, my comment reeked of jealousy. I had been wasting too much time glancing toward the other boat.

"Shit, little girl. I've been standing here a few minutes, and you've had your sights on that sloop more than the brass you're pretending to polish."

Doubling my efforts at rubbing, I tried to make the plaque shine. I added it to the boat a few days after my dad died. Had the makers rush the order.

"I'll get it cleaned before they return. Besides, I needed to keep an eye out in case they're ready to return."

He laughed an almost sadistic sound, and I knew he didn't believe a word I said. "I'm going below to finish cleaning my kitchen. Let me know when you're ready to pull the anchor 'cause that's when they'll be ready to sail home." He glanced across the water at them once more. "That Archie boy ought to be tired when he gets over here."

Ugh. Deep down, I knew Gilley was right. They were obviously having fun. Maybe I *was* jealous of those girls, but I'd dive into shallow water headfirst before admitting it.

I polished the brass while staring out in the opposite direction of the party. The wind died down some a few minutes back, and we might have to motor in to make it back in time. Normally, I preferred to sail, but right now, I didn't care one way or the other.

Those two had more fun with all the women fawning over them than sitting here baking on my boat. It's surprising they didn't come with their own entourage of mostly naked females. They probably did everywhere they went.

Why couldn't I get them off my mind? Glancing into the white clouds over the water, I tried to remember the last time I went to a party with friends or, more importantly, single men. If it took me that long to think of it, too much time had passed.

Partying with rock stars had never been an option until today. My mundane life, browned skin, and barely-there tits, along with mediocre looks, told me I wouldn't be invited to one either. Why ask me to attend when they could have all the beautiful women around them that they would ever need?

These guys were H. O. T. hot, stupid rich, and rockers. Women lined up for blocks and then paid to see them perform, and probably all forked over even more money to get up close and personal with them after the concerts.

Thinking back, I tried to remember if I'd ever gone to a rock concert. Some girls in high school invited me to go a few times, but my dad always needed me on the boat. I wondered if it was his way of keeping me out of trouble, knowing he'd used that excuse for other adventures I wanted to go on.

Good job, Dad. You did have a way of keeping me close while instilling in me a love for sailing. If not for him, I don't know where I'd be after making one tremendously bad decision in my early teen years.

Water under the bridge now. He was taken from me way too early, just like my mom.

Life hadn't been too kind to me, and I had to grow up sooner than most. What he did leave me was this boat and the ability to support myself if I kept her in top shape. I continued to run the soft cloth over the brass, trying to do just that.

I heard a loud laugh and looked up as Arch came from below deck with a woman after him and one before him. He swatted her on a bare cheek directly in his face on the steep ladder.

"Owe, Arch. That wasn't nice." I heard her squeal and then laugh hyena-like. My eyes rolled with her sound. *Fake. Fake. Fake.*

"Women like her give us all a bad name," I said aloud to no one before noticing the time. We needed to leave as soon as possible to make it back to the docks on time. Thinking someone would notice me, I began moving my arms all over so they'd know it was time. They didn't.

"Hey, Gilley. Throw up my whistle, please. It's time to go."

I watched the silver metal pass through the opening in my direction. Catching it, I blew a long, loud sound. It hurt my ears, but the entire boat of beautiful people turned my way as I started the engine to begin the process of pulling the anchor.

Not having time to watch for them, Gilley and I retrieved the hunk of metal. I opened the bow hatch, and we stored it for another day. Using the big ship's wheel, I steered the vessel in easily beside the girls, hoping not to do any damage. Waves and swells tore boats up all the time.

"Time to go, guys. I'll move in beside their boat," I called across the water. They stepped on board after each girl took selfies, hugged, kissed Arch, who was more willing than Wix, and whispered who knows what in both men's ears.

Arch grumbled after hopping below to get a beer and hit the head. I wanted to laugh at him but thought better. It surprised me that he hadn't tried to piss over the side at some point. Lots of guests did after drinking all afternoon. He seemed the kind to do something like that.

When Wix settled back in his bench position, I pushed the lever forward, sending the boat ahead easily. Staring at the open water, I asked, "Have fun?"

"Sure. It was okay. They were entertaining." He eyed me as he commented, "What about you? Enjoy the hour off?"

"I've been busy doing maintenance on the boat while y'all played with your little friends." My words poured out before I thought better of them. My caustic tone had sarcasm written all over it.

"Played with our little friends? That's rich. You make it sound like we were in the sandbox with shovels and buckets unless you were loosely quoting *The Godfather*."

"Just calling it like I saw it. Jailbait y'all's usual MO?"

"Not that it's any of your fucking business, but yes, they all were legal, except the chick I spent the majority of the time talking to. She was seventeen. You going to call the police on me?" His caustic tone matched mine.

I needed to back the fuck off from this line of questioning. He was right. It was none of my business what either of them did, but his taunting words pissed me off.

"Nope. Don't plan to. Let her daddy call them. That's his job, not mine."

Wix stood abruptly and faced my side with me facing the ship's wheel. "You saw us the entire fucking time, Bardot. I saw you watching me, and you know damn well that nothing happened with me. So what's your fucking deal?"

His words never rose above a normal volume, but the anger behind them burned me just the same. His eyes felt glued to my head, and I saw them each time I dared glance in his direction. I tried to be more discreet with my spying. Obviously, an epic fail on my part.

I needed to make amends for my rudeness. Not only did I want to, but he could ruin me with bad reviews. Our booking agent might drop me if that happened with such a high-profile client.

Finally allowing myself to look directly at him, I

began the crawl to apologizing speech. "Look, Wix. I'm sorry. It's none of my business what you do. We don't even know each other. It's just that I despise when young women make themselves look like bimbos, especially for men like you two."

"Men like us? What kind of men are we, Bardot?" His feet never moved, and his lips were only inches from my ear.

The warmth of his breath sent a chill down my arm, and once again, those damn little wisps on the back of my neck rose to attention. *Why did I let him have any effect on me?* I didn't know this guy. He was basically a stranger, and yet, being near him overwhelmed my senses.

"What's going on, you two? Little love spat already?" Arch palmed his friend's shoulder and squeezed it.

"Wix, dude, didn't you see the green glow from the top of Ms. Midnight's head while we were gone? If it'd been yellow, I'd swear she was signaling Batman."

"Shut the fuck up, Arch," Wix hissed.

"Don't fucking know how you missed it. She had her own laser light show going on over here."

"Arch!" He growled the word this time.

"Good thing she's not some badass knife thrower in her downtime. We'd have some explaining to do with all the bloody fucking bodies on the other boat."

"I said shut—" But before Wix finished the statement, I leaped over him to get to Arch. The dipshit backed up, laughing as Wix's strong arms wrapped around mine, preventing me from getting to his friend.

"Looks like she's ready to do damage," Wix barked out between laughs.

"Damn straight I am. I wasn't glowing while you two fuckers were gone. That was called manual labor. As if you would know one damn thing about actually working for a living," I shot out over my captor's shoulder. "But no, you parade around on a stage like entitled gods in front of a bunch of wild, screaming women all night, acting all high and mighty because you know they can't get to you. Bodyguards do your ass fucking dirty work keeping them away, so you can live to do it all over again another day."

Unlike Wix, my voice got louder with every word. I'd had enough of these two prancing around here acting all badass.

"Tell us how you really feel, Bardot," Arch shot back at me. "Seems like you've got a pretty fucking good gig going on here, sailing around on Daddy's boat every day, suckering people out of thousands of dollars while you enjoy yourself. He let you do this, or do you sneak around while he slaves away behind some corporate job?"

My breath squeezed out in a slow escape, along with the anger. Wix put me back on my feet, knowing Arch's words hurt.

"My dad's dead and buried, asshole." These words

sobered me in a heartbeat. Relaxing my strained muscles, Wix let me go.

I stepped behind the wheel, thankful the boat hadn't gone too far astray after I finished my tirade. Men sucked. And why did they bring out the worst in me?

Wix plopped back on the bench, and the other went to the bow to lean against the mast watching as the late afternoon sun began its descent into the water. I didn't see Gilley until I glanced down from behind the wheel. He'd heard it all. Hell, everyone in the harbor probably did. So much for a dazzling review. I'll probably have to find another city to work from now after I spoke my mind.

As I drove the boat back through the narrow channel under the bridge, the words I used against him tossed around in my head. *Why did I allow him to get to me?* My bitterness stayed tucked away most of the time, so why did it have to jump up and bite me in the ass with these two aboard?

No one should have to live a life like I had. It was fucked up in so many ways through a long list of tragedies, beginning when my mom died. She loved me fiercely. She took care of my dad and me so we knew the meaning of family and unconditional love. That is, until someone ran a stop sign and took her from us. We blinked, and she was gone, leaving us both wondering how to survive without her.

I used the following years doing all I could to get

my dad's attention. Or someone's. My dad dove into work unless we were sailing. While we were on the water, silence passed between us like two monks who'd taken a vow. Words were only uttered as a necessity. He used them to teach me everything about being on the water as a fun way to spend the afternoons together. Afterward, his lessons came as demands—formal instructions like a naval captain.

He taught me how to captain a boat and maintain it. He made sure I went to school, did my homework, and ate something. Emotions never came into play. I began to think I was a freak for feeling sad about losing her.

I missed her every single day.

When I tried to talk to him about it, he gave me a hard look and walked away. Was this the way adults grieved over the loss of a loved one?

Other things in life I had to discover on my own. Sadly, I gained this knowledge from the wrong people while he was away on business when I was only fourteen. Those lessons cost me more than anyone would ever know. They turned to dark secrets never to be shared.

He dealt with my situation but never spoke to me about it. He told me to go see my school counselor. No way in hell would I talk to Mr. Randall about my problems, my situation, or the aftermath. Those words were better left unsaid to anyone outside my dad and me.

Shaking my head to clear old memories away, I watched Arch basking in the last warmth from the sun. He lived like he didn't have a care in the world. Did anything bother him? Did he have demons like the rest of the world, or was he too busy living his life to worry about them?

Letting a guy like Arch push buttons he had no business toying with was on me. I knew better. I knew the consequences.

So why did I allow it? *Dumb move, Bardot. Really dumb move.*

Then there was Wix. His overwhelming effect pushed buttons inside me—those that have been dormant for years now—and a place they still needed to be.

CHAPTER 8

WIX

As I watched the boats glide in and out of the channel from where I sat on the deck, it afforded me a view of the easy life some lucky bastards lived here on the Texas coast.

Was it truly that much different living on a boat than on the bus? Tight spaces, always moving, no clutter to interfere with your life. Yes, the boat was hands down the better of the two.

I tried hard to keep my eyes off Bardot, not wanting to incur her wrath again, then I remembered it didn't flare-up until Arch pushed too hard. Prick never knew when to stop. I loved him, but sometimes I wanted to knock the shit out of him just to shut him up.

Bardot handled the boat with such ease I'd never believe someone as young as she appeared to be, had in them. Her sense of movement and direction were planned and executed through the narrow slot and into the opening of the lake west of the bridge.

A wall of cool water sprayed over the bow after a long cigarette boat caused a wake, making *Miss Midnight* fall into the trough left by the narrow boat. Luckily, Arch received most of the salty mist, making me wonder if our captain purposely turned into the rolling water to aim it toward him.

"Damn, that's cold," he yelled and moved back to the cockpit, sitting behind our dark-haired navigator. Making sure they didn't go at it again, I moved to sit beside him. A well-timed pop on the back of his head when needed tended to shut him up, too, but I knew Bardot would never do that to him, even if she wanted to.

"Hey, Ms. Midnight?" Arch called.

"Yes? Can I do something for you?" Her reply was curt and formal.

"I'm sorry for what I said earlier." Arch ended with a sheepish grin he reserved for apologies. He tended to throw out his panty-dropping smiles for the babes he spotted in the audience or at meet-and-greets, so this one looked completely sincere.

Since our drummer rarely considered others' feelings, his words caught me by surprise. He took what he wanted and gave little in return, especially to women. So, him apologizing meant a hell of a lot more than she'd ever know.

"Thank you. I'm sorry, too, for overreacting. It takes a lot to get me so riled up. Guess I've been on edge lately, and you ended up catching the brunt of my rage."

When she turned and genuinely smiled at him, my jaw almost hit the floor. There was no doubt she was beautiful, but with her lips arched up and a hint of color from something shiny, she took my breath away. Her true smile made my heart take an extra beat. Arch's lack of response said he noticed it too.

"All I ever want when I bring newbies aboard is to allow them to have the experience they're looking for. You guys seemed tired when you boarded, and I felt you both needed a relaxing, lazy afternoon. I never meant to spoil it with harsh, unnecessary words."

As she finished, she turned back to her job, steering into the yacht club's harbor where we boarded. Considering our limited knowledge, we helped her moor the boat as much as possible, which wasn't much. Our help wasn't necessary as she and Gilley seemed to know what to do on their own.

I found myself hating that we were already in the slip, tied up, and needing to get off.

"You have another group coming aboard today?" I asked as I watched her lash up sails and complete her work around the boat. Gilley made noises down below, readying his area.

"No, we're done for the day." She moved up front to the smaller sail. "Most people have work on Monday morning, meaning they don't want to take an evening cruise." Our conversation flowed easily with questions and answers she gave while continuing with her work. Neither of us attempted to get off the boat while she moved around with easy steps.

When Gilley stepped up from the cabin, he had a bag and a small ice chest with him. He watched Bardot for a second and then turned to us. "You two staying or going?"

I glanced at Arch, lifting a brow in question. We had the night off, so there was no need to rush back downtown. He hit me with a sly smirk.

"Is it okay if we hangout here for a bit? I mean, we don't want to keep you from doing something, but if you're going to stay, we'd like to enjoy the quiet for a while longer." I watched Bardot's face as I spoke to read how she might reply. I figured out early on that her expressions and eyes gave away her true feelings.

When I had her wrapped up tightly against me, keeping her away from the dipshit, her eyes were on fire, and her face almost matched. The strained muscles she fought with almost got loose in the heat of the moment. For someone so tiny, she packed a punch inside her I never wanted to be on the receiving end of.

Bardot looked up at Gilley and nodded her head. "Sure, you can stay. I have some more cleaning I need to get done before I shut everything off and go home."

The big man turned and gave a look that put the

fear of God into both of us. Neither of us was confident we could take him, even with two-to-one odds.

Arch stood, offering his hand. "Don't worry. We'll make damn sure the little lady leaves here safe and sound."

Gilley eyed Arch for a full minute before taking his hand to shake. "I'm not worried about her. Worried about you two. She'll put you down in a heartbeat. You ain't figured that out yet?"

As Gilley let Arch's hand go and turned to me, I wanted to hide my hand behind my back. I played guitar and needed my hands, but then so did Arch on the drums. Not wanting to look like I was a pussy, I shook his hand and was happy when I pulled it back intact.

"Beer and soda are in the cooler along with some leftovers from earlier, if y'all get hungry." His head tipped to the captain once more before turning to walk away. Glancing back over his shoulder while he lumbered up the walkway, he glared at us for a brief second. I knew he didn't trust us and said so with that look as if we didn't catch his drift from before.

"Nice guy..." Arch smirked and commented but quickly added, "... for leaving us drinks and snacks." He covered his dumbass blunder quickly.

"Yeah, I love him. He's been a lifesaver for me on the boat." Bardot's eyes followed Gilley to his vehicle as she wound ropes into tidy rings and loops, barely moving from her position.

"We can help," I offered. "If you'll tell us what to do."

"Ha-ha. Me tell y'all what to do." I knew she joked from the slight grin on her lips. Those lips had to have been the death of some poor schmuck—plump, pink and always shiny from the stick she kept in her pocket. I shook my head to remove the image. The last thing she'd want is me moving in for a taste.

Arch jumped to the upper deck and glanced down at her. "You know, I haven't even been below. Maybe I should check it out. Got a bed down there?"

"Yes, there's a birth down below. I told you about the head when you boarded."

His arms spread out. "There's a huge fucking urinal all around us."

"Gross. I try not to think about that." Her nose turned up, making a funny face.

"Now, what kind of guy wastes the opportunity to piss in the ocean by using a restroom?" he called on his way down the steep wooden steps.

"Me, I'm that guy." He knew I had because no fucking way would I get off this big-ass boat just to take a leak.

"Pussy." He ducked under the deck.

"Dumbshit," I yelled at him, laughing, and heard a name replied, but it was muffled from where he stood.

Bardot snickered. "You two always like this?"

"Yeah. We've known each other forever. He's always been a clown but can get carried away and let his fucking comments overload his ass."

She nodded as she continued her rope coiling. "I haven't had a close friend like that in forever." Her words came out barely a whisper, as though she wished it but didn't quite know how to make it happen.

"Out here on a boat all the time makes a social life challenging, huh." My words were more of an observation than a question.

"Being on a boat alone is a solemn life. That's one reason I'm happy having Gilley around. He seems hard, but he's a good listener."

"He always that protective?"

She lifted a shoulder. "I guess. Never really thought about it. The two of us spend our workdays with strangers. Occasionally, someone who charters makes a return visit. Usually, they either decide they hate sailing, get their own boat, or try a different size or maker."

Bardot kept her feelings close, but when she spoke about sailing, her face lit up like a billboard for a new club. I enjoyed how expressive she became when the subject excited her.

"Makes sense. Must be a huge investment. I'd want to try out a bunch of damn boats before dropping a wad of cash into something this massive. Your dad leave you the boat?"

I knew this would be a touchy subject, but we'd already ventured into the territory when she announced he had passed away.

She exhaled a heavy breath. "Yes, he knew I could handle it, and it's a great way to support myself."

"Right. After today, there's no doubt you can fucking handle it." While it seemed like a lot for someone her age, her dad's confidence in her skills amazed me. My dad still had a shit ton of doubts about my profession, even now that Copper Crowns was successful.

"If all else fails, I can sell the boat and use the capital to do whatever I want." She patted the boat like most people would pet their dog or cat. Her attachment to it gleaned in her eyes when she continued to rub her fingertip across the fiberglass.

"I have so many memories on this boat with him that selling it might kill me. It's all I have... left of him." Her voice broke mid-sentence, saying all I needed to know. The two of them shared great times. It made me wish I had those kinds of memories to hold onto.

"I'm sure you do." We sat in silence for a few minutes. Music drifted across the water from a bar in the harbor but not loud enough to ruin the moment.

I knew Bardot had dealt with hard times in her life. She had to be around my age and had already lost both parents but managed to successfully make it on her own. Not many young people faced a situation that difficult and came out on top as she had.

"So, when you're not on the boat, what do you do?" I knew so little about her other than boat information, so this seemed like a good segway.

"I have a small place close by. My dad and I lived there before..."

Before he died. I got it.

"That's where you live. What do you do for fun?" I saw this question made her uncomfortable as she began winding the ropes again, even a few she had already completed.

"I don't know. What do other people do my age for fun?" Her eyes never met mine when she spoke, and her face remained impassive.

"Go out with friends? Go to concerts? You know, like Copper Crowns' concerts?"

She laughed. "If you're fishing to know if I've seen the band, the answer is no. I'd have to go into Houston to see y'all. I rarely ever go into the city. Too busy and too much traffic. I'll take boat traffic any day."

"Then we need to fix that. You need to be at tomorrow night's show."

"Damn straight she does," Arch chimed in, climbing back up the steps with three beers in one hand and a monster-size bag of chips in the other. "And her sweet ass needs the fucking VIP experience."

"No, I really don't," Bardot quickly added her opinion.

"Yep," he popped the P. "You need a limo ride to the venue, T-shirts, a shitload of merch to take home."

"For damn sure," I added.

Once he finished handing out the beer, he wrapped

his arm around her shoulders. "Our captain needs a full-access backstage pass, photoshoots with the band, hang out with us before and after the concert, watch from the side stage, and the after-fucking-show party needs to be epic." He squeezed her shoulders tighter.

I watched as Bardot's eyes grew larger the longer Arch's list went on.

"Uh... I think I'm good right here, but thank you for the offer."

"Nope. We won't hear of it. The show is tomorrow night. You got a cruise scheduled?"

Staring into space, she shook her head. "We don't do cruises on Mondays."

"Then it's settled. You're coming," I announced. I pulled out my phone and called our tour manager. "Jones, we need the works for backstage for one." Holding the cell away, I asked, "You want to bring someone?"

Her face turned a sickly shade of white before she slowly shook it back and forth. Since we'd already covered her lack of friends, I should have known better than to ask. Mad at myself for pointing it out to her, I smiled to cover up the blunder.

Turning back to the phone, I added, "Yeah, the works too. She also needs everything we got for merch. Want her leaving there being the biggest fan ever. See if you can round up some of the opener's merch too. We're going to broaden her listening while we're at it." I ended my call.

"Ms. Midnight, you ready to rock and roll?" Arch used his long neck as a mic, shouting like we were on stage already.

CHAPTER 9

BARDOT

By the time the two crazies oozed off the boat and poured themselves into the back of the limo for a return trip into the city, my senses were blown, not to mention the fact they left the Harleys sitting dockside. They told wild stories of rock-star life that were the makings of the next most-watched documentary for Netflix.

I felt as if I'd learned some inside tracks of lives in the music business. Honestly, I couldn't understand why anyone chose to live that life. It sounded too intense twenty-four seven. They rarely had time for themselves, much less for anyone else. How could they continue living that way forever?

The idea of never having a family made memories of my own creep in. I'd had a family to belong to, and look where that got me. *Nowhere.* No one to run to when I needed someone. No one to check on me daily to make sure I was still alive. If the brokerage firm didn't call to relay messages about upcoming cruises, would I even be missed?

Gilley would eventually come looking for me, but he tended to leave me alone on our days off. Those stacked up during the coldest winter months.

"Stop it, Bardot," I uttered to no one. "Think about the good time you just had."

It felt good to laugh hard for a few hours—no boat to care for, no clients to entertain. Instead, three friends enjoyed an evening on a boat. Gilley would have to stock up on beer before Tuesday because those two put away more than I thought humanly possible. Enough to offer to send a service to deliver more to the boat. Naturally, I turned them down, not being able to forget they were guests, even if they were my guests and not the charter company's guests.

I drank a few but knew my limit when it came to drinking. Besides, I had to drive home. It wasn't far, but drinking and driving was a no-go for me. Not even buzzed. Getting a DUI came with all kinds of horrible consequences like losing my captain's license, something I couldn't afford.

As I laid in my bed, it was much later than usual. Good thing I didn't party often with guys like those two. Or never, in my case. They seemed to enjoy taking it easy as much as I did when they finally wound down. That made me wonder if they were only able to destress with alcohol.

Not that drinking mattered all that much to me. I watched people drink daily, but past experiences told me I never wanted to become that person who needed a drug to relax. While most people didn't see it as a drug, I knew better from watching how it changed people's behavior as they drank away their afternoon.

After the tales they told, I knew their lives might sound fun, but the pace was unbelievable—always on the go, moving from place to place.

They thrived on it. Their faces, when they spoke about their shows, said it all. Downtime came in the form of riding the bus from stop to stop. No wonder they insisted on seeing some of the cities this time around on tour. Not to mention getting under their bandmates' skin living in such close quarters.

For short periods of time, Dad and I lived on the boat. We quickly decided we both hated it. Too much togetherness, especially being a teenager during the majority of that time. At that age, everything I did annoyed him, and I couldn't understand it at the time. Now, I knew exactly why. *Hormones.*

Unless we were relocating to another area along the coast, we tried to keep an apartment. He spent his time on the boat during the day while I stayed at the apartment to go to school. Thank God for online homeschooling. I doubted I would have a diploma if those didn't exist.

Dad fought for me to go to a campus for school. He understood I missed out on the typical high school years—sports, dances, and friendships—but you can't miss what you don't know. He knew and begged me to go, but I resisted and won out.

When I was younger and my mother was alive, we had a real home and kept a boat in the harbor. Mom made it a home with frilly curtains and decorated walls, mostly consisting of my activities growing up.

They both worked for NASA, which took up a huge amount of property west of the lake and harbor. I eyed the complex daily going in and out of the harbor. Jobs like theirs proved hard to come by, but with the degrees they earned, working there made sense. My dad never pushed me to go to college, and my mom always assumed I would. After losing her, getting a degree never came into question.

When I attended elementary school, events kept me busy. She made sure I was involved in all the right kid activities. My soccer team won the trophy one year. Then I took piano lessons—epic failure. And my Girl Scout troop sold cookies. But her death put an end to all of that.

My dad tried in the beginning, but he miserably failed to follow through. I lost interest in all things kid related. The days of sports, dance, and school friends quickly went by the wayside.

Both of us suffered through the grief stages, at least some of them, in our own way. My school counselor begged him to put us in counseling, but somehow he missed the memo. We did the best we could.

By the time I made it to high school, I managed to find a whole new group of friends to hang with. Or maybe they found me floundering around with nowhere to fit in or no one to commiserate with.

These people explained how not to get caught sneaking out, drinking, tagging buildings, and with their guidance, we found trouble wherever we went. The nights freed me from thinking about what could have been my life. Left to my own thoughts became dangerous. I entertained dark ideas about life and my existence.

Dad started spending more time at the boat until late into the night, so he never knew what I was doing or where I went. He didn't seem to care anymore, and naturally, I took advantage of his lack of interest in me or anything, for that matter.

A few nosy but well-meaning neighbors tried to intervene on my behalf. He told them it was 'none of your damn business' and sent them on their way. That's the closest any adult got to telling me what to do for many of the years when I needed it the most.

After Dad had his say, no one bothered with what I did, where I went, or who I was with. The few old childhood friends drifted away, and my new friends taught me about a life I never knew existed.

Now, Dad was gone, I was alone, and short of Gilley,

there was no one around to concern themselves about me. Getting to that point, though, Dad and I dealt with some pretty harrowing nights and scary days.

Even as I grew older, nightmares came and went. For the most part, I believe I did okay for myself. I thought I remembered being happy living that life until people like Wix and Arch came along. They asked questions I didn't want to think about the answers to.

The stories the guys told of their lives made me stop and think as I lay in my bed alone.

Was I meant to be alone forever?

Was I happy living this existence I'd built for myself?

I rolled over and picked up my phone to see the time. Four thirty in the morning shined at me from the home screen. My sleep came in short spurts, and I knew this was too early to get up, but tossing and turning and wishing for a different life proved useless.

Throwing back my covers, I slipped into the kitchen and turned on the K-Cup machine for hot water to make tea. As I dug through my tea stash, a Sleepytime tea bag stood up in the back, so I grabbed it and waited for the water.

With more time to think, I remembered the upcoming show tonight. How was I supposed to attend a rock concert on my own? They assured me a car would be waiting at my door at six this evening, making the trip downtown easy enough. What was I supposed to wear to something like that? Leaning back, waiting, I pulled up Copper Crowns' concert pictures on my phone.

My tired eyes stretched open wider than ever. "Seems like the less, the better, might as well be naked." There was no way in hell I'd ever wear clothes that made me look like these women. Even if I owned the skanky garments, which I didn't, wearing something similar out in public was never going to happen. I couldn't decide if I'd be more embarrassed or self-conscious, constantly pulling down the short skirts.

Swiss cheese came with fewer holes, and the tops had less to them than I wore in a swimming pool. Those who donned a dress obviously wore nothing else. With the stretchy material clinging to their bodies so tightly, nothing could squeeze between their bodies and the snug spandex. How did they even walk?

Then I noticed the shoes at the end of their longer-than-life legs. No fucking way. The last thing I wanted was a visit to the ER with a broken leg or ankle. Can't exactly operate a boat with a leg in a cast.

After sugaring my tea heavily, I went back to bed. I continued to scroll through pictures until I passed over photographs of Wix. His arms rested around women well over six feet or their shoes put them up there. Blonde Barbie dolls, every single one of them. Their hair looked perfectly coifed to hold loose beach waves or flattened to be stick straight. How in God's name did they keep either in the humidity around here?

Glancing at my open closet door, knowing nothing in it would work, I realized I needed to call and cancel, but neither of them left a number to reach them as they precariously jumped from the boat. Not that they were exactly in any shape to remember to do so, much less recalling their own number.

Wix's jump surprised me based on his words and actions of the day. Drinking had made him bolder too.

When I thought about the evening, I smiled to myself. The two band members entertained me for longer than I thought possible. Wix continued being the less boisterous, but when he did add to Arch's stories, he gave little away as to his sexual escapades.

Arch thrived on telling stories, and his mate seemed more than happy to let him. It sounded as though it was that way in their days before the band too. Wix's backstory offered a more ominous tone. What little he shared, that is.

His friend shared everything, leaving little to the imagination, especially when it came to women. As he spoke, I watched the facial expressions Wix made. Where Arch was an open book, Wix was locked as tight as a seam in the boat's hull. I wondered what caused him to keep it all contained.

Life on the road with the band began like typical guys pulling pranks, drinking to excess, and finding the way between a women's thighs however possible. As the few years rolled by, they appeared to become more jaded to shenanigans and random hookups. At least, Wix did, since his stories became less about drugs, drinking, and sex and more about venues, music, and writing.

I wondered if Wix took relationships more seriously or maybe he'd been hurt a few times. Arch didn't act as though relationships were a necessary part of life yet. Love 'em and leave 'em needed to be tattooed on his damn forehead.

A smile crossed my face thinking about it. "Arch, one night only." I stretched my arms out like a billboard should read this whenever he came to town.

The sound of my phone vibrating pulled me back to reality. Rolling over to get it, I saw an unknown number pop up. I normally sent them to voicemail but decided to answer since it was still too early for most phone calls.

"Hello." My word was hesitant.

"Hey, this is Wix," a soft, quiet voice drifted through the phone.

My heart skipped a beat, causing me to suck in a breath. I knew attending this show was never going to happen. Good thing I hadn't spent hard-earned money on something I'd have to return because where else would I wear concert clothes?

"Hi, uh... how'd you get my number?" This, *this* was the first thing I wanted to know? My palm smacked my forehead.

"Had my tour manager call the boat booking company explaining I left something aboard the boat. Sorry, it was the only way they'd divulge CIA secrets."

"Ha, little white lies, huh?" Another smack to the head. "So, canceling tonight's VIP for me?"

"What? No way." His voice came across louder and with more force that bordered on anger in his tone. I heard him take in a long breath and let it out. "I, uh... we just wanted to make sure you were going to show up. Didn't want to arrange it all if you weren't planning to attend."

"No, I want to see the band play. I'm excited about the show." My face stretched into a wide smile with my white lie. I probably should try to be more aloof but whatever. I did want to see them perform, even if going already had my stomach doing somersaults. What to wear remained a battle for after this call.

"Great. We told the band we had a special guest attending tonight."

"You did? Why? I'm not someone special. I mean, I am, but not like another rock star or anything," I blabbered on and on, my anxiety skyrocketing and trying to get the better of me.

"Damn right you are. We had a great day and a better evening on your boat. I'd do it again if we were going to stay around longer."

"Can that be arranged?"

He laughed a dry tease into the phone. "No. Sorry to

say, it can't."

The letdown from a dream come true might have caused me to crash and burn from one too many tumbles.

After a few minutes, I heard myself yawn before I could stop it, and so did Wix. I guess the tea I chose did its job.

"Okay, sleepyhead, go back to sleep. Sorry I woke you."

"No, no. I wasn't asleep."

"Oh really? Your yawn says otherwise."

"Honestly, I wasn't. I kept waking up, so I made tea to help me sleep. It kicked in quicker than I thought it would."

"All right, go to sleep. Maybe you'll dream of me, Bardot. Night."

I said goodnight to a dead line.

CHAPTER 10

WIX

We sailed smoothly through sound check, considering Arch and I were late. Jones sent Elias, one of the roadies, to bang on the bus door to wake us. Lucky him, catching all the venom Arch spewed when he finally crawled to the door.

"What the fuck, dude?" Arch's scratchy words poured out.

"The fuck is 'get your lazy asses up and get to the sound check.' Those are your tour manager's words, not mine. You don't like us doing it, so come on."

Elias was one of the few guys who would stand up to band members to get the job done. Most of the guys pussied out when it came to creating a scene, especially at our doorway. Not him, though. He treated us like we were his employees instead of the other way around.

Fuck, I hated being hungover. Always did. This morning failed to be an exception, but hanging out with Bardot last night made it all worth it. I felt sure none of us had laughed that hard in a while, and sitting on her boat ticked it up a notch on the fun scale.

"Dammit, why'd we do that to ourselves?" Arch barked out while trying to wash the taste out of his mouth with something green beside the sink.

"Oh, you know... sounded good at the time." I snickered. "Always sounds better when you're staring at someone like Bardot."

"Yeah, she's hot and fun, but is she hot fun?" He looked at me and waggled his eyebrows.

I stopped walking down the short hallway to the front and looked back at him. "What the fuck, dude? Is there a difference?"

He caught up to me and clapped me on the back. "Shit, bro, if I have to fucking explain it to you, you're worse off than I thought."

"Shut the fuck up and hurry." I stepped down into the stairwell of the bus with him on my heels.

"About damn time," Trotter yelled through the live mic, sending loud words reverberating through the venue. He followed it with hard strums across his blood-red Stratocaster. He treated her better than some people treated their own child and knew how to make it sing on her own as though his fingers were simple to hold it in place.

"Yeah, yeah. We're here, aren't we?" I picked up my bass and strapped it around my body, low and ready.

Crowns' rhythm guitarist, Kenzo, answered me with, "Some of us stay the fuck ready," and he launched into a riff Trotter normally played as lead guitar. Both played their parts in our band better than anyone Arch and I had ever performed with.

Other guitarists paid them mad respect for their abilities to create the badass music on our albums. But live music, well, it brought out a whole other side to them. That shit was un-fucking-believable. When the audience poured out the love in a show, it fed their need to show exactly what their guitars could do.

Trotter and Kenzo went head-to-head many nights on stage, but when both men and women cheered for them, the two created music together that most guitarists never achieved in their lifetime. I felt so damn lucky to be part of the sound they created, and so did Arch. The four of us had a vision when we started, and we're still chasing that vision every fucking night.

"One, two, three, four..." Arch cracked his drumsticks together, leading us into the first song we used to warm up and any last-minute tuning of our guitars. While we worked on the sound, I watched Kenzo drop paper on the floor for the roadie responsible for our set list, which he promptly taped down by each of our marks on the floor.

Kenzo finally announced, "Works for me," after we played the intro to a few more of our songs while the roadies did their final shifting of equipment and taping down cables and X-ing marks for us on the floor. He spoke into the microphone that flooded the auditorium with a deep voice.

Women loved it when he said words directly into the sound system that way—lips hovered all around the mic. He always dropped his tone at least one octave, if not two, and made himself sound like Crash, an old seventies DJ our parents mimicked. The low gravel tone melted panties almost as well as that panty-dropping smile he gifted the audience with when he finished.

The dude loved playing to the audience followed by the three of us shouting out some smart-ass remarks. We yucked it up with stage banter that drew in comments from the crowd. Doing so reminded us of when we played our fair share of dark dive bars. Some remarks back then let us know we had a long way to go to reach real fame, but we still got a kick out of it.

Handing off my bass to Raul, our guitar guy, I messaged Jones to remind him to get the pass ready and in place for Bardot. While I played the tunes this morning, I found myself constantly drifting back to last night.

Wonder if she's going to have fun being here tonight? I wanted her to like being around the madness we existed in daily. A new world would be opened to the golden-eyed beauty.

The solemn life she'd adopted on the water rated polar opposites from us. Why did I even give a shit? It's not like we have anything going for us at this point. I've never even considered settling down or even staying in one place long enough to grow roots but Bardot seemed stuck for life.

> **Jones:** *Yeah, man, got it handled for you.*
> **Me:** *Thanks.*
> **Jones:** *Been a minute since you asked for a pass.*
> **Me:** *Yeah.*
> **Jones:** *Just saying.*
> **Me:** *Chick's never seen us before. Making new fans.*
> **Jones:** *Right...*

Jones' comment was spot-on. I rarely ever asked for passes for women. Why bother? Enough of them found a way into the after-parties, and if we spotted one in particular we wanted, the security guys took care of getting them backstage for us.

Bardot wasn't one of those women. She made that pretty fucking clear when we went over to the other boat.

"What's with the shit-eating grin on your face?" Arch asked.

"Just thinking about how pissed Bardot was last

night when we got back from the other boat."

He nodded in agreement and let out a low whistle. "Dude, that girl rushed from zero to pissed in the drop of a fucking second. I thought she might try to hurt one of the women." He slid the drumsticks into his back pocket, and we returned to the bus. "Damn good thing we didn't ask to bring one or two back with us." His lips raised in a grin.

We stepped on the bus to find Jones sitting at the table working on his laptop. Before closing the screen, he tapped a couple more keys. "Okay, you're all set with this new girl for tonight."

Arch turned to me with a strange look. "I thought she only scored some tickets to the fucking show. Didn't know you planned more with her."

"I told her she'd get the VIP treatment for her first show."

"I said that before and it's still a good idea, since it'll probably be her only damn show, you know, since we take off tomorrow morning for New Orleans and all," Jones butted in.

I faced him with an exasperated look. "Dammit, I know we leave in the morning."

Jones enjoyed constantly reminding us about leaving. It was his subtle-as-shit way of keeping us from accumulating women along the way. Not that I ever did that anymore, but since some of the band did on the first tours, he felt the need to slip in digs here and there. Saying we accumulated a lot of 'things' along those first tours that created problems later looked more like *The Bachelor* collected willing women for their show.

He made sure we understood the old adage of love 'em and leave 'em. Hanger-ons only caused trouble. Groupies found their own way from show to show these days—no help from the band needed.

"Honestly, I was surprised when you wanted to go with Arch on a fucking boat anyway, much less find a piece of ass on one," he commented, looking up from the screen.

My head shot up, and I glared at him. "This girl isn't just a piece of ass, so don't refer to her that way. She's not like that."

Arch sprawled out on the couch with a bottle of water. "Naw, dude. She is *not* like that *at all.* Pretty fucking straight-laced as far as females we hang with go."

"Does this sound like a relationship kinda woman?" As I got water from the cooler, I felt Jones' eyes follow me, waiting for a reply.

"No one said a single fucking thing about anything like that, Jones. She's a nice woman who might like our show and hasn't ever been to one. Hell, man... she didn't even know who we were when we got on the boat. Thought we were from a badass motorcycle club or some shit like that."

This caught his attention. "A fucking motorcycle club?" He pushed up an eyebrow. "You two?" He threw back his head and laughed. The distinct feeling I was the butt of his laughter hung on in my head.

"What's so hard to believe about that?" Arch asked as though he were offended by Jones' comment. "We rode in on the Harleys you rented. Remember we had to leave them at the dock?"

"It takes a helluva lot more than riding a Harley to be in a club, dumbass," Jones commented as he typed a reply to a text that came through on his phone.

"How would you even know anything about it, Mr. College Boy?"

Without taking his eyes off his phone, he replied, "My brother's in one in New Orleans... that's how."

"No shit?" Arch's question sounded like he didn't know whether to believe Jones or not.

"I'm telling the fucking truth, bro. He's in something called NOLA Defiance. That's all I know too. He told me the less I know, the better."

"Dude, that's fucking awesome." Arch clapped him on the back.

"If you say so. Those people aren't the kind you want to be involved with. They're a fucking tight-knit group who look out for their own and no one else. Seems like someone's always getting killed or put in jail from one or another of those types of gangs."

"You mean like fucking Jax Teller kind of mean dudes?" Arch continued. Arch refused to let it go. I knew him, and he'd want all the details he could get.

"Hell no. That's some made-up shit for TV. Jax

Teller was a pussy compared to the shit that NOLA deals with."

"No fucking way. Teller was a badass. Killed his mom for dissing his old lady. And dude had all the women on and off the show hot for him."

Wanting to lighten things up, I said to Arch, "Bro, if I didn't know you only batted for one team, I swear you had a boner for Teller too."

"Fuck, you say. Bite your damn tongue. I only want the Egyptian pussy. You know... hairless."

Everyone in the band enjoyed harassing Arch about his sex addictions. He gave horndog a whole new meaning.

"We get it, but we've had this discussion before, dipshit. They aren't from Egypt. They're fucking Canadian cats," I informed him *again.*

"Yeah, but it sounds more authentic calling a bald cat Egyptian than Canadian."

"You're so full of shit." I laughed before drinking my water.

"Okay, that's enough. We all know which fucking way you swing." Jones calmed Arch down. "I'm just saying if all it took to belong to an MC was owning a Harley, there'd be so many it'd be nothing special."

"MC? The fuck is that?" I asked.

"They call themselves a motorcycle club, not a gang. MC... get it?" Jones informed us.

"Doesn't have any power behind it like calling it a gang does."

Jones shook his head and stood, collecting his paperwork and laptop. "I can see I'm done with work with you two jokers."

I stood and made my way back to my bunk. "Nothing to worry about with me. I'm getting some sleep. Barely got any last night."

Before I climbed in, I caught sight of Arch raising his hips off the couch, mimicking the deed, when he said, "Hell yeah, he's gotta get his rest for tonight."

I picked up a bottled water stuck in the side of my bunk and threw it at him, popping him right in the nuts.

He screamed, holding his junk. "You fucking douchebag." He bent over in pain.

"Serves you right if she's not that kind of woman,' Jones told him as he climbed off the bus and shut the door behind him.

I turned over on the narrow bed and pulled out my phone to play some music.

A text waited from Bardot, surprising me.

Bardot: *Hey.*
Me: *Hey yourself.*
Bardot: *About tonight...*
Me: *Right, it's all set up at Will Call. Come early if you want. I'll send someone around for you to bring you back earlier.*
Bardot: *Uh, actually...*
Me: *Don't even think of backing out. The*

limo will be there to get you at six.

Bardot: *But what if I have to work?*

Me: *You said you weren't booked.*

Bardot: *Sometimes there are last-minute trips.*

Me: *You have plans.*

Bardot*: I know but I need to make money too.*

Me: *Then I'll rent the boat out for the night and you won't have worry about it.*

Bardot: *NO NO NO*

Me: *:) I'll see you when you arrive then.*

Bardot: *Ugh, OK. I'll see you later. What about Arch?*

Me: *Fuck Arch. He's busy.*

I smiled to myself as I sent the last text.

He WILL be busy.

I'll make sure of it.

CHAPTER 11

BARDOT

While waiting for the car to arrive, it gave me time to wear a path on my apartment floor. Why in the hell did I agree to this? More than likely a last-minute charter would call in, and the scheduler would give it to someone else. I puffed out a hard breath. Not that it mattered as Gilley had plans for the night anyway.

A text came through letting me know my ride waited downstairs, so I hooked my tiny crossbody purse across my shoulders and locked the door behind me. Thinking about the wreck I left in my bedroom from trying on every stitch of clothes I owned made me angry with myself.

"Good evening, Miss," the older man said as I approached the fancy-looking old-lady car. Sleek black and longer than my entire den, the Mercedes sat crossways in the lot. He opened the door for me, and I slid in across the soft leather before buckling my seat belt.

My door shut, and I watched the man walk around and get in the front seat.

Did he do this kind of thing all the time for the band?

Pick up strange women for them to show off at concerts?

"My name is Joseph. I'll be taking you to the concert, and anywhere else you and Mr. Stoker will go tonight."

"Thank you, Joseph." The words almost stuck in my throat since I said it like I was some kind of rich bitch talking to the hired help. A slight throat-clearing cough happened spontaneously.

"Please feel free to open the small refrigerator. A bottle of champagne is chilling and ready for you. Or you might choose some water if your throat needs something less carbonated."

His formal speech made me smile. "Thank you." I leaned down and pulled out a mini water bottle and took a drink. Thinking about what I was getting into, I decided having some bubbly was a good idea. Just one glass to take the edge off.

The bottle was half the size of a normal champagne bottle, so I finished it off as Joseph zipped in and out of traffic into Houston. "The champagne was good, Joseph."

"Very good, Miss Bardot. Happy to hear it was to

your liking." He grinned at me in the rearview mirror.

Miss Bardot sounded so strange when he said it out loud. I couldn't remember hearing it said that way before. If people addressed me, it was just Bardot or Miss Bohen, but that rarely ever happened, either.

Before I found myself thinking about my mother, Joseph turned into the parking lot, announcing we had reached our destination. "We're quite early with the traffic so light this evening. I've been instructed to take you to retrieve your pass from the ticket window first."

"It's no problem. I can get it myself and find my way around."

He turned and looked at me. "No, ma'am, I'm afraid I can't let you. Mr. Stoker gave me very specific directions. I'm to retrieve the pass, drive you around to the buses, and deliver you directly to him and only him."

I raised an eyebrow looking at Joseph in the mirror. "Oh really?"

"Yes, ma'am. He didn't want you to get, uh... sidetracked by anyone else along the way."

Sidetracked, huh? What was he afraid I'd do? Or someone else, for that matter?

"Okay, we wouldn't want Mr. Stoker to get mad now, would we?" I replied in the best formal voice I could muster. Mr. Stoker would be hearing about this. Did he think I wasn't capable of finding my way around a big building or something?

Deliver me to the devil himself, Joseph, I thought to myself.

I put the VIP pass lanyard around my neck. All kinds of other tags hung from the clasp. Joseph slowly picked his way through the people before coming to a gate that allowed us behind the scenes and away from the fans trying to catch a peek of Copper Crowns. Loud screams began on the other side of the gate behind us as the car stopped.

"Who are they screaming for, Joseph? I don't see anyone."

"I believe that would be for you."

"Me?" my voice said in a higher octave than usual.

"They probably believe someone from the band is going to get out of your car."

"Wow, are they going to be disappointed," I whispered since Joseph had stepped out to get my door that faced a row of buses.

When the door opened, high-pitched screams got louder and louder until I stepped out. One very pointed, "Who the fuck are you?" greeted me when Joseph shut the door.

"Do you think I should wave or give them a one-finger salute, Joseph?"

He looked back at the crowd and then at me again. "I believe I'd do neither, ma'am." And he smiled just a little with the answer. "One never wants to play down to the level of besmirched hot air, Miss."

It took everything in me not to laugh out loud at his

word choice, but I stopped myself. Instead, I followed his advice, kept my head down, and stayed on his heels to one of the huge buses. The nondescript outside served as a façade for the elaborate inside.

Rolling down the highway, no one would suspect the luxury I discovered when I raised my head to see what lies down the length of the huge home on wheels. Most houses I visited didn't hold a candle to this place. Leather furnishings, quartz counters, and even a chandelier hanging over the table greeted me.

With wide eyes, I stood staring at the finery these guys lived in daily while my meager apartment had the basics. If this was what Wix expected when he came to see me, he'd be sorely disappointed. Rock-star lifestyle mimicked a few of the vessels in the harbor. Mine was nicely rigged out but not elaborate as the true yachts that slipped in for overnight stays on their way to bigger and better places.

Arch jumped up from the sofa. "Lookie who we have here, guys. It's the one and only Bardot Bohen in the fucking flesh." Yep, Arch being Arch.

"Hi." I gave a little wave to the others sitting around the den area. They had to be the rest of the band and a few others.

A man with his hair in a bun stood and came toward me with his hand out. "Hey, I'm Trotter. Nice to meet you."

I slid my hand into his, and he shook it with gusto. "Happy to meet someone our boy, Wix, thinks is worthy of gifting a pass to. Doesn't happen too often these days."

All I could do was nod. His comment tumbled around in my head. *That's good to know.* There wasn't enough time to really think about it, though, as a dirty blond stood and almost touched the ceiling. His face looked like an Abercrombie model. Damn, how did all this hotness end up on one bus?

"Kenzo. Glad to meet you." He took my hand in both of his to shake it. I felt smooth skin until the ends of his fingers glided across my palm. The callouses scraped at my skin. He had to be a guitar player to have them built up so much.

"It's great to meet you all," I replied to the bunch.

Arch spoke up, but I caught sight of Wix coming from behind a door down the long hallway. "Oh, you're here. That's great." He came to the front and kissed my cheek in greeting, which took me by surprise.

"I was about to introduce her to Jones back there. He's the one responsible for getting your evening arranged for our boy here," the drummer informed us.

Wix gave Arch a look, and I wanted to laugh at them. I wondered what was with 'the boy.'

Jones waved from behind a table where he worked on his laptop. "I'd get up, but with all of them standing between us, I'd pay hell getting by. I'm happy you made it in plenty of time."

"Yes, thank you for arranging the evening for me.

Having a car pick me up turned out to be a treat." I grinned at Jones. He needed to understand how out of my realm a car was but that I appreciated him providing it.

"No problem at all." He returned my smile with one of his own that appeared genuine, if not flirtatious, with the tone he used as he delivered his line.

"You ready for a fun night?" Wix asked, leading me toward the back of the bus. I wondered exactly what he thought I was here to do, but when he opened the sliding door and a leather wraparound couch took up the entire back of the bus, I let out a breath I didn't realize I held.

I giggled out loud and nodded my head.

Giggled. Really, Bardot? Are you twelve?

"Yes, so ready. I'm already having fun and only took a ride in a limo."

"Great, great." He rubbed his hands together. "I wanted you to see how we roll."

Glancing around at the plush surroundings of sleek polished wood and marble, I couldn't help rolling my eyes. "How you roll, huh?"

"I caught that eye roll. I meant down the road. You going with a sassy attitude tonight?"

"More like smartassy," I added with a slight smile.

"Hey, I can work with that. At least I know you're happy to be here." He sat in the turn on the sofa that followed the curve of the back of the bus, leaving me to sit on one side or the other of him.

"It's more than happiness. I'm thrilled, with a side of anxious." With a shake of his head and a pat to his left, he indicated where he'd like me to sit. It felt like manipulation.

Before I had time to think, Arch yelled down the hall, "We can still see and hear y'all, you know."

Wix jumped up and closed the door, blocking the view in both directions. "Sorry about that." He slid back into the same spot as before.

"Damn, dude, you didn't have to close it because of me," Arch continued to butt in.

Nothing was going to happen between us. At least not before the show, so closing it made no difference.

"You didn't have to close it for me. I'm okay with them being right there where we can see them," I offered as a way out to the closed door.

"No, but if I didn't, they'd all eavesdrop on everything we say. Next, they'd be adding some dumbass comment, and then they'd be slipping back here to join us. I know how they work. They'd make it seem all fucking innocent when really, they planned it all along."

I turned toward him. "They like to be included in everything you do?"

"Every fucking thing," he responded by laying his arm across the back of the sofa and picking up a lock of my hair before running it around his finger and sliding the hair easily back out. Slight tingles shot up my scalp, making my body shiver without meaning to.

"Sorry. Does that bother you?"

My head automatically shook from side to side. When I looked up at him, I saw the deep gray had returned in his eyes. How did he do that?

"Your hair just looks soft and begging to be touched. Look what I got for my efforts." He reached down to pick up a coil the size of his finger. My hair had body to it that didn't require much to take the waves to curls. The constant humidity and sea spray required me to use lots of product, which I hated to spend money on, so pulling it into a bun was always my go-to.

"Yeah, blame it on my dad. He blessed me with this texture."

"Well, feel lucky because both times I've seen you I wanted to touch it. Didn't seem right on the boat." He took another crooked finger full of strands and curled it again, increasing the tingles, but this time, they ran straight down my spine. I don't remember this ever happening before.

I'd been with men and learned my lesson the hard way while I should have been gossiping with friends at sleepovers or attending birthday parties. With my mom gone and my dad to make decisions like that, I found a lot of bad things to get into and paid the price in the worst of ways. But I learned valuable lessons about who I was meant to be.

"We only have a few minutes before we'll have to be rushed inside. I wanted to have some time with you before the madness begins."

The darkness rambled around in his pupils. I didn't know what he expected, so I said, "Tell me something about yourself that we didn't talk about when Arch was around."

Wix responded by pulling the next few strands to get my attention. "Searching for dirt or stupid knowledge?"

"I don't know. Just something I might find surprising."

He turned straight forward and stretched out the long, lean legs hidden behind tight black jeans. "Let's see. I write most of the music for our songs. Kenzo writes the lyrics."

"I always thought it came together like someone wrote and sang it."

"Sometimes it does but not with this group of social misfits." We both laughed at this until he followed up with, "In a lot of bands, the lead singer and another member write lyrics and music. People assume since the damn front man sings it, he writes it, but that's bullshit."

Wix's tone told me how passionate he took the music, and it made me happy to see it. On the boat, he kept to himself and wasn't much better when we docked. He talked and added things to what Arch said but seemed reluctant to do much sharing.

"So how do you do that with a bass? Isn't it like notes and stuff? Do you play other instruments?"

He jumped up and opened a hatch above us, taking a regular-looking guitar out. Honestly, I knew so little about instruments. I only took a few piano lessons when I was young. Anything he told me, I'd probably believe. I'm not that trusting of people, but maybe I'll learn something from these guys.

But they're leaving tomorrow, so I'll add it to useless knowledge.

My black-haired hottie sat down, causing the tight jeans to stretch across his thighs. Ripped holes pulled but he must be all muscles because not a bit of skin came through the tears. He sat the wooden-looking guitar across his lap and started strumming across the strings but then stopped and turned the knobs on the end of the long bar under the strings.

"Why are the knobs all the way down the long bar?"

He looked at me like I spoke Greek or something. "What?"

I pointed to the knobs. "Aren't those to help tune it?" He nodded, still staring at me.

"Then why aren't they down there where the big part is? It would make so much more sense."

His eyebrows moved up his forehead like he was still trying to translate my foreign language. "I see you're not learned in the ways of the guitar, Padawan."

"What?" Is he making fun of me? "And what the hell's a pada-something?"

Wix almost fell off the couch, but his guitar was in the way.

Whatever, he pissed me off.

"I can leave if you're going to make fun of me."

"Sorry, sorry," he said as he tried to straighten his face. "You don't know guitar or *Star Wars*, huh?"

I stood and looked down at him. "Fucking forgive me for not being some music savant or talented or keeping up with stupid movie characters. There are a shit ton of things I can do that you can't. Put me in the goddam ocean with a twenty-foot sailboat and a compass, and I can find my fucking way to land. I bet your dumb ass can't do that." Each word got a little louder so that by the time I reached land, I was yelling.

Wix dropped the guitar, surprising me, and took a step toward me. "Wait, wait, wait... I wasn't trying to make you feel like you were dumb. You've just never been taught, that's all I'm saying. I bet you could master it if you took lessons. You're super talented on your boat and can make lots of strategic moves at one time that the guitar would probably be a snap for you."

"Well, what if I don't want to play a guitar?"

"That's okay too. I'm just saying you'd probably be great at it."

I turned toward the door. "Maybe I should go."

"Oh, kiddos, you already having a lover's quarrel back there? We hear her yelling at your dumb shit from here."

"Shut the fuck up, Arch," we yelled in unison while my nose almost touched the door and him right on my back behind me.

I spun around. When did he get so close to me? His hands reached out to steady me or stop me from going. I don't know which.

"Look... I'm sorry, okay, Bardot? I never meant for it to sound like I was making fun of you. I just never... never... knew anyone who didn't know about music." Warm palms and long fingers held my biceps, keeping me close to him.

There was no escaping from the situation without pushing him, and I found myself not wanting him to move away from me. I stopped with my back against the door and slowly lowered his mouth to mine.

The kiss happened differently than I pictured it in my head. I couldn't throw my arms around his neck and pull him closer. He held me wedged between him and the door with strong arms keeping me still. I might have felt trapped, but since I wanted it to happen, the situation seemed more domineering than I thought Wix would be.

Behind closed doors, though, who knew?

What I did know is it ended way too soon.

His smooth lips pulled back, and he watched my eyes as they rose up to meet his. The turbulent clouds moved back and forth between mine as if he only dared to look at one at a time.

I realized my labored breathing sounded ragged, so I tried to calm down by holding it. That lasted about three seconds because when I didn't breathe, he took my lips again, but this time he let go of my arms and moved up to my cheeks. Fiery hands shifted my mouth where he wanted it, and I let it happen like my head was free from my body.

He held me in place and slid his warm tongue over my bottom lip before nipping it.

He wanted in.

But did I want to offer this invitation?

Did I dare allow entrance now?

Too soon.

Way. Too. Soon.

CHAPTER 12

WIX

"Dude, let go of your girl back there already. Time to go," Arch interrupted the moment.

I glanced back down at Bardot and realized I still had her against the wall.

"All right," I yelled back, mostly because I hated that the dumbfuck ruined the moment. Holding Bardot this close and feeling her warm body against mine made me want to stay here forever, but I knew it was only a brief encounter. She responded as though she enjoyed the kiss. I mean, hell, she didn't push me back or try to slap me.

When she looked up and smiled, I knew it was all okay *for now*. I never really knew with a woman like Bardot. It had been a long time since I was with a woman who came to me because of me and not because of the band.

"Guess we better open the door," she spoke softly. "He'll probably be banging on it if we don't." And she smiled again

"You're right about that. He sure knows how to ruin a minute, huh?"

She nodded and moved her hand to the latch, flipping it open, so I moved over and let her pass before me back into the hallway.

"About damn time. You two are gonna make us late for the show." He laughed as he said it because we're never late when we are *the show*, which was a running joke among us. Someone always made us *late*.

Jones stepped on the bus, looking down through the middle directly at Bardot and me. "You ready?"

"Sure thing, bro. Let's do this thing." I moved forward, pulling Bardot behind me, and the others fell in line behind her. The last thing I wanted to do was let go of her in the melee about to happen once we stepped off the bus. We never knew exactly what to expect except that a shitstorm always occurred somewhere before we reached the stage.

I didn't want Bardot to be scared off before we strummed a single chord. Our after-parties had a way of causing unsuspecting guests to freak, so I definitely didn't want anything to happen before our set.

The fans didn't disappoint. Particularly females. Between the posters, loud screams, and vulgar offers of various body parts these women were willing to sacrifice to get their hands on any of us, I was shocked to turn and see the beauty with me still smiling. Maybe this shit shocked her speechless.

Our next steps were my least favorites. I loved our fans, but sometimes they made me hate this business. Their enthusiasm for all things related to the band caused some to act like the biggest damn fools. There was nothing some of them would stop at to get to us— ripping clothes, baring breasts, dropping panties to throw—and this transpired nightly.

Some people had no shame, and it showed when we took one step toward performing a show. All of us, including Jones, had become accustomed to it, but I knew Bardot would never understand them. Even with the little bit of her background she'd shared so far—and I wanted to learn more about—nothing about her screamed groupie. She possessed more self-respect than they would ever have.

When we entered the back doors and the guard slammed them behind us, we stopped long enough to make sure everyone made it. More than once, one or two of us got captured by a wayward fan who managed to slip past the bodyguards. Jones nodded, and we continued down the long hall to the rooms designated tonight for Copper Crowns.

The guard opened the door to the first room, where we found a crowd gathered around the spread laid out for us to nosh on. The opening band stood around waiting and looking eager while the second one played their hearts out on stage. No doubt, the newbies had been hated on by other big bands. We invited them to stay if they wanted to hang out and talk.

We experienced a lot of negatives opening for bigger bands when we were virtually unknown. Some were nice, but others were the worst dickwads to all of us little guys. They refused to allow us even in the room with snacks much less drinks. If we were lucky, someone would hand us a bottle of water when we came off stage. Jones handled that for us back then.

The entire band agreed without any arguments that if we made it big, we'd treat our opening acts like they were as important as we were. Who knew when that shit might come back to haunt you? Nowadays, when we happened to be at a festival playing with acts equally as popular, we made a point to call them out on their shit. All of us would laugh about it on the bus later.

Little things like that stuck with you. We wanted the respect that came with earning it, not because people knew our names.

One guy, who looked like a teenage version of myself, came over with his hand out to shake. "It's great the band let us in here tonight."

I took it and gave him the bro hug. "No fucking problem, dude. We were there once."

"Yes, I guess everyone is in the beginning."

Noticing right away he couldn't take his eyes off Bardot the entire time he spoke, I decided introducing her might prevent a situation later. These guys would be opening for us for a few weeks, so maybe their paths would cross again. Houston was their hometown which left the possibility of their meeting again. Not sure how I felt about that.

My eyes turned to her. "This is my girl, Bardot."

"Oh, hey, I'm Cameron. Uh... Cam." He put out his hand for her too.

Shaking it, she uttered, "Nice to meet you, Cam. You're from Houston, right?" He nodded. "I'm from Houston also. Well, Kemah."

His entire face lit up like neon in a roadside bar window. "I'm from Seabrook. Damn, we're practically neighbors." Just what I feared happening. *Cam* was enamored with the first look.

An easy laugh floated from Bardot. The stars in the dude's eyes needed to be extinguished, but I didn't know how she felt about me staking a claim on her.

She let go of the hand I was holding and put her arm around my waist. "Yes, we are, Cam." Her head bounced as she looked over his shoulder to the other two guys with him. "How about the rest? They from the Kemah area?"

"Yeah. Uh... we're all from around Clear Lake."

"You go to the Lake, Creek, or one of the new high schools?"

He instantly deflated. Poor sap. Without even knowing it, Bardot pushed him into the kid's section. *Good for her and me.* In a heartbeat, these guys became nothing to worry about. Thank God because I'd hate to resort to a fucking beatdown over her at this point.

"Uh... Lake. They went to Creek." The look on his face said it all.

"Great. Surprised y'all get along since they've been rival schools forever."

"Yeah, none of us were that big on school. More like social misfits."

"Hey, that's like a band, right?" Bardot turned to me, thinking to impress me with a band's name.

I pulled her to me and kissed her forehead. "Good going, sweetness. Yes, Social Misfits is actually a Christian band from Miami, I think."

"Y'all play with a Christian rock band sometimes?" Wide eyes stared at me with her question.

"That would be a big *hell no*, but we have run across them at festivals. They're popular in the south, and since they're rappers, we wouldn't be booked together. But I have to say, the things you know surprise me."

"Hey, I'm not a total music loser. The boat does have a radio and Bluetooth speakers."

Arch walked up behind Cam. "Making new friends, Bardot?" The dumbass had to address her instead of me.

"Yes, I am." Her light and happy tone made me feel good because all I wanted was for her to see the best side of the business and not the seedy side. Backstage had a way of showing the worst of bands and the damn groups who circled them.

"These guys are from my area of Houston. Maybe they'll play somewhere locally, and I can see them live," she said, looking between Arch and me like she wanted to rile us up.

Arch stuck out his hand, "Hey, I'm Arch. Friends with the lovely Bardot already, huh?"

"Cam." He nodded over his shoulder. "That's Clark and Ethan." The latter of the two raised a hand and waved.

"Great. Hate like hell we missed your set, but I'm sure we'll catch ya in a couple of days. Got a lot of fucking time to hang around and hear shit over the next few weeks."

We all nodded in agreement. "Listen, Bardot and I are going to the dressing room. Good to meet you three." I nodded at them all.

"That's code for a lot more shit's about to go down in the other room, but don't forget we all need to get ready." Arch wiggled his eyebrows.

"You think like a damn fourteen-year-old, Arch, so shut the fuck up." I gave him a pointed look before swinging Bardot around and heading for the door.

Sweet laughter came from Bardot as I shut the door behind me. "That was pretty funny back there."

"What? That I called Arch out on his shit or that you put the children in their place as far as you're concerned?"

"I did not. I was making conversation and trying to make them feel comfortable around 'Copper Crowns.'" She air quoted. "Being in royalties' presence must be intimidating for young, new bands." She plopped down in the center of the couch, leaving me no choice but to sit close to her, which I was more than pleased with.

"We try hard not to come off as a bunch of douchebags, especially with new bands. We were there, and we damn sure remember the people who treated us like we were dirt under their shoes."

Emerald eyes cut to me before turning her body and bending her knee toward me. Without knowing it, she erected a barrier between us. My need to touch her grew the longer we were together, so this wouldn't work to have something between us.

"I wish everyone in the boating industry felt the same as your band. Getting ugly looks and being talked down to is still the norm for me. Not a single week of my adult life have I spent not trying to prove to someone that I'm more than competent to do my job."

"That's harsh. Seems very unfair since you have mad skills when it comes to that boat."

"I know, right? But I'm telling you, sometimes it happens daily that someone asks me about my credentials for being the captain, especially after they see Gilley down below."

I picked up a curl again and wound it around my

finger while she spoke. Her almost black hair and mine were about the same color, but hers was soft and smooth, whereas mine had a more wiry feeling. Hers curled around easily, and if someone tried, they'd have to force mine to make a curl. And then there was the shampoo she used—warm vanilla and citrus. I couldn't decide which it was, but either way, it left an impression I wouldn't soon forget.

"Don't you have a license or some official shit like that?"

"Of course. I have a skipper's license and several different levels of it. It all depends on the length and weight of the boat."

"And you've spent all this time acquiring them only to be questioned like you're a kid?"

"Yep." She popped the P, making her look young and cute, but I'd never say it with the information she was sharing. "No matter how far women have come, we still have to fight in a man's world, and I'm willing to stand up for the few of us who are in the nautical world. Anyway, I don't want to think about boats tonight," she admitted. "The opening act isn't going to be with y'all for long?" She turned her body back to face forward, which allowed me to move in closer to her after I wrapped my arm around her shoulders and rested my hand on the smooth skin of her arm.

"No, they're only coming for a month or so. I'm sure it'll be a financial burden for them to stay out too damn much longer. That's usually the kind of shit that stops new bands until they get signed by a label."

"So, Jones doesn't rep them too?"

All I wanted to do was kiss the words out of her. The longer she talked, the less time we had alone.

I leaned in close to her ear, speaking softly. "No, he only works for us now."

Bardot slowly turned her head toward me, and our lips drifted closer together as she licked hers. We'd kissed already, so this shouldn't surprise her. I wanted more than just the feel of her sweet, gentle breath wafting across my face.

We met in the middle when her lips slid across mine. God, so soft, so smooth, so warm. My tongue slid to the seam keeping me out, but this time she allowed me a quick entrance.

It took everything in me to not pull her in my lap and do dirty things with her, but I don't want to have to stop before we even got something started. Her heated tongue danced around with mine, twisting and licking. I savored every second of the feel of her.

With her arm wrapped around my neck, she deepened the kiss, surprising me. I was down for it, so I pulled her in closer. I loved how her skin was soft but taut under my touch. I wanted under her clothes, but now wasn't the time, so I settled for ending the kiss and worked my way down her neck, dropping gentle kisses along the way.

When I reached a spot below her ear and bit down easily, she gifted me with a faint moan that caused my cock to twitch hard behind my zipper. I knew it was headed to a full-blown hard-on and fast, but I couldn't get close enough to her like this, so I gently tugged where my arm rested around her waist. She responded by climbing over, straddling me. *Damn, I liked the way she thinks.*

"Knock, knock," Jones bellowed, barging into the room, causing Bardot to practically leap to her feet in front of me. Her green pupils dilated and were sexy enough to make me want to pull her to me again. Dammit to hell and back. What's with the fucking bad timing these people who call themselves my friends have.

"Sorry, lovebirds, but we need to finish up in here and be ready. The second act just counted off their last song. It'll only take a few minutes for the team to trade out the few pieces of equipment, and they'll be ready for you." The rest of the band slipped behind Jones. "Chop, chop, get moving." The six of us crammed together in one room.

I hated it when he used that antiquated expression. Wasn't it politically incorrect with all the other phrases that were outlawed?

"I need to go," Bardot stated and headed for the door.

Stopping her midstride, I pulled her back to me. "No, you don't. We're not going to do anything special. Maybe change clothes or something, but..." I looked around at the others, and no one responded. "See, no one's even changing for the show."

Bright green eyes glanced around the room. "Don't y'all have stuff to say and ritual type, weird shit to do? Oh, and guyliner? I've read rockers like to use it."

The four of us looked around at each other and busted out laughing. "What the hell, Bardot?" Arch gets out between taking a breath and laughing. "Are you shitting me? We're not AC/DC." Another round of hysterical laughter began.

"Okay, okay. That's enough. You do need to warm up your vocal cords, guys," Jones announced, ending the best laugh we've shared in a long-ass while.

I looked over at her beet-red face and felt guilty for laughing at her. This woman was so out of her fucking element with us, but she gave it an honest effort to fit in.

"Knock it off, assholes. Bardot worked hard to be here tonight. The least we dumbfucks can do is make her not feel like an outsider."

CHAPTER 13

BARDOT

God, I hated being pushed outside my comfort zone.

Mixing it up with these guys went so far from anything closely related to that small space. When Wix told them not to make me feel like a stranger, I knew he understood. Socializing with these guys took my life to a whole new level.

"Oh, come on, Bardot. We were only fucking around. If you're gonna hang around with our boy here, you better learn to take the fuckery that comes with the band," Arch jokingly stated.

I knew right then he spoke the truth. Their lives compared nothing to mine. *So did I even want to pursue anything with Wix?* Not that he indicated there'd be anything more than what we've shared so far. *Do I want more?* Decisions about where this might go needed to be determined before I ended up being the one hurt. Believe me, I saw hurt written all over this situation if allowed to happen.

Glancing down where our hands linked, Wix's fingers squeezed mine before I faced him. I felt him anticipating something from me. An answer. A response. A letdown. Does he care enough to be disappointed?

My eyes trailed up his arm to his beautiful face. Damn, he melted panties with that look. But what about me? *Did he melt mine?* Yes, I believe he did. Not five minutes ago.

"Now fuckery is something I can get on board with, guys," I answered them with a grin.

This earned me another round of loud cackles and guffaws. "I knew she was A-fucking okay," Arch added.

"The only drawback is if shit's dished out, be ready to receive it too," I amended my answer for the rowdy group.

"Bring it, little girl."

"Bring. It. On."

"Paybacks are gonna be fun."

I wasn't sure who said what, but the three band members commented at once while we laughed together. Wix pulled me forward and wrapped his other arm around my neck, drawing me in close to his body, then stuck his other hand in the air for a high five which I gave him.

"You won them all over in one sentence, babe." He kissed my forehead and hugged me tightly.

"Bonding's over, dudes..." Jones informed us, "... and dudette."

Trotter spoke up first, "Ain't nothing about her that resembles a dudette, so she's gonna need her own band name."

"She does, but she has to earn it, so we'll be listening and watching," Kenzo added.

A nickname sounded fun, but who knew how long I'd last around them? I wasn't going to be their new groupie. With my job being full-time almost year-round, our visits would be few and far between if there were going to be any outside of Houston.

I needed to give this a lot of thought before I allowed myself to become invested in whatever *this* was. *Once bitten, twice shy.* I had the bitten part down to a fine science, thanks to my teenage days of monumental mistakes.

I would never allow myself to become caught up in those types of problems again.

Never.

***

The guys worked their way to the stage, moving through the groups of people while Jones led me to the best spot to watch, perched on a platform above. Scaffolding hugged the sides, back, and above the band's heads with various equipment. It all looked overly technical, so I knew someone designed or engineered all the sets for the band. That person had a difficult but probably rewarding job once the show kicked off.

Jones introduced me to people along the way responsible for making the show happen, even the guy on the platform I climbed to stand on. Kyle paced along one side with a headset, two different radios, and a phone attached to him. With him busy, he had no time to talk to me, and I didn't dare interrupt him. Who knew how many people he had speaking to him at once?

An announcer walked to the microphone at the side of the stage once all the new pieces of equipment found their place for Copper Crowns.

"Our headliners don't need an introduction because it's them you paid the big money to see." The audience laughed in agreement. "So, let's hear it for Copper Crowns."

My eardrums felt pierced by the loud screaming from the enthusiastic audience. No doubt female voices carried for miles away from the venue. As I looked out across the sea of faces smiling at the band, I realized all of them probably knew more about the guys than I did.

This many women and men took the time to listen to their music, seek out their concerts, and pay to see them perform. Never had I been to a big venue like this to hear a band, and yet, here I stood, watching thousands of excited fans eager to finally see them.

A wave of considering myself 'one lucky girl' ran through me, and it only took until I stood above four hot-as-hell guys looking out to finally realize maybe I've been hiding away from the world.

Had I clung to the boat for too long, and for what? Security? Anonymity? Refuge? Fans from one area of Texas paid big money for tickets to enjoy one night of fun while I worked to alienate myself from society.

What price did I pay for it?

Losing my parents cost me more than I ever knew until this moment. The toll for their absence was steep, but then so were some of my bad decisions when Dad was still alive. Those choices hurt us both in ways I never dreamed until it was too late, and his time was up.

Maybe I should have tried to be a part of something other than the water after he left me. Salt sea spray became all I knew, but why hadn't I taken a minute to see other things?

An overwhelming yearning for my dad hit me as I stood still beside a stranger.

"You okay?" Kyle asked aloud, but I had to read his lips to understand.

I nodded at him. The sound deafened me, so there was no reason to try talking. He spoke into his headset again, and I heard Arch count off the first song with his sticks hitting the beat.

What began as screaming fans calmed down to the music of their first song, one I was familiar with.

YouTubing their music helped prepare me for the moment, but nothing compared to listening to the melodious sounds of Kenzo and Trotter.

"Your first time to see them?" my platform companion asked, leaning in close to my ear. He had ditched his headset. His part in the hard prep work must be done.

"Yes, and it's amazing. Live music sounds so much better, don't you think?"

"They put on a fucking awesome show. If you're only going to see one this year, this was the band to see."

"You're a big fan?" I replied without taking my eyes off Wix.

"Who isn't?" His face lit with an easy smile. "But yeah, I've worked with these guys for a while now. And you?"

"Just a new friend of the band." After I said it, his smile turned to a knowing look I didn't appreciate. I knew I'd answered the question wrong. He assumed I was some new slut they planned to enjoy after the show.

"And by that, I mean... they invited me after spending time on the sailboat I charter and wanted to share this experience with me as I had mine with them." My explanation was a mouthful of knowledge, and once more, here I was explaining myself to a man. *Again.*

"That sounds exciting, bet the guys loved it." His

gaze hung onto my face for longer than necessary. "Hey, I didn't mean anything offensive. It's just that they rarely have anyone up here, so it made me think you were someone, uh... special." He did a great job of backtracking to cover his ass. Wix explained the women before to me, but Arch was a different story. He had a manwhore reputation I didn't want to add to.

"I'm here at Wix's request. He loved sailing." Yes, I reached for this, but Kyle didn't need to know that.

"Sounds like a wonderful way to spend a lazy afternoon to me," he added. "I was on a big boat ages ago when I lived in Texas."

I nodded as the sound from the floor grew louder. Kenzo walked to the microphone and started talking for the first time between the third and fourth songs.

"Hello, Houston fucking Texas." Screams and yells bombarded the arena. "We're so damn happy to be here tonight in your great city. It's been a minute." More screams. Trotter strummed across his strings, adding a funny sound.

"Yeah." He nodded at Trotter. "We always find Houston exciting, and we meet the best people here." Trotter turned, looking up and straight at me, which caught the attention of the small section of the audience who could see me. Thank God it was only a few.

This earned the guitarist a series of drumbeats from Arch and some deep twang sounds from Wix.

Who knew each instrument had its own way of talking? That's exactly how it came across, as though each one replied to the lead singer.

Following that break in the music, the band performed almost nonstop. Trotter or Kenzo announced a few songs along the way for people like me, I'm sure. The audience knew their music, and Kenzo even invited them to sing along with them on a few choruses.

I couldn't wrap my mind around how that must have felt to perform before thousands of fans who all knew the words as the band struck the notes. What a feeling of pride the guys must gain at each show. Nothing in my life even compared to the experience. A quiver moved down through me from simply thinking about it. Notoriety gave them a sense of importance and belonging, something I hadn't had in a few years.

Before I knew it, Copper Crowns worked their way off stage after their second encore. They handed off instruments to the roadies and waved at their wailing fans. Kenzo, Trotter, and Wix threw pics into the crowd before Arch lobbed two sets of drumsticks as he was the last off stage.

Two females fought over the last stick, but one quickly gave up in an effort to catch Arch's eye.

Hmm... she must have known he often picked someone to come backstage.

Her loud yells and a piercing whistle made him turn to spot her. His head tipped to one of the security people, and the drummer pointed at her, earning herself more time with the wild drummer.

I'm not sure if Kyle knew or not, but him letting me go down the steep ladder first made me feel better. The last thing I wanted to do was climb down with my butt cheeks in his face if he went first, and I followed. The short jeans skirt I considered wearing would spell disaster right now.

My feet didn't touch the floor when I came to the last step because strong arms came around me and tugged me into a hot body. I circled my hands on Wix's wrists and felt the heat rising from him. Playing bass guitar might seem to have no physical aspect to it, but what seeped from him into me was pure male body heat.

His body vibrated like the strings of his guitar as he wrapped around me from behind, and I wasn't anticipating that feeling. If Wix still had it strapped to him and he placed me between him and it before strumming a chord, I knew my soul would throb. Tremors would start in my core and allow him to play me like a love song.

Until he finally allowed me to slide down his ripped torso, my body felt suspended in the air. Hot pleasure built inside me with every slow inch he allowed me to move. My heartbeat grew faster, louder in my ears until I thought I might experience a heart attack on the stage floor.

When my ear passed in front of him, he latched his

teeth on the rim and let it tug ever so slightly as my feet made contact with the floor.

We heard a throat clearing, making us realize Kyle had waited to jump down from the ladder.

"Sorry, dude. Just happy to see my girl here. Thanks for taking care of her up on the platform." Wix stuck his hand out, the two men shook before someone called Kyle's name, and he took off to do his job.

"Well, what'd you think?" His voice was soft and undemanding, but warm breath fanned across the sensitive skin he'd awakened with the raw scraping of his teeth. He spun me to face him.

It took a second before my brain registered that he'd spoken, but the fire inside me kept me from answering for several beats. My eyes blinked in slow motion with his stunning face staring at me. The turbulence in the gray orbs created feelings I didn't know existed between a man and woman and certainly never in me.

His cut jaw, high cheekbones, and kissable lips no doubt captured the attention of all the women he encountered. And yet, I stood attached to him by strong arms and a look that held me immobile.

Not other women, but me. *Me*.

"I... I... I thought it was the best I've ever heard or seen."

He snickered. "Oh yeah? How many have you heard or attended, Bardot?" he repeated back to me.

He burst my bubble with the embarrassment I felt

since we both knew I had attended so few in my life.

"Sorry, I didn't mean to cause that beautiful shade of pink to heat your skin and work its way up your neck, but I gotta tell you, watching it happen created all kinds of other thoughts about you up here." He tapped his head. "And maybe the other head too."

I swallowed the remaining liquid, making it difficult to respond to him. Blinking back thoughts I didn't know what to do with, I simply gave him a ghost of a smile.

Jones, once again, interrupted by barking orders for the band to move to the room for the meet and greet backstage.

"Come on. I need a minute before facing another crowd." He released my body but grabbed my hand and pulled me with him as the entire band moved off the backstage area and into the same long hall we'd come in from.

Another new experience awaited me involving his fans.

My heart fluttered a bit when I realized I'd do this while attached to him.

CHAPTER 14

WIX

"Kenzo, Trotter, Wix, Archie," fans yelled out like they always did when we passed them in line, waiting to get inside the large room.

Taking Bardot into the dressing room with us, I glanced at her as we all changed into clean T-shirts without sweat drenching them. Everyone in the band took the time needed to keep in shape. Under the stage lights, performing drained you if you weren't in top shape to handle it.

We knew of plenty who turned to drugs to keep up the pace. A line of coke here and there became common when we toured with other bands. Outside of smoking a joint or downing a handle of liquor, our band decided to lay off the drugs from the start. Watching other bands burn out early in their careers or spend months out of each year in rehab told the four of us all we needed to know.

Some mornings I woke up and thought just a quick hit would make my fucking life so much easier, but then I remembered friends in the business and how they ended up. Those ideas went by the wayside. We worked too hard to get here. One wrong bump or swallowing a pill could take it all away.

Arch pranced around the dressing room showing off for Bardot, who hardly looked at him, making me laugh.

"What?" Arch asked.

"If you're trying to impress Bardot, just fucking stop, bro. She's seen your weak-ass pecs before."

Saying her name caused her to look up from the phone she played on while we cleaned up to meet our fans. "What?"

Arch took her question as an opportunity to jump. "What?" He faced Bardot. "I was just sprucing this body up to show our fans we cared enough not to stink up the room. Your fucking boy over there couldn't keep his eyes off this body." He motioned up and down his torso. "I mean, I realize it's a hell of a lot to take in for some people, but damn, dude, you've seen me butt-assed naked." Arch intentionally flexed and showed off the six-pack he'd developed.

My eyes rolled, and I threw a waded-up towel at him. "Stop showing off, dipshit. She's seen you shirtless before, remember?"

"Yeah, I know, but sometimes females need a

second look to capture the full concept." He flexed his biceps. "See, Bardot. These guns always get the ladies."

Bardot finally spoke, putting my friend in his place. "And just like the first time... not impressed, Arch. Only this time there's not a boat full of barely dressed minors to see you."

Her comment caught Kenzo's attention. "What the fuck, Arch? Minors? You want to risk going to jail? You know the rules about teendoms."

"Couldn't make me touch one these days." Arch hung his head. "Damn, that makes me feel fucking old."

"For a minor, you are old. Now get ready. We need to go," Kenzo stated as he reached for the doorknob. "Our adoring fans await, sir." He ended in the worse English accent ever spoken.

The other two filed out behind Kenzo with Arch looking dejected. Bardot stood and followed the leader, but I grabbed her hand and swung her back to me with a strong pull. She fell into my arms, right where I wanted her.

"Perfect," I uttered before my lips landed on hers in a hard kiss. I'd waited long enough. The entire time I played on stage, I thought about what I'd like to see happen when we were done.

With the adrenaline running high from the set, I wanted nothing more than to push her up against the wall and fuck her into next week. Hard and fast. Give us both something to look forward to more of later.

I reached under her thighs and pulled her legs around my waist before backing her into the closed door with an "oomph." Her back hit the wood, and she deepened the kiss. Our tongues danced around while we quickly explored the body parts we could reach on each other.

My dick strained against her warmth as we pulled and pushed to get the friction we sought. We broke the kiss, and I made my way down her neck to her collarbone. Her head leaned to one side, allowing me better access as she dug her feet into my back, trying to get me closer to her center. It would never happen with all these clothes on, and dammit, we didn't have time to remove enough for me to do what I wanted right now.

A knock on the door caused us to look at each other, our breathing hard and labored. "Well, fuck. Guess that was our personal invitation to the party," I spoke while nibbling down her neck.

"Pick up where we left off later?" Bardot whispered, surprising me with her boldness.

"Hell yeah, we will," I said with a smile.

She unlocked her ankles and stood, then straightened her clothes. Her hands had been in my hair, but fuck it, I didn't care how it looked. Let them think what they want for fucking up a good time.

"Mirror?" She moved across the room to look at herself when she spotted it. I moved in behind her and put my arms around her, staring at our reflection.

"What I wouldn't give to have you right here, babe. I want to watch you in that big-ass mirror while I fuck you from behind and tease your clit until you scream obscenities, my name included."

Her fiery eyes gazed at me through thick lashes, and I knew she was down for my suggestion without saying anything in return. My lips caressed her neck before I pulled skin in my mouth. Needing to leave my mark on her now caused me to grind my hardness into her peach of an ass.

"No, don't leave a mark where others can see it," she complained, slapping a hand around her neck.

"Where would you rather I put it?" I wiggled my eyebrows.

Her face turned pink, but before she could voice her answer, Jones yelled through the door he popped open. "Stop whatever it is you're doing and get your ass to the party." He slammed the door behind him.

Reluctantly, I let her go but took her hand in mine as we left the dressing room. I knew the shitshow we were headed into. After-parties were part of the package, and I hoped it wouldn't prove too much for Bardot.

"You ready for this?" I raised my eyebrows and questioned.

She mirrored my look. "Should you warn me ahead of time?"

My eyes scanned her hot body. As many males as

females would be inside, everyone looked to pick up someone for the night. Bardot wasn't one of them, and with her around, neither was I. Nothing stopped aggressive groupies. If it meant they earned a notch of sleeping with a rock star, they were down for sharing.

"Probably so but take it as it comes. Just remember at the end of the night, you *will* be leaving with me."

Her head bobbed while I threw open the door. Music blasted louder. I knew my brothers preferred it low-keyed, but the partygoers wanted the sound loud. Damn, if they didn't get their way every fucking time. Sometimes I wondered if these people wanted their eardrums bursting to make us get closer to have a conversation. Closer led to touching, and touching always got out of hand in some fucked-up way.

The door closed automatically with our bodyguard, Duke, standing beside it. Pulling Bardot closer to me, I wrapped my arm around her waist, leaving no space between us. My message needed to be sent loud and clear, even if I had to lay a big wet one on her in the middle of the room.

Leaning into her ear, I whispered, "If you leave my side, make sure one of the guys or Duke is at arms' length, please."

Bardot turned and looked hard at me before she scanned the room, locating each band member. *Smart girl.*

"Planning your escape?"

"I'm not a Boy Scout, but I'm always prepared," she

informed me with a cute smile that gave her a mischievous look. "Maybe I have other plans." This time her eyebrows wiggled up and down. *Damn, this woman did everything to keep me hard.*

We moved over to join Arch and a busty brunette standing by the food table. "Dude, you two need to meet Val." He gestured in the woman's direction.

Bardot stuck her hand out, expecting the cat-eyed vixen to respond, but Val never took her fucking eyes off me. Rudeness was never attractive in my book, and I knew Arch hated bitches at these parties.

As soon as he saw her lack of manners, he pushed her away from him. "Find someone else to fuck. I'm not it," he announced loud enough for everyone in the room to stop what they were doing and stare. The disrespectful phony should know with that announcement, her chances were over with any of us. If she was lucky, she might attract a roadie to have sex with her, but my brothers knew what his announcement meant.

We didn't make a step because Arch's words told Duke what he needed to know. Before I could turn to him, the guard clamped his meaty fist around Val's arm and escorted her out.

"What the fuck?" she yelled at Arch.

Duke whispered directly in her ear and opened the door, sending her to the hallway before slamming it in her face as she tried screaming down the house. It served her fucking right for treating my girl like she was nothing because right then, she was everything.

"No one likes a mean bitch at our parties," Arch told the two of us. "Have some respect," he yelled toward the door.

Bardot watched the scene play out without saying a word. The look on her face as she dropped her hand beside her was enough. I knew she wasn't used to being treated this way, which is why I didn't want to attend the party, but the radio station sponsoring the event wrote it into the contract.

"Sorry about that, Bardot," Arch addressed my beauty. "I'd never let her cling on if I'd realized what she was."

"It's okay. I just wasn't expecting it."

He looked at her with a wary eye. "Me either. It's definitely not a perk of the business. But hey, the night is young, my friend. 'The night is still young, and so are we,'" he rapped Nikki Manaj's lyrics. This caused the whole room to burst into the talented rapper's song's chorus for a loud sing-along for a couple of minutes.

Arch dropped the words to the rap by taking a long draw from his longneck. I knew the look he gave Bardot since I'd given it myself. Her innocence to the ways of these women willing to do anything to get into the after-parties made him think for a change.

Aside from the contest winners or radio executives, beautiful women did whatever it took—sucking dicks, public sex, kissing unknown rivals. Nothing mattered to them. Why would they lower themselves to have no self-respect in the name of getting laid by a celebrity?

We grew tired of it after a few years in the public eye. Our boredom didn't stop us from getting all the pussy we wanted, but we tried to be more selective these days. I realized when I met Bardot that she'd never fall into the category groupies were in.

"Let's make the rounds and leave," I told them both, so my girl wrapped her arm around my waist this time and held on. Arch fell in behind and joined our brief conversations as we made small talk with people clustered together. Talking to groups made this chore go faster and kept some women away.

As we worked our way toward the door, Jones appeared behind me.

"You trying to slip out of here?"

"Hell yeah. I've had enough," I informed our manager.

"You need to try to stay at least an hour. Have a drink, get something to eat... whatever it takes." He kept his eye on Bardot most of the time he spoke. I knew he wanted me to mingle with the guests without her, so I appeared available, but tonight I sure as hell was not. I invited her here, and I'd be leaving with her.

"Bardot, don't you want to get something more to drink and snacks?" Jones had the audacity to ask her directly.

"No, she doesn't," I answered for her. "She's here with me, and I don't want her exposed to these fucktards, especially alone." I never took my eyes off Jones, who had pissed me off with his suggestion.

"She won't be alone. I'll hang out with her while you shake a few hands," Jones continued.

I knew better. The minute my back was turned, he'd ditch her to make another contact. The man did a great job with the band, but sometimes, he went too far. It looked like tonight would be one of those times. I rarely kept women around or invited specific ones to come to these, and he knew it, so he should have been more agreeable.

"What the fuck is your deal, Jones? You know she's my guest."

"Right, but you have obligations tonight to other people as well," he replied in a matter-of-fact tone as his eyes roamed the room.

"Oh yeah? Well, fuck that. We're outta here." I turned, nodded at Arch to let him know we were out, and moved us toward the door.

Jones took notice of our departure and stopped us. "Wait, wait. I'm sorry I came on a little strong. The band really needs to meet one guy before you take off. It's truly important."

I didn't respond, and neither did Arch. "Come on, guys... just one man. Won't take five minutes."

Arch and I exchanged looks and decided we could do one handshake. Jones did all he knew to keep us successful, so we needed to spare him the time. I pulled Bardot with me, but Jones stopped us.

"Let's have Bardot wait there with Duke. He'll keep a close watch on her."

I felt my eyebrows shoot up without even trying. What did he want us to do that she needed to stay behind?

"Five minutes, please," Jones begged, which was a first. This dude he wanted us to meet must be something important for our manager to stoop to begging.

Bardot spoke up this time, "It's fine, Wix. Go on. I'll wait right here." She pointed to the open spot beside Duke. "I'm sure I can entertain myself for five whole minutes." Her lips tipped up at the ends, making her face light up. *Damn, this woman killed me with just a look.* What was that all about?

"Duke?" I pointed at him. "Watch her for me."

"I'm not an errant child, Wix. I don't need a babysitter," she interjected before Duke could say a word.

Duke nodded, and I knew he understood, so I leaned in and pecked her on the lips. "Be right back."

"Let's do this thing and get the fuck out of here," Arch told Jones.

"This guy has a tremendous opportunity for the band to do something new."

"Oh yeah? Like what?" I asked.

"Yeah, what haven't we already done in the biz?" Arch interjected.

Jones looked us over as we approached a man in a

custom suit tailored to his body. The dude was the only one dressed formally for an after-party.

"Mr. Knox, this is Wix and Arch from Copper Crowns." The man stared at us as though we were aliens but then smiled and put out his hand to shake ours.

"Mr. Knox owns Paradise Productions. He flew in from Austin to meet the band."

"Great to meet you," I replied. Arch did the same. I didn't have a fucking clue who this guy was, but Jones had a boner for him for some reason.

"Men, good to finally meet two members of the band. My daughters are huge fans, and they're the ones who actually came to me with the idea that might be very beneficial for all of us. The girls have been looking for a project to take on since their last was extremely successful."

I didn't have a clue what Mr. Knox referred to, so I simply nodded and smiled before glancing at Jones. The poor dude looked like he was about to blow his load on the spot.

"The band is more than willing to sit with you and your daughters to discuss the possibility of making a docudrama about their rise to the top of the rock-star royalty, Mr. Knox."

Jones' sentence quickly cleared up the mystery. He'd wanted to do some movie shit with us for a while. I assumed it would be done with clips from our tour and maybe a small number of fill-ins from us but not an entire docuseries. That shit could take weeks or months to pull off. Something would suffer as a result, which is exactly what the four of us had explained to Jones.

Now here we were making small talk with a producer. *Fucking Jones.* He knew better than to corner us like this.

Arch finally spoke, "Yes, Mr. Knox. The band needs to meet with your company and see what this plan looks like for Copper Crowns."

His comment took the monkey off my back to come up with something intelligent to say about a project I wasn't ready to get behind.

"Great, gentlemen. I look forward to it, and so will my girls. Always trying to please them." His smile spread across his face. No doubt, these two held Daddy's heart.

And now we not only had to suck up to this guy, but we'd have to please the daughters too?

Did Jones just fuck us over or what?

CHAPTER 15

BARDOT

As Wix and Arch talked with an older man dressed out of character, considering the others in the room, I leaned against the wall watching. The guy looked ready to address a boardroom full of big wigs and too formal for my taste. Give me boat shoes and tank tops any day over some stuffy suit, even if it looked designer-made.

"You know the boys long?" Duke asked without turning his head in my direction. His job was to keep the band members safe. I noticed he'd rarely taken his eyes off them as he scanned the room, anticipating trouble before it happened.

I moved closer to avoid yelling over the talking and music. "Just a few days. They did an afternoon cruise on my boat."

"Oh, right. I drove them to pick up their bikes, but

they insisted they could take it from there. Must not be too many fans hanging around the docks."

"No, at least not in the yacht club where we moor the boat." Duke made it sound like my baby lived in a shipyard or something, so I set him straight. "That doesn't mean Arch failed to find some on the water, though." I snickered, remembering the boat full of bikini-clad females he spent quality time with.

"Right, I understand. That man can find women anywhere he goes."

Turning to him, I cocked an eyebrow. "Oh, he did more than find them."

Duke laughed at my comment, causing several in the room to glance in our direction. Obviously, he knew the guys well.

Does he spend every moment with them when they tour? That had to be intrusive on their lives. I wasn't sure I could live under someone else constantly watching me.

"What about you? You been with the band a long time?" I asked, not really caring, but small talk seemed like the right thing to do. The band's security didn't know me, so it was easier for me to engage in twenty questions than him.

He ran his palm over his smooth head. "Yeah, I've been with them since before they were a band. We met as kids. Went to school together. I chose the Marines while they drove their neighbors to drinking with the noises they made in the garage before working their way up to a few local dive bars."

"Thank you for your service. I'm sure you learned a lot about watching people who might have it out for this wild bunch while you defended something far more important." I respected the women and men who gave their time, and lives in some cases, for volunteering to serve. That form of commitment required more bravery than I could muster. Not for something so important.

"You're welcome, and yes, I did learn a lot about guarding another person's life in the Marines, but I never thought I'd be using it for these guys." A smile ghosted his lips. "I was lucky they brought me on when I returned. The band's fan base blew up about the time I got out, and they realized after a few mishaps they needed security."

"Lucky timing for everyone," I added with a smile. It made me feel more at ease talking to Duke. Maybe we both felt somewhat out of place in the room full of important people.

Wix whipped around and headed back to us, leaving Jones and the other three talking. The news must not have been what he wanted to hear—the anger on his face stood out as he worked his way through the crowd toward me.

When our eyes finally connected, his look changed to a smile that lit up the room, stretching wide across his face. Heads turned and followed him back to where I waited, making me feel like I'd won the jackpot for the night.

Yes, bitches, he's going home with me.

"You ready?" he asked as he slid his arms around me and gave me a hard kiss for everyone to watch and be jealous of. All I could do after he broke it was stare at his deep gray eyes since he stunned me into silence from the power of the kiss.

I finally came to my senses enough to nod my head in agreement. Thinking was completely out of the question. No one should have that type of power over another with a simple kiss, but there I stood, wrapped in strong arms, navigating the depths of his turbulent stare.

With his voice barely above a whisper, he uttered, "I can't wait to get you alone." And with that, he turned to the crowded room and, in full force, announced, "My girl and I are taking off for the night. See ya down the road." He took my hand, waved at the group with the other, and we slipped out the door.

We made our way through the long hall, Wix holding my hand in one and his phone in the other. He fired off a text and then looked at me. "Car's on its way." All I could do was acknowledge him with a smile, my body still on fire from the kiss he'd laid on me.

"Did you get some bad news back there?" I finally asked, coming to my senses.

We reached the outside door, where he pushed it open only enough to see outside, looking for our ride.

This move obviously meant to scan for fans who might prevent us from sneaking out of here since Duke didn't follow us to the door.

As it closed, he turned to me. "Yeah, it was news, not sure how good, though. A media company from Austin wants to do a docudrama about the band."

"Austin?" That would put Wix close to me for a longer time. I needed to decide if this was a good thing for us or not.

Wait, Bardot, we are not *an* us.

When did I start thinking like that? We'd *never* be an *us.*

"Yeah, with access to huge, big-ass warehouses in the old airport. They shoot a lot of videos there nowadays. I've been reading about some that are made and then presented at South by Southwest. Like a Sundance film or Cannes or something."

"Oh, I've heard of that. It's a huge Austin event with movies, books, music, and other media. I've been told by some clients to avoid Austin at all costs during South By. I had to look up what South By meant." Listening to clients talking helped me gain a lot of outside knowledge since listening to the news and reading useless shit on the internet never made my list of time-wasters.

"Yeah, they usually just spell out SXSW in print, though." He peeked through the doorway again. "Where's our fucking car?" His impatience gave me other ideas.

I urged him toward me until he stood close enough for me to find the tanned skin of his neck, where I began leaving soft kisses moving up to his face. He stopped what he was doing and pocketed his phone. My mind raced through all types of things we could be doing besides waiting patiently while my libido grew more impatient by the minute. Wix had a way of ramping it up and then letting me down in a heartbeat. *Was this a new kind of foreplay?* Not a fan if it was.

With my arms around his neck, I tiptoed closer until my body lined up to his, then kissed and nipped my way up his neck. Little love bites always started a frenzy in my body, so I prayed it did the same for him.

I don't know what got into me with Wix. Maybe it was the fact I hadn't had sex in forever and, if truth be told, never had great sex, but something about him said a night with him would be all that and more. Like stuff-that-dreams-were-made-of more. Like wake-up-in-the-middle-of-the-night-breathing-after-I'd-run-a-marathon more. Damn, I needed this. I needed him. Tonight.

Before anything else happened, we both heard the car driving up. Dammit. But I planned to continue right where I left off in the hallway, minus any prying eyes.

Wix opened the door, and I stepped in, slid over a smidge, and waited for him to join me. As soon as he closed the door, he barked at Joseph, "Take us to the—" he stopped and looked at me. "Where do you want to go?"

My mind went all over the place. "I have options?" I threw him my sexiest smile. At least in my mind it was.

Wrapping his arm around my shoulders, he pulled me closer to him. "Sweetheart, there are always options." His eyebrows wiggled a few times, causing me to smile even more.

"Well?" I needed to know what he thought our choices were. In my mind, we could go back to my apartment which wasn't the first place that sounded like fun. There was always a hotel nearby, seeing as we were in downtown Houston. Then there was the band's bus, but that might be limited on space, and others might barge in. I didn't want that to happen, so the bus was out.

He gave me a quizzical look, and I knew he considered all the things I rattled off in my head and maybe more. I had limited experience in this game, so who knew what he could come up with?

"Do you have an early cruise tomorrow morning?" he asked.

"No, I purposely took that charter off the books when I decided to go to the concert. I... I didn't know what time I'd get home. I mean, who knows how long bands play at their shows." My voice stammered through the explanation when I realized I rambled from a slight case of nerves.

A beautiful smile lit up his face. *God, he was too hot for his own good or my own demise.*

"How about we go to the hotel room I have for the night? It's close by, and you seem kind of anxious. When you're ready, we'll take you home."

I felt my left eyebrow move upward. "When I'm ready? What if... what if I'm never ready?" It was a ridiculous question, but he rolled with it.

"Mmm... good to know. I might never tire of you either, so you'd be kidnapped and stowed away on the bus with us. You should know, though, the bus can get rank sometimes with all men on it."

"Eww. No, I'd rather be aboard my boat surrounded by water and clean air than stuck with a busload of testosterone and sweat." I wrinkled up my nose, making Wix laugh hard.

"Okay, that settles it." He hit the back of the driver's seat. "The Laura Hotel." The driver tipped his head and made his way out of the parking lot, leaving us at the mercy of streetlights barely illuminating the inside of the limousine off and on through the darkly tinted glass as we passed under them.

I wanted to climb him like a mast but tried to focus on the road ahead until I felt him watching me. His warm hand moved to my chin and he turned my face to his. "What happened to that girl in the hallway?"

"Oh, you know. She didn't know if you liked being mauled in public, so she decided to hold off until we got to the hotel."

"Now that's a shame because I really enjoyed the aggressive Bardot. She's quite unusual when she's not being herself. Did the music excite you?"

I felt his hand trace downward from my cheek while one finger continued along my jaw and down my neck, ending between my breasts, causing the peaks to stand at attention, waiting for his next move.

"Ye... ye... yes, it did. I mean, some of the songs sounded like they were made for sex."

"That they are." He moved around to face me. His voice was deep and rough, probably from the performance, or maybe he was as excited about our time together as I was. "Sometimes when I wake up in the middle of the night from a, uh... *vivid dream*, I'll record lyrics or hum a melody on my phone." He kissed down the line he traced with his finger, starting over at my chin and stopping at the hollow of my throat before descending lower to my cleavage.

Damn the shirt I wore. Why didn't it button? His smooth tongue slid down between the tops of my breasts, making my need for him grow that much stronger.

We both realized the car sat still under stronger lights when a knock sounded at his door before springing open by the hotel doorman. Wix let me go and stepped out, only to offer his hand to help me.

Leaning in, he whispered in my ear, "Guess we were a lot damn closer to the hotel than I thought."

I smiled, thinking the same. Good thing I didn't

climb him like I wanted to.

His soft voice warmed the skin on my ears. "Yeah. Not enough time to do anything we'd be regretting right now, especially since the dude opened the fucking door so fast. He might have found us in a compromising position. Social media would love that."

My eyes cut to him, and I felt my face heating up since that's exactly what would have happened if I carried through with what I wanted to do.

"Why, Bardot, were you thinking of compromising me in front of my fans?" he asked with a concerned look. His words scared me. My head jerked around, thinking people were watching us. We'd only had a taste of it in the venue, but who knew what would happen here on the sidewalk in front of this five-star hotel?

Luckily, no one stood around other than the few bellboys who watched every step we took to the doorway. They recognized Wix but didn't bother us by coming forward to talk to him. I knew this hotel saw many celebrities when they came to Houston. Society news staked a claim here often to report on important visitors who chose to stay there.

"This is a nice hotel," I told him. My heart raced as I spoke in anticipation of what the rest of the night held.

"Yeah, upscale places are more than accommodating when it comes to celebrities who might mention them or bring the press. Free PR always makes them happy to have them."

I wanted to laugh at his comment. He used them instead of including himself in his statement. Was this him trying to come off as humble, or did he really not consider himself important enough to attract a crowd?

"Oh yeah, right." I nodded, finally thinking of something other than the guy who had my hand. "Hey, where are the others?"

"What others?" Wix asked as we moved past the concierge desk toward the elevators.

Finally realizing we were the only ones here from the band, I replied, "The rest of the band and all the other people who travel with y'all."

"Oh, they're all on the buses. They may leave after it's all loaded."

My mouth dropped open, and Wix pulled me into the elevator, where he stuck his room card into a slot below the buttons. "Wix, why aren't you on the bus too?" My voice climbed an octave.

"Because, sweet Bardot, I wanted you all to myself tonight." I felt myself slowly being backed up against the wall where he captured my lips with his own in a kiss that caused my toes to curl. When he finally pulled away, only to work his way over to my ear, I asked, "But don't you need to go with them?"

"No." That's all he said before he bit down on the skin just below my ear, licking his way to my collarbone with the tip of his tongue. My skin lit on fire until his teeth bit down. I knew tomorrow when I saw the marks, this night would flood my head with sweet memories.

And that this would go down as one of the best nights ever, if not *the* best.

CHAPTER 16

WIX

Every glance in Bardot's direction made me want her more. Something about this woman called to me more than any other woman I'd been with. Her strength to move forward in her life after losing her parents at an early age amazed me. Where most people would have been lost, she buckled down and kept trudging ahead. Her ability to run her boating business showed her determination to live life on her own terms. No way in hell would I have risen to her level under similar circumstances.

We tumbled into my room, pushing and pulling each other in a frenzy to get inside, remove our clothes, and get to know each other more intimately. My need to be inside her had my throbbing cock straining behind the zipper of my leather pants I always wore on stage.

I ended up ripping her shirt. Who cared? I'd buy her another, but right then, I couldn't stop myself. She peeled my pants down my legs before pushing me backward on the bed to get them off my feet. Damn leather.

"Why do you wear these things?" Her words came with a struggle and rosy cheeks, but I didn't know if it was from exertion or need. In my case, it was definitely need.

"Management likes them. Says they make me look good under the lights. They're supposed to be cooler or some shit like that." I pushed with my other foot, trying to help her. "God knows our stylist always makes sure they fit like a second damn skin."

Finally, we're both down to our skin. I propped up on my elbows and saw sweet Bardot standing between my knees looking at me. What a vision. Waves and waves of thick dark hair framed her beautiful glowing face, the color making it more pronounced. I couldn't take my eyes off her. More than that, her perk tits with dusty pink nipples stood out, begging to be adored.

My voice dropped an octave with desire trying to consume me. "Come here, Bardot." I curled my index finger, beckoning her to me. Her eyebrows rose slightly as she placed one hand on her hip, followed by her eyes drifting downward to where my thick cock masted, waiting for her awareness. The hard shaft strained to be the center of her world.

When she had her fill of looking me over, I again crooked my finger, but this time she placed her knee on the end of the bed and began a slow crawl up me. Her hands gripped my ankles and rose inch by inch, slipping past my knees, then thighs, where she squeezed the strained lateral muscle that mimicked every other muscle in my body.

Her face hovered, looking down at my aching cock as it twitched to capture her attention. Warm breath blew over it as she exhaled, and I thought I'd lose my battle to wait, take it slowly, and let her lead for a bit.

"You're killing me, sweets." She grinned as she sat back on her calves. *Little minx.*

With her hands kneading the lats she seemed glued to, her face turned more serious. "You think this is torture?"

"Yes, both of my heads do." My words caused her to grin again.

"Then just wait until I do this." Her hands, hot from the rubbing and squeezing, wrapped around my length and gave it a tight tug up and down.

My eyes rolled back for a second. *Keep it in check, Wix.* "Death by anticipation, Bardot. It can kill a guy, you know."

Her fisted hand repeated the action. "Oh, you think so? I was unaware anyone died from delayed gratification. I've read what guys like to do to women because it makes the climax so much better for them. You know, like edging?"

Listening to her talk made matters worse. I could *not* take her bringing me to the brink and not coming. I'd die a slow, horrid death.

I grabbed her hand and helped her continue the physical torture by squeezing down harder as she worked my cock over. If she wanted this to happen first, who was I to let her down? I knew I'd still be hard after coming on her hand.

Bardot had other ideas, though, as she leaned over and tongued my head around and around while we tormented the shaft together. I moaned loud enough to be heard in the lobby.

"Does it hurt, Mr. Rock Star?" The innocence in her voice made me open my eyes and stare at her.

"No, but it sure makes me want to take your control away and finish this tor—"

Before I finished the word, her mouth took me in and descended downward until I felt the back of her throat. Before I could voice my surprise at her ability, she withdrew and did it again, swallowing as she pushed the rigid flesh further back. What the fuck?

"Ooohhh, baby. Ohhh. Ohhh. Ohhh. Oh my fucking God. What are you doing to me?"

The tongue-lashing she gave me was unlike any other I'd had before, and I'd been with a lot of women. Who taught this girl to do that trick? Bardot had some explaining to do, but that had to be later. Right now, my eyes only had whites showing, and my entire body responded with muscles clenching and releasing in places I didn't know would do it.

"I can't take it, Bardot. I'm gonna blow in your throat if I don't pull out."

She moaned something as she sucked down hard, and that was it. I came so hard as the upper half of my body rose off the bed in a way I know I looked like I was doing crunches. My abs contracted with each powerful stream that gushed out. I honestly had no idea what Bardot was doing because I was too far gone mentally to even be able to notice.

All I knew was when she popped off me, another rush came through my body from the sensitivity my dick still felt. There was nothing left to jet out, but no one told my dick that. I felt like I was going to have another load to bust.

A shiver crawled over my body before I opened my eyes. *What the fuck?* I wrapped my hand over my eyes and rubbed them with my thumb and index finger. Talking seemed out of the question. There was so much I wanted to say to her, but her actions fried my brain.

Not being able to speak yet, I stuck out my hand and waved her upward, needing her smooth skin on mine. The bed barely moved when she crawled beside me and rested her head on my chest as I wrapped her under my arm and around her back, pulling her in as close as I could. Her foot slid up my leg, but she was careful not to go high enough to touch my finally deflating dick. Guess she knew exactly what she did to me with that surprising performance.

This girl held so many mysteries inside her.

Where did she learn to give head like that?

Who taught her?

Because I don't think the internet gives up that kind of information, even on the best porn sites.

The problem is this girl is no porn star. She's too reserved, too quiet, too something. I don't know what, but it's not triple X-rated by any means. Usually, I didn't care what women did before I had them, but Bardot presented me with so much intrigue now, I needed to know more.

Her background would have to wait for now. She'd just blown my mind, and now it was my turn to catch her up with me. I turned and kissed the top of her head before moving my hand under her chin to look up at me. The gold streaks stood out from the green, and up close they radiated the golden veins I hadn't noticed before.

"We're going to revisit what you just did to cause me to black out that way, but right now, I need more of you." I leaned down and connected our lips, hers swollen from before, but I licked around the edges of them, seeking entrance. She complied with my request as I rolled over on top of her sweet naked body.

The skin-to-skin contact was like nothing I'd felt before. My body gave a slight shiver from the touch for the second time. My entire body felt like she had injected me with the power of a bolt of lightning. It wasn't normal. In any other instance, I'd think she'd done something wicked to me, but I knew better.

Ending the connection, I kissed, licked, and bit my way down her neck, over her collarbone, and rubbed my body down hers until I reached the swollen peaks waiting for me to adore them. I let my tongue circle the outer edge of her nipple, grinning as it responded by pebbling into a harder peak. Squeezing the plumpness of the smooth flesh, I sucked down on the needy nipple while continuing to circle it with my tongue.

My teeth wanted in on the action, so I scraped them over the taut skin as I pulled off the peak with a light bite. Not enough to cause much pain but enough she knew I'd been there. Her body twisted and strained upward as I caught the other between my lips and showered it with the attention it needed. Definitely one of her erogenous zones. She responded to every touch I made, from breathing my warm breath over the skin to nipping at the tip with my teeth.

"Wix, you're driving me crazy. I'm gonna need you to get on with this." Her hands moved to my shoulders, and I felt her pushing me down and snickered.

"But your tits are perfect. I want to make sure they're taken care of."

"Hey, I'm glad you feel that way, but I want more."

My hand slid down her skin as I moved off and over

to her side, never allowing our bodies to part. "I love your skin, Bardot. It smells amazing, and the softness... I can't even think of words to describe it."

"That's great. You smell good too. Now, can you, uh..."

It took a lot not to laugh at her eagerness, but I wanted to touch every inch of her. "You know, babe, I want to get to know every single spot on your body that causes you to react the way you do when I nip at these beauties." I kissed the peak right in front of my face.

"Okay, I'm good with that, but maybe later. It's been a long time for me, and I really want you."

I traced a light touch down her taut stomach, circling her navel as I nibbled on the skin below her breast. Sliding my tongue down her body, it followed the same path as my fingers. They skimmed lower to the dark, trimmed patch leading to the promised land.

With nips and bites, I worked my way down, stopping to look my fill before slipping my finger in to find the bundle of nerves that poked slightly out of her lips from swelling. "Someone's anxious to have attention too."

"You think?" Her words left her on a groan as she pulled her opposite knee upward. "Please, Wix. This is torture."

My tongue lapped at her clit as my finger moved lower to circle her entrance. "Woah, someone *is* ready for me." I glanced back up at her, but her eyes squeezed tightly together. I knew exactly what I was doing to her, but after the blow job she gave me, she deserved some torture too.

Bardot whisper-groaned, "So ready, please." I felt her bent leg shake a little as I worked her over with my tongue and fingers. Inserting two into her tight channel, I moved over her attacking her clit with sucks and lashes from my tongue. This caused her to writhe and grab the low headboard above her as though she was hanging on for dear life.

My fingers moved in and out with all the molten fluid slipping from her, so I added another finger, scissoring the tightness open more. Turning them upward, I found the rough patch I sought, sending her upper half off the bed with a scream.

"No, no, no. I can't take it."

"Hmm... most women would say yes, yes, yes, sweets." Her channel contracted with my words.

"Fuck me. Fuck, *fuck*, *FUCK*," she yelled out.

I picked up the package on the bed and rolled it on without taking my tongue away, allowing her to come down from the high she floated on. Replacing my tongue with my dick, I moved it up and down the slick crevice, spreading the lubricant needed to move inside her.

Slightly pushing inside, she cried out, and I stopped. "Sorry, I'll take it easy. You said it had been a while. I don't want to hurt you, Bardot."

A protective feeling ran through me. I'd never want

to hurt her, especially not with sex. So, I eased in some more, but she wrapped her legs around me and pushed her hips forward, sending me all the way to the hilt.

"There, the pain's over. Now we can get to the good stuff." She eeked out on a breath.

I knew she wasn't a virgin, but the amazing tightness felt like she was making me wonder how long it had actually been. Thinking about her having sex with someone else caused me to plunge deeper and harder, wanting to make her only ever remember me. She was mine, and I refused to share her with anyone else.

"What?" I said out loud.

"What, what?" she asked as I continued my pleasurable blitz on her pussy.

"Thought you said something I didn't hear. You're so tight, babe. Makes me ready to come again fast and hard."

"I'm not complaining. Fast and hard is good with me."

Who was this girl? She loves what I'm doing but hasn't had sex in a while. *Why would she purposely not have sex when she clearly enjoyed it?* More thoughts for later.

I flipped us over where she straddled me. With my hands on her hips, I helped her move to give us what we both wanted. She rotated her hips, making me touch every possible part of her, especially the spot she wanted the most.

The spasms on my cock told me she was close, and I fought coming with everything in me, so I moved my hand to where we were connected. Touching her as she slid off and on me felt unreal. I spread my fingers on each side of my dick, feeling her skin stretch with each deep dive.

"What are you doing, Wix? That feels... that feels..." she choked out.

"Amazing?"

She bounced up and down, grabbing her beautiful tits since I had my hands full. My other hand left her hip and moved to her clit to work it over.

"Oh yeah, right there. Right theeerrreee," she screamed. "God. Oh God."

Her pussy convulsed on me, and that was all I needed to let go. I put my hands on her hips to hold her still as the condom filled.

Bardot finally fell forward. I wrapped her in my arms, holding her close. Neither of us moved. I couldn't or didn't want to let go of this connection. Of this minute in time. Of what we'd just experienced.

This complex creature presented me with a craving to spend more time to figure her out. At that moment, I realized our time together was going to set events in motion in a direction I never saw coming.

My mind told me beware.

But my body said differently.

CHAPTER 17

BARDOT

Damn, that was intense

I laid next to Wix, wondering what the fuck just happened.

Even if it had been a long time, I never remembered sex feeling like that before. Granted, he possessed talents and skills the few guys I had been with lacked, but still, that rated as some otherworldly type of sex.

"You okay?" he asked in a low, almost whispered voice after disposing of the condom.

"Yeah, you?" I felt his head nod before he replied with a soft, "Yeah."

A few seconds elapsed before he continued, "Don't think I've ever had anyone ask me that before after doing the deed."

"Anyone, huh?" I knew what he meant, but it

sounded funny as if he'd had sex with random sexes.

"Well, not anyone." He blew out a breath. "Any female. I'm not into guys at all, and I don't even like to share women with them."

"Good to know because I'm not into being shared either."

A soft laugh came from him, so I moved over some and rolled to look up at him. "Just saying, I'm not down for a threesome or an orgy or any of that wild shit."

"Yeah, like you said, good to know." His voice had gained some substance, and I knew he'd recovered. "So, what's going to happen now? I don't have much experience with this one-night stand thing."

"That's also good to know. I'm all for crawling between the sheets and sleeping. It's been a long day for the both of us."

"Works for me, too, considering I have the day off tomorrow or today since it's two in the morning."

He pulled up and leaned into me, kissing me senseless before crawling off the bed and sliding back the covers from under me. Returning, he stretched them over us before wrapping me in his arms again while I rested on his chest.

"Just so you know, Bardot, that had to be the most intense sex I ever remember having. Like... never before do I recall sex being so intense. I'm still trying to wrap my head around the experience."

"Yeah, I know what you mean." I thought it was just

me, but hearing him talk about it made those feelings even more real.

"Not that I'm complaining or anything. Just, well, it was deep and powerful, maybe even extreme. I'm not even sure I have the right words for it. I'm going to need to do that again, maybe to see if the words come to me."

"You're the songwriter, Wix. I sail boats, remember? If you're having a hard time with words, then I won't even try to find them, but you have to know, all those words you said, I'm right there with you."

"That's definitely not all your good at, though." He snickered and kissed the top of my forehead. "Not at all."

"I'll take that as a compliment of the highest order, then."

"Night." The easy word slipped from him as his eyes closed, telling me he was already asleep.

Going to sleep was the last thing on my mind. The exhaustion was real from all the hot sex, but my head drifted all over the place. His words led me to believe he looked at me as some young, innocent girl.

If he only knew what my life was like as a teenager and the trouble I got myself into, he'd be running the other way. I was anything but innocent. I honestly thought after the blow job I gave him, his idea of my younger self would change. Apparently not, though, from his comments.

True, I wasn't all that experienced in the actual sex act because of the consequences that followed it, but it didn't mean I was all that naïve either.

My fingers traced the lines of his tattoos decorating his chest as I lay there remembering my former life. The one I led when I had a dad who loved me unconditionally. My dad and I had a great relationship, but I needed more in my teen years.

The friends I chose to hang out with weren't good for me. I allowed them to lead me down paths that got me into trouble. Problems that adults needed to solve, not some kids who lived doing what they wanted, when they wanted. We all had parents who lived comfortably, not rich but nowhere close to poor.

Our troubles came because no one suspected what we were really up to. The sex, drugs, and petty crimes were just to see if we could get away with them. And for the most part, we did. At least until we didn't, and our parents were called.

The old busybodies tried hard to tell my dad, but he didn't listen. Lying here, looking back on our bad choices, I knew my problems came from losing my mom. I missed her so much, but I refused to let my dad in on that piece of information.

He hurt enough for both of us.

They were soulmates through and through, and I searched for someone to give me the same type of love she gave Dad. I needed to feel I had a purpose and wasn't just looking for a hookup. I wanted my own soulmate because if I could find someone to help fulfill those needs, I felt like I'd make it. Or maybe I wanted to show my dad he could make it too.

Someone out there waited for him to make himself whole again. Not that he was looking because he wasn't back then. Every time I mentioned it, he told me it was too soon to consider looking, even after several years had passed.

Now here I am at twenty-five, living a solitary life. I failed to find that someone back then, and I doubted I would now either.

As I watched Wix sleep, he looked peaceful and completely at ease. Gone was that stage persona he kept up while he talked to the fans and friends in the room backstage. The guy he portrayed on stage was long gone. From the moment we stepped into the limousine that brought us here, he turned it off.

I grinned to myself, thinking about him dancing around on stage in his tight leathers with his bass strapped low over his hips. He twisted and turned as he played the line that held the song together, along with Arch beating away on drums. Sure, Trotter and Kenzo attracted more attention than Wix and Arch, but their abilities kept them all together on a song.

Kyle explained all of that to me as we watched them from above. He viewed them for different reasons than I did, but he kindly gave me band lessons to help me understand. Maybe if I ever got to see

Copper Crowns play again, I planned to work on using the knowledge to understand what each guy brought to their songs.

Watching them tonight mesmerized me to the point I didn't care what they did. I liked however it sounded, however they moved, and however they sang and played. It was all right with me.

What I didn't like stood below them screaming and yelling their names. Lingerie flew on stage, landing at their feet. I watched Wix kick a bra across the stage to Trotter. He bent, picking up the lace and held it high, gaining more noise from the crowd before throwing it offstage to one of the roadies. What a job he had, catching bras and panties while Kenzo wailed on his guitar.

My smile grew wider.

All in all, this night rated as the best of my life, but now it was over.

Tomorrow Copper Crowns played in another city. More screaming fans, more underwear to dispose of.

Thinking about this made my smile fade.

I closed my eyes, remembering Wix standing on stage below me, his beautiful face looking at all the women.

I felt my eyes fill up with warm tears before I drifted off to sleep.

***

Something slowly moved across my leg. I barely felt it, but it was enough to pull me from the deep sleep I rarely enjoyed. When it happened again, I swatted it.

"Damn mosquitos," I muttered before drifting back off.

Feeling it again, I sat straight up.

I hated those pesky insects, but they loved me—an annoyance of living on the coast. Opening my eyes to search for it knowing I'd never go back to sleep until it was dead, I realized I wasn't in my bed or apartment or even on the boat.

"Looking for something, sweets?" a deep, scratchy morning voice asked.

Realizing I wasn't alone, I pulled the sheet up, covering my nakedness and then remembered who was with me. As I brushed my hair back from my face to see, I glanced over my shoulder at the god-like face smiling at me.

What a way to wake up.

Seeing that face every morning would make it worth it.

A dark five o'clock shadow covered his chiseled jaw, but his eyes caught my attention first. The light gray surrounded by thick dark lashes looked almost unnatural. I wondered if he changed contacts before I woke. They presented a huge contrast to the dark, stormy orbs when he hovered over me last night.

"How... how long have you been awake?" I managed to get out.

"Long enough to see you calm for a change." His warm hand made its way up my bare back. His slow ascent upward riddled my arms and legs with goose bumps. The tingle it left behind made me pull the sheet tighter to me.

"I'm calm a lot."

He sat up beside me, wrapping his arm around my back, resting his hand on my hip. "Cold?" he asked with a grin. He knew exactly what he did to me.

I shook my head and leaned over on his shoulder. "No, you know what you do to me when you use that calloused finger on me."

"Oh, you mean like this?" He ran his hand under the sheet and found my bare breast, making a ring around the nipple to make the skin taut and ache for attention.

A hard breath sucked in me as he continued his torturing circular motion, and a shock of desire shot straight between my legs.

Wix pushed me back to my pillow. "I think these are begging for attention, and I'm more than happy to help them out." Warm lips overtook one nipple before teeth lightly scraped the taut peak. He applied just enough pressure to make my entire body light up with a fire of need.

"Morning sex?" I asked.

This was all new to me since I had never stayed the entire night with a partner. Sneaking out before they woke up to do a walk of shame wasn't really my style, but it happened once in a great while. Hell, sex happened once in a great while.

"Morning, noon, night. I'm not picky when it comes to having you. Besides, why waste good morning wood?" He kissed down my body, holding the covers up as he inched his way down my body between my legs.

He looked like a model with the white sheet creating a hood over him, framing his gorgeous face. His dark hair peeked around the edges of the sheet, appearing perfectly messy from sleep. The gray of his eyes darkened with each word he spoke between the various forms of worship he left descending lower and lower over me.

This was happening again.

He knew exactly what to do to ruin me for any other lover.

I figured he'd hound me with questions after my performance last night, but apparently, he had other ideas. Never wanting to rush this because God knows it was incredibly hot, and I needed to figure out a way to get out of there when we were done. Those thoughts had to wait since my brain failed me while he paid attention to all the right spots to push me over the edge to oblivion.

Answering questions and confessing my past didn't work for me. We were temporary, and he didn't need to know.

I carried my shame, my mistakes, and those were

something I planned to keep to myself.
   Forever.

CHAPTER 18

WIX

Slowly, my hand worked its way over to the other side of the bed to not wake up my girl. It stopped with that thought. Bardot wasn't my girl, but she was better than some random I usually ended up with. Having her here all night after choosing to stay while the rest of the band left for Austin told me that.

The band worked as a unit, especially on tour. If one went, we all went. Only this time, I decided to spend more time with Bardot. The guys would give me shit about staying when I landed today, but I didn't give a flying fuck what they thought about my choices when it came to her.

Rising on my elbow, I realized the bed was empty. "Hey, you in the bathroom? I need to take a piss?"

Nothing.

My feet hit the floor in an instant. Where the fuck

was she? "You order us some coffee, sweets?" I asked, thinking she was in the living area of the suite.

When I located my jeans from last night, I pulled them on as I rounded the corner and looked across the bigger room.

Empty.

"Bardot?" My voice grew louder now so she'd hear me no matter where she hid.

My words echoed in the hollow void of the entire space.

She had left.

Snuck out while I slept like the dead.

A yellow sticky note stuck out on the black countertop, calling to me to understand what she had done.

> *Wix,*
> *Thanks so much for the perfect evening and night. I'm so happy we got to spend more time together before we both get back to our real lives. I wish you well and continued success with Copper Crowns.*
> *B*

"What the fuck!"

She leaves me a damn thank you note for our date?

Who does that?

It sounded like something you'd send your grandmother for taking her to dinner or something.

We had a lot more than a fucking dinner. Is that what she actually thought our time together was, one goddamn date?

"Where's my fucking phone?" Flipping over everything, I finally located it in the bedroom on the floor by the bed.

The lock screen opened, and there were several messages from the guys and one from Jones but nothing from Bardot. Guess she said all she had to say in the note she so kindly left me. I picked it back up and read it again.

"Shit, shit, shit." I've never been dismissed so easily by a woman before. It's like she let me off the hook for the morning after by sneaking out in stealth mode. Did she really think that's how I fucking roll? Kick women out of my bed when I was done with them.

Flopping down on the bed, I saw myself in the huge mirror on the wall across from the foot of the bed. If only she were still here, we'd put that to some good use about now, but no, she fucking left me.

Her perfume scent lingered on the sheets and me, and that needed to go. I'd scrub it away and forget about Bardot. That's what she obviously wanted.

A vibration in my hand alerted me to a new text.

Arch: *You alive?*
Me: *Hell yeah. Where are y'all?*
Arch: *On the bus still headed to Austin.*

Jones hoped you were going to make it. Told the fucker you were tied up.
Me: *No, I'm free now. I'll hop a plane asap and see you there.*
Arch: *Where's hot sweetpants?*
Me: *Don't call her that. She's home.*
Arch: *Already? Dayyyuuummm. Bum lay?*
Me: *Fuck off. Later.*

I send a text to Jones.

Me: *Send a car.*
Jones: *When.*
Me: *30.*
Jones: *Done.*

As I stood in the shower, all I could think about was how relaxed we seemed hanging out. The time flew by with no worries. At least that's what I thought. Maybe Bardot didn't enjoy herself the way I did, or maybe the whole band life overwhelmed her. Not everyone thrived on the attention the way we did.

Our time together wasn't consumed by band shit. The night was the two of us laughing, talking, and getting to know each other. She acted like sharing much of her life freaked her out, so I backed off on asking anything about it. With my life being pretty much an open book, I told her whatever she wanted to know. No point in fabricating information with the internet.

"Dammit," echoed off the shower walls. I turned off the hot water, still angry with her and at myself for not making her feel like I wanted to spend more time with her before I had to leave for Austin.

She took the day off. The two of us could have spent the whole fucking day doing whatever she wanted or nothing at all. I was down for both of those options.

"Fuck it. I'll call her and put her on the spot for ditching me."

No, she made the decision, and I had to honor that. If she wanted more, she could damn sure get in touch with me. She had my cell number. It wouldn't take that much effort.

***

The plane touched down in Austin, and the attendant had me deplane first and exit through a different door inside the terminal. Flying commercial stopped being an option because it caused problems with security, but this trip wasn't planned enough in advance to schedule. The last thing I wanted was to cause a scene in the airport.

A car waited for me through a side exit, and I ducked inside. Duke sat behind the wheel. "Oh, hey, bro. Thanks for coming."

"The night go okay for you? No problems?" He

jumped right to the point even if he had no idea where my head was at.

The flight only lasted a little over an hour, but it gave me enough time to think about all the things Bardot and I talked about during our short time alone. She held back on me with some of her secrets in life, which was okay with me at the time, but now I wanted to know everything about her. These secrets kept her at arm's length, and that wasn't something I was comfortable with.

If she built walls to protect herself, I wanted to know why. For her to hide behind them and keep me shut off, they must have been deep scars that hadn't truly healed. Normally, dealing with some random chick's drama wasn't my problem, but with Bardot, I wanted to help heal them.

Shaking my head at that thought, I looked up at Duke in the rearview mirror.

"You okay, Wix?"

"Yeah, I'm good." I turned to watch out the window as we navigated the traffic on a major freeway. "Are you sure we're not in LA?" I asked, changing the subject.

"Yeah, I was told before I left the hotel to plan for extra time on this freeway or find an alternate route."

"Great." The Texas sky looked like I felt—dark and rainy. I didn't need some girl making me feel like this. My emotional state didn't need to rest on her, but joining up with the band would take care of that.

"Hold on. We're going to take a little detour."

I felt the SUV jump over a curb and go through a slight ditch. We turned and took off down a side road through a questionable neighborhood.

Duke's driving had me laughing before we got close to the hotel. "Shit, dude, we weren't in all that big of a hurry."

"Yeah, well, I'm not that fucking patient to sit in traffic." I saw the smile on his face in the mirror and laughed again.

"I'll remember that when I'm the one in a hurry."

Duke turned one last time, and I looked out to see a back door in an alley. "Uh... where the fuck are we?"

"This is the door we took the rest of the guys through earlier to avoid people." He typed on his phone as he talked. My door opened, and a concierge stood waiting for me to enter.

"Welcome to the Hotel Archer, Mr. Stoker. We hope you'll enjoy your stay here. If you'll follow me, please."

I felt my left eyebrow raise at the welcome this guy gave me. I felt like I was walking into a real five-star hotel. I didn't care at this point. Just get me to my room.

"About time," Arch barked at me when I walked into the big living space we were apparently sharing. I looked around at the huge common room connecting the suite together.

"Damn, Jones. What kind of a place did you book for us?" We stayed in nice hotels, but this was over the top. Two stories, four bedrooms, and a conference room seemed extreme. Cheap bastard never minded spending our fucking money.

Jones piped up, "Mr. Knox booked this on their dime." He looked at each of us before continuing, "So don't trash it up like some of you have done in the past."

Arch laughed. "You know that was so far in the past, I don't even remember where we did that shit."

Trotter weighed in by adding, "Yeah, bro, we hadn't had that kind of fun in forever."

"I remember the havoc you four wreaked, considering I'm the one who had to answer to the suits from the label. The shit I had to put up with for months answering for you dumbasses doesn't need to be repeated. Just take it easy on tearing shit up, please."

"We outgrew that the first time 13 Recording's accounting deducted the money from our sales. The label's money guys can do whatever they want," I finally told them all. "Can we live a little cleaner than the bus?"

The other three nodded. "It's the least you can do since Paradise Productions is coughing up the funds," Jones ended that line of conversation. "You may as well unpack some. We'll be here a few days."

"How the fuck are you managing to get us time away from the tour to do it?"

"We lucked out. The date in NOLA had to be

canceled after a huge storm damaged the venue, and nowhere else would hold that large of a crowd. Plus, we had three days off after it. Basically, you lucky fuckers have six days off to deal with the terms laid out by Paradise—"

"Yeah, yeah. We'll see," I interrupted. "You know, Jones, it would've been great if someone had run this shit by us before agreeing to anything."

"Hey, don't talk to me about it. Talk to 13 Recordings. I got a call from them during the Houston show and was told to follow through with whatever Knox wanted to try."

"That's fucked up, and you know it. We aren't actors." Trotter's tone told me he wasn't happy about doing a documentary either.

"Right, someone should have informed us that big fucking decisions were being made for us regarding *our band*," Arch agreed with the rest of us before turning to point his finger at our manager. "Jones, you damn well know we hate the suits making our decisions."

Jones stood up to Arch. "Did you not hear me say I didn't have anything to do with this? 13 Recordings, you know... your label... told me to have Copper Crowns in meetings with Paradise Productions in Austin. They said to make it happen, so I did. The timing worked out anyway with no show." He rubbed his hand down his face and let out a deep breath.

"Look, what do you have to lose by listening to

their idea? It might turn into something great for the band. Maybe you'll gain thousands more fans from it. Documentaries are being made all the time about great bands," Jones concluded his plea.

"Yeah, washed-up or too-old-to-make-music bands. Not like Copper Crowns, who's just hit their stride at the top," Trotter uttered while walking over to take Arch's arm. We all knew when Arch got pissed, something bad followed. Having Jones bow up to him only spelled trouble, and Jones knew it.

Kenzo finally decided to join the argument since that's what the conversation had become. "Hey, I don't see what the big fucking deal is. We've only been to Austin one other time to play the big festival, and we only saw the park where they held it. They call this city the live music capital of the world. We'll have some time to find out why."

"Hey, maybe we can do an impromptu show at a small venue while we're here. You know, like jam with another band or find an open mic night and surprise the hell out of the audience." Thankfully, Arch calmed down when he suggested this idea might work.

"I'm with Arch," Kenzo added, then turned to our manager. "Jones, find us a chill venue all on the d-low and make sure it stays that way. We can slip in the back and take over the fucking stage at the last minute. Need a band that can do our kind of sesh."

Jones' face finally broke into a smile, telling us he was good with our idea. I hoped it all came to fruition since our itinerary had been highjacked by a storm. But my first thought was I'm only a short plane ride away from the woman I'm not quite ready to put behind me.

Hopefully, she'd feel the same way.

CHAPTER 19

BARDOT

"Gilley, the next charter is heading down the dock. You ready for them?"

"Bardot, when have I not been ready for people to board?" His words held a smile to them. Never had he had a problem with having his end of a charter ready to go, but I still liked to check in with him before clients stepped on the boat.

These people looked normal. Why did I think that? Did I expect every charter to glide in on Harleys, wearing leather and sporting tattoos? I can't deny that keeping Wix off my mind proved difficult.

Not having heard from him since I left the hotel room bothered me more than I cared to admit. How hard was it for him to shoot me a brief text saying he had fun, or see ya later, or—

"Stop it, Bardot. You were just another meaningless

overnight guest to him."

"You say something?" Gilley's head peeked out the hold, staring at me.

"Talking to myself. Sorry."

"You've been doing that a lot lately. Care to share what's going on?"

"Nothing's going on. I've had a lot on my mind."

"Yeah, ever since you took a day off to spend time with the rock stars."

My head whipped around so fast to look at him. Were my distractions so obvious that Gilley even noticed? Dammit! I couldn't allow that to happen. People on my boat were my responsibility, and if I'm worrying about someone else, something bad could occur.

I needed to put a stop to thinking about Wix.

It happened.

I enjoyed it.

It was over.

Enough said.

Move on, Bardot.

"Hello, welcome to the *Miss Midnight*. I'm Bardot, and I'll be your captain for the day, along with Gilley, who'll see to your needs and provide you with the best culinary delights you'll ever have the pleasure of eating."

Yeah, poured that on a little thick, but oh well.

***

The last person waved from the end of the dock before stepping onto the parking lot to find his car.

"Glad that's over," Gilley mumbled for my ears only "When they stepped on board, I thought it would be an easy afternoon, but oh, hell no. Couldn't happen that way, could it?"

I watched their car back out and exit the lot. "Funny, I thought the same thing. We never know, though, do we?"

Even if I wanted work to keep my mind from Wix, waiting on three people, hand and foot, didn't happen the way I pictured the afternoon. They were here to be catered to like royalty. King Charles probably asked for less while on a sailboat.

"Maybe we should write it into the damn contract that clients are expected to pour their own wine when it sits on the table directly in front of them. I don't mind climbing up to pour when I'm not preparing their dinner, but every fucking time they reached the bottom third of the glass was a bit much." Gilley huffed as he wiped down the tabletop still resting between the benches.

His comments weren't too far off the money. Some people couldn't do enough to help, and some acted as though we were servants put on the boat to wipe their asses for them. This charter was the latter.

The best thing about being occupied with menial chores for these jokers was not having time to think about a certain rock star who rolled into some new city and prepared to perform.

A flash of a memory from standing on the platform hit me as I stepped up to the top deck to work on storing the mainsail. I looked down into the water below and saw turbulent gray eyes staring back. Only he was on stage, his bass hanging in its perfect location, his foot tapping ever so slightly with the beat Arch banged out on the kick drum.

Dark hair fringed his forehead to emphasize the windows to his soul. The water's reflection showed me storm-like orbs drilling me with passion. The same passionate way they did when he was hovering over me while coaxing me to a height I never thought my body was capable of reaching.

"Bardot?" Gilley's calling brought me back to reality. "Girl, you're gonna fall off this tub if you keep glazing over. You need to call the guy and see what's up before something serious happens."

"No, I wasn't thinking about him," I lied. "Those entitled asshats today got to me. I need to put the day behind me and move on to tomorrow's job."

Gilley climbed out of the galley and sat on the bench to work on removing the table. "Bardot, at least admit to yourself the dickweed has you twisted up in all kinds of knots."

"That's not true," I quickly replied, a little harsher than necessary. The two of us rarely talked about our dating lives. Occasionally, we traded stories about day-to-day events or past events with our relatives but never with those we spent time with after hours.

"The fact you jumped to tell me what's what says it all, chica. Do some soul-searching when it comes to the guy and act on it. Nothing's going to get resolved in your head until then."

His words spoke volumes more than he knew. My mind seemed to be consumed with Wix. I asked myself a thousand times over the past few days why I snuck out on him. Not once did he imply he might want a quick getaway after the best and only morning sex of my life.

But he didn't bother getting in touch with me either. I needed to see he wasn't into me that much, or my phone would have been blowing up with messages or calls, which it was not.

"How bad would it be if I called him?" I asked, using my best nonchalant voice while fastening the last bungee around the sail's cover.

"Hard to say. Some guys would be happy you took control of the situation. Others, not so much." As the big guy moved to the steps to his lair, he looked over his shoulder, "Me, I like a girl to do a little of the chasing. Just a little, though. Don't go all *Basic Instinct* on him. That shit's not good on any level, even if Sharon Stone was smokin' hot."

"Ha-ha." As if I would. Stalker tendencies never resembled anything in me. After my turbulent adolescence, I didn't care enough at that point. Like zero fucks to give. Too many bad experiences jaded me to life by the time I reached my eighteenth birthday. Escaping to the sea became my only refuge.

But that happened years ago. Hadn't I punished myself enough for all my wrongdoings, all the trouble I put Dad and myself through? These thoughts played on my mind often when I allowed myself to get down, so I kept busy. With Wix on my mind, the list of ideas blossomed into better, more pleasant areas.

Waking up my sexual side after that one night with the rock star caused my brain to conjure up all sorts of sordid adventures. Guys had spank banks, I had adventures. Needless to say, my rarely used guybrator—a term I lovingly named it—saw a lot more action. My imagination ran away when it came to Wix. Those stormy eyes, his beautiful tattoos, the body of an Adonis. It wasn't necessary to stretch the truth when it came to him starring in my sexcapades.

Before it might have been a Hemsworth or a Skarsgård, but now I had my own reality to pull from since Wix left me with memories I knew would never be forgotten. Obsessing over someone I spent the night with made mouthwatering memories.

"Enough of that, Bardot. There's work to be done," I mumbled out loud.

Gilley stepped up with a box of items he handed off to me. "Eat this tonight or tomorrow. For all of their demands, they ate very little of my cooking. Pissed me off too. I worked extra hard to please them for nothing."

I eyed him and smiled. "Not for nothing. I get the best dinner on the lake, free of charge."

He laughed, staring at me. "There is that. At least I know you're getting something good out of the afternoon." Taking a long step, he landed on the dock beside the boat. For as big as he was, his jaguar movements fooled strangers who encountered him. Maybe he was a jungle cat in his first life. His quiet pace amazed me.

"You got plans, little girl?" A name I hated from anyone else but him.

"Other than devouring my dinner that already has my taste buds tingling? No. There are some movies I've been waiting to see." I held the box up to my nose and took a deep sniff. "Damn, it smells good."

He waved and started up the docks to his car. "See ya tomorrow then."

I returned the gesture and finished putting the items I planned to take home beside the box. Before I finished, my phone buzzed. The screen lit up with Hot Bass Player, the words he stored his number under while we were at the venue. Laughing at his choice that day, he informed me he refused to be an unknown number in my phone.

I slid my finger up to see the text.

Hot Bass Player: *Hey.*

That's it? After all this time, all he said is 'Hey?'

How did I reply to that, not sounding desperate?

> **Me:** *Hey yourself.*
> **Hot Bass Player:** *Whatcha doin?*
> **Me:** *Leaving the boat. Finished my charters for the day.*
> **Hot Bass Player:** *Oh yeah?*
> **Hot Bass Player:** *Plans for the evening?*

His hesitancy between texts made me wonder where his head was at.

> **Me:** *Not really. Eating leftovers Gilley made. Watching movies.*
> **Hot Bass Player:** *Want to come to ATX?*
> **Me:** *Haha. Just like that, huh? You know that's like four hours from where I'm at, right?*

What the hell? He doesn't bother calling or messaging, and he now wanted me to drop what I was doing and go to Austin? I don't think so, Mr. Rock Star.

> **Hot Bass Player:** *I'll send a plane for you. You can be here in less than an hour.*

My phone rang before I thought of a reply. Did he honestly think I'd want to climb on his fancy-ass plane and come to him? *Hey, mister, if you want to see me, come to Houston.* His jet service for women ran in both directions.

"Hello?" I answered. I knew it was him without looking, but I tried not to sound like I was excited.

"Sweets, I need to see you."

His words and tone caused my eyebrows to raise almost to my hairline in disbelief. Every word he uttered reeked of desperation, something I coached myself not to mimic. Part of me wanted to believe he longed for me as I did for him.

"Then come to Houston. I'll pick you up at the airport." Needing me to pick him up was laughable since he traveled in a private car everywhere, but I wanted him to see I was at least willing to see him.

"Can't. We have a small show tonight. It'll be late before it ends. I... I... I'd love for you to see it. Listen, Bardot, there aren't enough words to say how badly I want to see you." After stumbling over the words, I felt like some sincerity stood behind his words. But was I convinced?

"Uh-huh." Maybe he was playing me here? Or maybe an impulsive booty call?

"Listen, I'm sorry I haven't called or anything. You ran out on me, and to tell the truth, it pissed me off. I thought we'd had a great time together, then I wake up, and boom, no Bardot."

"I didn't want you to feel like you had to spend the day with me or see me home. The band waited for you to do whatever it is y'all are doing in Austin. Me being there would keep you from going early." My words tumbled out quickly like they were prepared ahead of time. They were anything but.

All the way back to my apartment, I thought about why I really took off with only leaving a note behind. Deep inside, I knew we shared a connection. It rattled me more than any guy had ever, even back in my dark days.

"Bardot, that wasn't the case at all. Yes, we met with the prick's execs from Paradise when we all got there, but I didn't have to be onsite. For what we did, that shit could have been handled with a conference call."

Seriously doubting his words, I considered my reasons for escaping while he slept. Not that I had anything to complain about, but facing him after several rounds of the best sex ever, sent a tiny shock through me. I lacked experience in this area, and dealing with the unknown scared me. My life since I became an adult had a routine—a plan. Introducing him into it messed with that plan.

Wix had the power to change me, change my life, and alter my design. I lived a controlled life created by my own outline. Him waltzing in could wreck it in a heartbeat. My world revolved around the water with charts to plot a course, one I could register if need be.

His lived inside a hurricane that drifted where the wind wanted to go.

A storm like that might sink me to the ocean's depths with no lifejacket in sight.

CHAPTER 20

WIX

Bardot's way of thinking seriously fucked with my head. I wasn't used to having a female on my mind constantly. Since I realized that having a different woman every night was no longer how I wanted to live, choosing someone became more important to me. But was this how it was going to be if I found someone I truly wanted?

Everywhere I went now, I wondered whether Bardot would enjoy being here. Moving around in Austin, I found myself wondering if she had been here. What did she think about the shit that went down on Sixth Street? Had she gone to the big-ass music festival we played a few years back? Did she shop and eat along Capital like a tourist or barhop through the numerous bars all over the city? Hell, had she ever even been to Austin? She didn't seem to have gone too far from her Houston haunts when we talked about doing things in the city.

I realized I knew so little about her and another reason why we needed more time together. She had to come here if I was stuck waiting for decisions to be made for the band, which only pissed me off. With her here, I had something else to focus on.

"Babe, please come to Austin. I need to see you, like today. Please."

What the fuck was that? I never begged a woman for anything. Even to myself, I sounded like a pussy. Wouldn't the guys get a great laugh if they heard me?

"I don't know, Wix. It's asking a lot for me to just up and leave my work."

She didn't sound too convincing with the harsh words. Like she was trying to convince herself and not me.

"We'd have a great time. And we'll get you on a plane the minute you say you're ready to head home." If I had my way, it wouldn't be until we left here. Now that was asking too much.

"Like if I could come for the day, you'd be okay with it?" Her words came out sounding like she didn't even believe her request.

"Sweets, I'd love for you to come for several days, but if I can only get one, then I'll take it." She needed to understand how much I wanted this while secretly hoping one day wouldn't be her choice.

"Well... I guess I could come for overnight. Like,

leave here after my morning cruise and then come home the next evening? Would that work?" A touch of excitement in her voice, finally. This idea looked better and better.

"Hell yeah, it works. Are we talking tomorrow since I know you wouldn't say yes to tonight?" I snickered into the phone. "Hey, I had to try."

As much as I wanted a long night of wrapping myself inside her proving how needy I was for that sweet body, I decided to be happy she had agreed. The batshit craziness of it all was I didn't just want to get her here for sex. I truly wanted to spend time with her. Something drew me to her more than any other woman I'd been with. Her back story intrigued me. The girl had a guarded past I needed to learn more about.

"Yes, I'll be finished with the early morning cruise by eleven. We're doing a brunch instead of lunch. The whole damn group wants to see the sunrise, so I've got to be ready too freaking early."

"Yeah, that's nice, I guess." Her work was important to her, but having her with me was my priority. "Can you be at the airport by noon?" My words proved my eagerness if she hadn't already gotten the message.

Bardot's delayed reply made me wonder if I'd been too pushy. The last thing I wanted was to scare her off. Maybe this was too new, too soon. She shared with me about rarely dating, so I needed to remember that because there was a reason for it.

"You're pushing it. Is this how your uber fans act?" She laughed at her own joke. "How about thirty extra minutes for the drive? I can make it by then." Giggling, I detected some enthusiasm, stoking my excitement.

"Yeah, yeah. That's perfect. I'm already looking forward to meeting you at the airport," I replied.

Damn, dude, calm down, I had to remind myself.

"Sounds like a plan. I'm going to let you go so I can get home and pack before turning in early. Getting up at the ass crack of dawn makes me tired just thinking about it."

"I get it. That's never something I think about, especially on tour. Too many late nights in a row for us." Spending time in the hotel lets us dial back our internal clocks but only slightly. We'd be on the road again soon, and getting ourselves back in performance mode took a toll on everyone when we constantly went back and forth with it.

"Right, I'm at my car now so... talk soon?" she asked.

"I won't call again because I want you ready to go when you step off that boat tomorrow. Sweet dreams of me, Bardot." My voice dropped a full octave with my last sentence. I wanted to make sure I was the one on her mind when she went to bed tonight.

I'd gotten my way, and the dreams I had would abso-fucking-lutely be about her.

***

When I walked into the suite's living area, Jones sat nursing a cup of coffee with Kenzo and Arch.

"Morning, sunshine," Arch spoke first. The dude could go from zero to awake in a split second. I could not. He received a grunt as I headed for the room service tray with a pot of Columbian gold waiting for me. I'm not talking drugs either, I'm talking the actual good stuff.

Jones took my response as an invitation to start talking. After all our time together, he should know better than to hand out anything I needed to remember before I had a sip of coffee. But no, shit vomited from him anyway.

"Today we're going to sit down with Knox again. He's had time to try his idea out on some producers there at the studio."

"Great," Kenzo's low voice groaned.

"About that," Arch began. "I think they should send a cameraman or photographer with us and film all our remaining tour dates. They can put their producers on splicing it together to make a mansterpiece of goodness staring Copper Crowns."

"What the fuck, Arch?" My eyes peeled in his direction over my mug.

"What the hell is a mansterpiece?" Jones asked what we all were thinking.

"You bunch of losers. Keep up. A mansterpiece is a work of badass manliness, which is exactly what we are." His grin left me still wondering what the fuck.

Jones looked at him for a second and then continued, "We need to show these guys that the band is serious about making something worth viewing. Something the fans will download, share, and repeatedly watch."

"And why do we need that?" Kenzo spoke up. I finished my first cup and stood up for another. This line of shit sounded like something I needed a clear head to talk about. These dumb fucks might have us jumping through hoops to satisfy them. Fuck that. We'd paid our damn dues at smokey clubs and backwoods dive bars.

Leaning against the counter with my hands around the full mug, I listened to the conversation taking in all the information before speaking. Kenzo said most of what needed to be said, but I wanted to back him up with more. Jones had to understand we were not all about pleasing another group of fucking suits. We had a label and meeting their demands was enough work.

As I moved to the big-ass sectional, sat, and propped my feet on the glass coffee table, I leaned back waiting my turn to add my opinion. Usually, I made my thoughts known, but it was still early.

Jones continued trying to pick and choose all the right things to say to convince us this was for the good of the band. I drained my cup and placed it harder than necessary on the glass, happy it didn't shatter.

"Stop," I finally spoke up. "Hold the fuck right there." I stood to make my point known as I towered over Jones in the small chair. "Who exactly do you work for, Jones?"

He cleared his throat. "I'm always working for Copper Crowns. You know that. I want to bring you guys to another level of fandom. I can only do that by working with other areas of the industry to offer more options for the band to get exposure. Most of your immediate competition has TikToks from every performance. We've yet to release an official one. The good thing is your fans post after most of them."

We all knew the truth in his words. We had worked with him since the beginning. He pushed us to be better, get shit done on time, and found ways to get the band out in the music industry. Lately, it seemed like he had a lot on his plate, though.

Jones' dad had a lot to do with his success, and our manager constantly tried to make more of us for that reason. Scott Savage's giant presence in the music industry lent a lot of credit to our brand. If he said it, the words became the gold standard for whatever he backed.

Even with Jones making his own name now because of Copper Crowns, he still felt obligated to prove himself to Scott. We all understood this, even though Jones rarely ever shared anything about his dad like he did in the beginning. Back then, we cut him slack and helped him appease his father, but now we were past that shit. We did what we wanted.

Yes, we still had suits at the label to give us some

directives but not as much. They knew we had become their platinum princes, but what we actually were was the best cash cows they owned. Sometimes I wondered if they looked at us like prostitutes and Jones was our pimp.

Jones did a lot more than pimp us out, though. He took care of us and led the band to bigger and better things. He kept us on the straight and narrow as best he could. That job rated up there as his most difficult one, especially in the beginning. Young and dumb was the only way to describe us then. Thought with our dicks, acted like dicks, and generally gave him grief, but Jones knew a good thing when he found it.

He had some shit in his family he didn't want to deal with, so he kept his act together to please Daddy. I wondered if Daddy was putting the screws to him now. This whole setup just didn't seem on the up and up to me. Too little information had been shared with us. Then boom, they expected the band to jump through hoops to do their bidding with a documentary.

"Whose idea was this to begin with? Who brought the plan to you?" This information would tell the band all we needed to know.

"I... well, the truth is..."

CHAPTER 2.1

BARDOT

With ease, I parked and walked across the tarmac toward the plane and the flight attendant, who waited at the bottom step for me. My backpack wasn't stuffed because I'd only be there one night, but it had enough to appear heavy.

"Let me take that for you." He held out his hand.

"No, I'm good." I barely smiled, glancing at the nice-looking guy. "I'm used to it from my job."

"Oh, what do you do that has you carrying twice your weight?" He returned an infectious smile back. Surely, he earned extra tips with that face, even if he was the only attendant on the plane.

"I captain a sailboat on private charters."

His head whipped around, staring at me. "What?"

"I'm the captain of a sailboat. We do charters from

Clear Lake into the gulf." As I finished my sentence, we reached the bottom step of the sleek jet. The outside had a cool paint job. I wondered if anyone who owned a plane could have their design on it. Was this the label's design on the side?

"That sounds like an amazing job. Sail around all the time. I used to sail when I was a kid."

"Then you know how great my job is." He nodded and ducked in front of me at the top of the steps leading me through the doorway.

The inside matched the sleekness of the outside with blue and tan seating lining the sides.

"You can sit wherever you'd like. You're our only passenger today," he said matter-of-factly, but all I could think was what a waste of money to send a jet just for me. Couldn't I just fly commercial? "Would you like something to drink? Champagne, wine, soft drink?"

"No, I'm good. I'm sure I'll be having enough to drink once I arrive in Austin."

"Oh, right. Those guys always have something going no matter where they are."

"You fly with them often?" He might share some juicy knowledge with me about my favorite bass player.

"No, only occasionally. They rarely ever fly because of touring, mostly using their private buses."

"Yeah, I guess that's true. It's a great bus too."

He turned to me with a knowing look—piercing

eyes and pursed lips. "You've been on their bus?"

Immediately, I knew where his thoughts led him. Another groupie for them to enjoy. A disgusted look was written all over his face. "Just to look inside while Wix changed his clothes. We were going out in Houston."

Yes, it was a lie, but I didn't care. He wouldn't question me. Did I need to defend my reputation with this stranger? Hell no, but I did anyway. The last thing I wanted was people looking at me like one of the many women who frequented the band's beds.

"Oh, sorry. I didn't mean to make it sound like that." His face changed, looking apologetic. "It's just, well... we get a lot of people on here to fly wherever the bands are. Sometimes it's family or friends, but often it's someone they want to spend more time with after just meeting at a concert."

"I'm sure you do."

"No, really, I'm sorry. I try not to be a judgmental prick with the guests. Sometimes the guests are a hundred times worse than the entertainers, though. Demanding and condescending, that is."

"Since I'm in the same type of service as you and the pilots are, you'll never hear that out of me. I understand your situation." As I sat in the plush leather reclining chair, I thought back to the day Wix and Arch boarded the boat. Arch's arrogance shone through until we got to know each other. Wix never gave off that appearance. Thank God.

He handed me a glass of water over ice. "I'm sure you do. I have to say... it's nice to have you on board. A breath of fresh air from the usual..." he trailed off, thinking better of using the words I know he desperately wanted to say.

Smiling, I thanked him with a nod.

"Buckle up. We'll be taking off shortly. I'm Shane, by the way. Just call me if you need anything at all."

"Thank you, Shane." He nodded and made his way to the galley. I felt the plane moving forward and double-checked my seat belt before leaning back. "Here you go, Bardot. Off on a new adventure," I mumbled to myself.

The plane rose sharply, leveled out, and before I could finish the water, I felt us descending. I knew it was a short flight, but the ride went by so much faster than I imagined.

The jet glided to a stop while I watched it all happen through the window. A big black car came toward the plane before the door opened. My ride was waiting for me. Shane unlocked a mechanism and pushed a button for the door to open and the stairs to fold down.

I gathered my backpack and stood, moving to the doorway. "Thank you, Shane."

"No, the pleasure was all mine to have you on board today." His lips formed a huge smile.

"I bet you say that to all the passengers."

He snickered. "No, actually, I don't. There are some

I'm happy to have off here, but you've been nice. Hope your stay in Austin is everything you hoped for."

"I'll be heading back tomorrow. Will you be here for that flight too?"

"No, it's my off day," he replied. "That's a fast trip to Austin."

"Yes... have to get back to the real world."

He smiled again. "I hear ya."

I turned and made my way down the steps to the awaiting car, where a female driver opened the door for me. "Good afternoon, Miss Bohen. I trust your flight was a good one." Her speech sounded formal and stiff.

"Yes, thank you." *Did I sound like that?* "Hope you didn't have to wait too long. Call me Bardot, please," I added, trying to sound more normal. I was a nobody on a fancy jet about to get into a small limousine. I understood why she felt the need to speak formally, but it bothered me.

"Oh, no, ma'am. I arrived as you were taxing down the runway." She shut the door behind me.

"Please, no ma'am either. Just Bardot. You know where I'm going?" The conversation flowed more smoothly now.

"Yes, ma... Bardot. I already have the directions on the GPS. I'll be your driver for the time you're here. Anytime you want to go somewhere, do something, or need anything, call this number." She handed a card over the seat for me to take. "I'll be waiting."

The card had Marcy Browning written on it. "I'm sure I won't need anything, Marcy. You'll have a lot of downtime with me. My visit will be very short."

"That's okay. Keep my card with you and know I'll be waiting." She smiled in the rearview mirror, and I returned it.

The trip to the hotel went quickly. I've been to Austin a few times and knew the airport wasn't too far away from the downtown area, but we quickly moved to the north side of the city instead. Austin's reputation for horrible traffic these days became clear when Marcy took shortcuts and back roads to get us to the Archer Hotel on the north side. She explained they were staying there because it wasn't too far from the studios they were working at this week.

We turned a corner, and before us stood a boutique hotel I'd never heard of, but it was obviously an impressive one. "Does the band stay here often?"

"I wouldn't know ma'am," Marcy replied.

I gazed out the window at the vertical sign extending down the exterior before we pulled up to the front, where tall sheet-glass walls greeted me. The building stood several stories tall, and the windows allowed visitors to take in a chandelier hanging from the multistory ceiling surrounded by a spiraling staircase. The posh entry offered visitors an idea of the elegance they were about to enter and spend some time enjoying.

Looking down at my clothes, I wondered if I

dressed correctly for this type of lavishness. Wix didn't say I needed to be ready for an extravagant night away. They may consider turning me away when I try to go inside.

"Are you sure we're at the right place?" I asked my driver.

"Yes, this is where they're staying. It's close to the studios where they are working and a lot of upscaled areas for shopping and dining. The Domain is only like a half a mile from here should you want to walk to it."

"I don't know if we'll have time to go shopping or out to dinner. He doesn't like to go places where he might be recognized."

"True, but Austin is used to having celebrities around town, so they usually leave them alone."

"That's good to know. The last thing either of us would want is being mauled by fans. He's told me some horror stories about it already."

"Yes, that's why they keep security guards on standby or with them at all times."

"Oh, right. I knew that. I met Duke when they played in Houston."

Marcy opened the door as I was speaking. Her eyes lit up when I mentioned Duke. "So you've met Duke too?"

She quickly looked down, but I saw her smile. "Yes, we've met a few times. Not that he ever remembers it, though."

"I'm sure he does, but he's always so busy scouting

the area around the band he probably can't comment."

"Anyway, this is where I was told to bring you. Don't forget to call if you need anything... anything at all."

"Thank you, Marcy, and I have your card right here." I pointed to my crossbody purse, where I stashed it.

Turning to the opulent entryway, I walked through the revolving doors and into the lobby. I had never seen anything like it. The floor-to-ceiling stacked stone fireplace had a low fire burning for looks because it was too hot this time of year for a fire, but it created the appearance of coziness in the area surrounding it.

The circular stairway boasted a huge mural of horses galloping across an open pasture. Not that many horses galloped anywhere around the Austin area, but it looked cool.

I made my way to reception and a young woman greeted me with a fake smile. Her job of welcoming people must have been getting to her from the look on her face.

"May I help you?"

"Yes, I'm here to see..." I stopped. Wix never said what I was supposed to do when I got here. He didn't tell me the room number either. Looking at the woman, I knew she'd never give it to me.

"Ma'am?" she asked.

"Just a minute. Let me make a phone call first." I turned and walked away from the desk, shooting Wix a text.

> **Me:** *I'm here in the lobby. What do I tell them?*
> ...
> ...
> ...
> **Wix:** *Don't tell them anything. Just come up. We're on the top floor in the penthouse suite.*
> **Me:** *Just get in an elevator?*

I turned around and saw the woman staring at me as if I were doing something wrong. The little hairs on the back of my neck stood at attention. She made me nervous even though I had every right to be here in this lobby. I came with a purpose, and being dressed down by the eyes of some clerk wasn't it.

> **Wix:** *Yes, get in the elevators and press the P.*
> **Me:** *OK.*
> **Wix:** *See you shortly :)*

I located the elevators just off the lobby in the hallway. Pushing the call button, I noticed a man come in and stand beside me, waiting too. When the doors opened, I stepped in and looked at the panel of buttons and found the P. As I pushed it, he stepped forward and pushed the 'close door' button.

"Where are you going?" His gruff voice startled me, making me even more nervous than I already was.

"What?" I turned and looked at him. "Why are you asking me?"

He pulled out a badge and flashed it at me. "Hotel security. Now, *where are you going*?"

"My friend is staying in the penthouse suite. He's expecting me."

The muscular, well-dressed man looked me up and down as though he was trying to decide if I was worthy of being a friend of someone who would stay in that suite.

"Maybe we should go back to the lobby and check with your *friend* to see if you should be coming up to see him or not?"

"I don't think so. I've done nothing wrong, and he told me to come on up." I felt my face getting red with anger by the second. That clerk sicced him on me. She watched every move I made while I messaged Wix, and now this big guy was here to follow through.

"No, ma'am. We're responsible for keeping our guests free of unwanted visitors. If the person in that suite wanted you, they would have told you about using the keycard necessary to get up to that level. Obviously, you knew nothing about it." He grabbed my upper arm and lifted me so my feet barely touched the floor.

"You're making a big mistake, and your *guest* isn't going to be happy about it. Plus, you're hurting my arm." He lowered my arm some but still enough to practically drag me back through the lobby to a door off the check-in desk area.

The woman from before followed us into the room. "I knew you weren't supposed to be here. The people in the penthouse suite want their identities held private so we don't even know who's staying there. Must be someone famous or very important."

"They are my friends," I shouted back at her. "Wix is going to be pissed when he finds out what you two have done."

"Wix? As in Wix Stoker? I knew it." She looked at the security guard. "Do you know who that is?"

He shook his head no.

"He's the bass player for Copper Crowns. Corporate didn't give out the information. They didn't want anyone knowing who was there." She pointed at me. "This is one of their groupies who figured it out somehow and wants a shot at getting to them."

"I'm *not* a groupie," I yelled at the bitch. "I'm a friend of his and the rest of the band. Call them and ask them. Or better yet, I will."

I pulled out my phone to call, and the guard snatched it away. "Guess she managed to get the number already. We may need to go ahead and call the police."

The woman nodded at about the same time my phone rang. As usual, I had it on identify caller mode to screen my calls on the boat.

"Wix Stoker calling," the robotic voice stated. "Wix Stoker calling."

"See, he's wondering where I am. Answer the damn phone." It felt like my face was glowing by now. She looked at the man and gave a curt nod, and he answered my phone.

"Where are you, babe? I'm standing at the elevator waiting." Wix spoke with a low deep voice into the phone.

"Uh... Mr. Stoker?" the security guard asked.

Wix's reply was anything but low and sexy. "What the fuck? Who the hell is this?"

"This is hotel security. We have a woman here claiming she knows you and the band and is trying to get to your suite, sir."

"You better not have harmed a single strand of hair on her head. Do you fucking hear me? Get Bardot up here *now*," Wix yelled loud enough we could all hear him through the phone that wasn't on speaker.

"Yes, sir. We'll be there shortly. In our defense—"

Wix cut him off. "You have no damn defense. She's my guest, and you fucked up big time with this."

"We'll be there shortly, sir."

"And you can bet your ass *I'll be waiting*." Wix drew out the last three words like a threat. I was nervous for them, but they had it coming.

The bitch behind the desk stood and said, "I doubt you'll be needing me to take her there." She tried to open the door, but his big foot stopped it.

"Oh, no. You're the one who told me to stop her, so you can explain to him why." He let go of my arm and grabbed hers. His manhandling seemed completely unnecessary, but now she knew how it felt to have her security goon taking people into custody as if he were the police.

The woman put the keycard in the slot above the floor buttons when we stepped on the elevator and turned to me. "You realize we were only doing our jobs. If a strange woman waltzed into their suite, we'd have been reprimanded for not stopping her."

"Yes, I get that, but you should have done a little more questioning and checking with the band before you decided to send Godzilla here to pick me up by my arm. Doesn't feel too good, does it?"

She rubbed her arm the same way I did mine when he let me go. "No, I don't suppose that was necessary, Edward."

"It's how we're taught to escort perps. What can I say?"

"How about you're sorry?" I piped up. "I feel like you'll be saying it a lot in the next few minutes." I looked at the woman. "Both of you will."

Part of me felt sorry for the two because Wix was going to be furious, but then they should have asked more questions before assuming the worst. Maybe we all learned a lesson today about dealing with people we didn't know.

Or dealing with famous people.

The doors to the elevator opened to an angry mob of guys.

The whole band stood at the doorway of the suite.

CHAPTER
22

WIX

The look on Bardot's face said everything I hated. I knew coming to see me was big for her, and it was taking her out of her element. The last thing we needed was a disaster like this. The glare she wore drove the point home like none other.

My head was muddled over this insatiable need to be with her while I waited for her to arrive. Nothing about this woman said we worked on any level, and yet, I couldn't let her go so fast. The desire to see what we could have if we tried hard enough stuck with me.

Now here we were, staring at each other, surrounded by the band. These guys stood by me through everything. They were my brothers, my family. The fact they knew me better than anyone else said everything when it came to the idea of holding onto one woman. Kenzo and Trotter knew what I felt, and I doubted Arch ever would, but it didn't make moving forward any easier.

Finally, Bardot broke the silence with, "We need to talk." She looked around at the guys. "Alone, please."

The hemming and hawing around us disappeared as I took her hand and dragged her into my bedroom in the suite. Shutting the door with a back kick, I kept my eyes on her. She looked ready to bolt at any moment.

I took both her hands in mine and looked straight into the glowing green eyes that captured my attention when we first met. "I'm so sorry, Bardot. I should have planned to meet you at the airport. This could have all been prevented if I had."

She took a deep breath and let it out slowly, as though she were trying to form the right words as she calmed down. The red color she wore when the group bounded through the doorway drained while the anger inside her subsided. Maybe it wasn't anger she felt, more like embarrassment or disappointment. *God, disappointment.* It was my worst enemy. The idea I disappointed her for any reason cut me to the core.

"We all make mistakes, Wix. I get that. But—"

"I'm sooo sorry, babe. Please believe me."

"But... I'm not sure this life is cut out for me. You live life on the expressway, and I live it at half the wind speed." She dropped my hands and walked over to the windows overlooking the downtown skyline in the distance. "Our worlds are too far apart to find a midpoint between us."

Closing the distance she created between us, I stepped between her and the bright sky. "No, they aren't, Bardot. We can both make concessions to meet in the middle. You know I'm willing to do whatever it takes."

"Oh, Wix, don't you see? We're brand new. I'm not even sure we are a *we* yet, and there are already issues."

"We are definitely a *we*, babe," I assured her.

She slowly shook her head back and forth. Tears welled in her eyes before spilling over her long lower lashes. "I can't do this to myself. I loved and lost too much in my life to allow myself to get tangled in a web that might blow away in a strong wind."

I watched as she walked to her bag and put the strap on her shoulder. "I can find my own way back to Houston."

"No, please, Bardot. Don't do this. Let's take a beat and talk."

She leveled her eyes on me. "It's easier to do it now than later. We had fun like I'm sure you're used to. Now it's time for me to let you go on to the next show."

I watched the door close behind her.

Letting her walk out of my life.

Probably for good.

And it hurt me more than ever before.

Maybe she was right, though. Ending it now kept

both of us from more pain than necessary before we both were in too deep.

So why does it feel like I watched my forever walk away?

BARDOT

"Where do I meet an uber?" I asked the bellman. As I cleaned my face up in the lobby restroom, I found a rental car available back at the airport. The thought of driving back to the boat hardly appealed to me since I'd have too much thinking time, but flying commercial at the last minute was too expensive.

The kind driver must have read the look on my face driving up to the front of the swanky hotel. He opened my door, where I threw my bag in, and followed it as quickly as possible. We reached the airport in no time, and my car waited in its assigned lane, making my getaway even faster.

The phone helped me get on the right roads, and I watched the skyline of Austin disappear behind me. It didn't take much time before I realized I had left more than a beautiful city in the rearview mirror.

Wix's face wrecked me as I walked out that door. He let me go easier than I thought he would, but then I could hardly think past leaving at that moment.

My heart ached as I walked out that door, but my head knew the decision was for the best. In the long run, it saved me so much grief and agony. I felt the warmth of my tears rolling down my cheeks.

Why did I do this to myself?

How did I get caught up in the excitement that quickly?

I refused to tune the radio to any stations because if a Copper Crowns' song came on, I'd probably turn around and drive straight back to him. That was something I couldn't do to myself or to Wix.

Would I haunt his dreams enough for him to make something happen between us?

Or would I not be able to let go and make something happen on my own?

CHAPTER 23

BARDOT

It would take about three and a half hours to drive from Austin to where the boat sat in Houston, depending on traffic. This time proved no different, except I didn't race down the interstate like I had somewhere to be. The fact was, I had nowhere to be, so I knew I drove home to the same situation I left in.

Alone.

All alone *again*.

No one expected me to message saying I had made it home safely. No one would call to check if I didn't send *that* message. People didn't keep me on their radar since I lacked that bubble of friends. My circle failed to exist and I pushed away anyone who wanted in.

Open farmlands east of Austin covered the hillsides as I rolled down Highway 71. With only crops burning in the hot Texas sun to watch go by, a constant reel played over and over in my mind of the look on Wix's face when I walked out the door of his hotel room. As I left, I knew the other band members of Copper Crowns would rally around their brother. It's what they did when one in the group found themselves out of sorts. The troops closed ranks around those in need, offering comfort through jokes, sarcasm, or sometimes even silence because being there was enough.

Brothers come together in a crisis. At least, that's what I'm told. As an adult, I never had that kind of friend, never a sisterhood—that someone who would run in to help, rescue, or comfort me. I shouldered problems on my own since my dad passed. This time would be no different.

I forced myself to slow down while driving through the small town of Ellinger, where I caught sight of a child playing off the side of the highway in a cluttered yard. Casted-off appliances and cars littered the area around the shabby house, only allowing for a small space for the young girl to play.

Naturally, the only red light in the town, known as the perfect pit stop between two metropolitan cities, stopped me, so I gained a firsthand view of her. With thin legs protruding from baggy shorts and her hair pulled into a ponytail hanging askew on the crown of her head, probably done by herself without a mirror to see the results of her efforts, her appearance said unkempt.

She played with a soccer ball, kicking it in a net and retrieving it only to do it again. No one noticed her efforts to strike the rubber harder or in various directions, but she continued anyway. I watched until she faded from sight in my review mirror.

Wondering if she ever had the luxury of a playmate, I began to realize that was my life. My choices made me kick my life in a net with no one there to watch or cheer me on, but just like this child, I did it over and over every damn day. Sure, I benefitted from the daily grind monetarily but to what end?

Why did I walk away from something that had the potential to change my life? played on repeat in my mind as I made my way closer to home.

My head felt ready to explode from the anger I aimed at myself until I rolled down the windows and blasted the radio on hard-core rock music.

"Why!" I screamed as loud and hard as I could with the rough, harsh sound. I needed the blasting and screaming to escape my thoughts. Taking in a deep breath when I finished, I felt a tad better but no more than that. Making stupid mistakes when I was a teenager happened constantly. I thought I had outgrown it until now.

Driving into the Houston traffic, I turned my tunes down and rolled up my windows. While others thought it entertaining to share their music with drivers and their passengers, I did not. The freeway took me past downtown, where the hotel stood that Wix and I stayed in the night the band played at the Verizon Center.

I thought back on all the fun I experienced on the platform high above the stage, watching Wix and the others doing what they did best—entertaining a crowd who loved them. As I stood there listening and the audience echoing the words along with them, I felt the love the band experienced at every venue. Their words touched the hearts and souls of their fans, as they did mine while I observed the four below me.

Nothing in my life gave me that kind of satisfaction, but I didn't need it to be happy, did I? My boat gliding through the salty water gave me all the happiness I desired. The problem always came back to being alone. What would I have to give up to find someone to share the joy with? Was I willing to compromise? Maybe that was my problem all along.

I hadn't had to concede my dreams to allow someone else's happiness in so long. Did I remember how? My dad never wanted me to sacrifice my ideas for his. He expected me to help, but anytime I planned something, he quickly found a work-around in my absence. Dad gave in to my dreams, and now to find happiness, maybe I needed to do that too.

Sure, I catered to my passengers, but it was my job to satisfy them. Their pleasure didn't change me in any way. I gave them what they wanted for a few hours and sent them on their way to the next adventure. Everyone who boarded my boat had different expectations, and I gave in to their whims, but nothing they did changed me.

Finding a partner, a friend, or a lover would change me. I knew this from my earlier life. I allowed people who called themselves friends to influence me to do things I'd run from now. I hid away the real me to have friends and boyfriends until it all came crashing down around me.

The difference between then and now is I had my dad to fall back on. Now I had me. Could I put myself out there without a safety net?

This line of thinking stayed with me until I rolled into the marina and stopped the car. I sat and watched as my boat bobbed slightly from a wake caused by another boat coming into the harbor. She looked perfect sitting there resting in the water, waiting for the next time her sails would unfurl with the wind and carry my passengers and me to the rolling waves of the bay or maybe even out into the gulf.

As I put the car in reverse to deliver it to the return location for rentals, I saw someone sit on the deck above the galley. I kept the lower location locked from anyone getting inside the hold, but it wasn't designed to prevent people from boarding and sitting on the boat. The security guards, who frequently checked over the area, would fail to notice anyone if they stayed still.

The man stood and stretched long arms over his

head. *What the hell?* I opened my car door and looked around for the guard but quickly realized he was nowhere around this side of the yacht club. Approaching a strange man on the boat might be tricky and dangerous. What would I do if he refused to leave? Maybe I should call the police and report him for trespassing. Boatowners paid rent for a location in the club as if we rented a house, so this person technically was breaking and entering my home without permission.

I never considered owning a weapon worse than a boat paddle, but right then, the thought occurred to me. I bit the inside of my cheek as I stepped out of my car. The only thing I knew to do was ask him to leave. Nicely. If he didn't, then I'd call the police, or maybe the guard would show up by then.

Taking a deep breath, trying to calm my racing heart, I quietly shut the car door and, with light steps, made my way down the gangplank leading to the floating dock. A keyed entry, I had the combination to, stopped me. Nothing appeared broken on the gate, so how did my trespasser get in? Better yet, why was he on my boat?

The longer I walked toward this guy, the madder I became. He would not get the best of me in this situation. The law stood firmly on my side.

When I stepped on the small wooden planks that led to the side of my boat, the guy turned, and our eyes locked.

"Oh my God, Wix. You scared the hell out of me.'
My hand laid over my out-of-control heart. "What are
you doing here?"

He stared at me like he was memorizing my face. I
brushed the wayward hair from my eyes and stepped
across to stand on the boat, which meant he looked
down on me from the upper deck. Damn, why did he
have to be so perfect? And those eyes. They sucked
me into his orbit without even trying.

In one smooth move, he sat, putting the two of us at
eye level. Reaching out, he took my hand and pulled
me between his legs, much closer than I needed to be.
His signature scent hit me with the fresh orange citrus
mixed with a delicious amber and musk as soon as he
got me closer to him. I knew the short distance
between us wasn't enough, but with the fragrance
wafting around me, my hesitation melted away with
the light sea breeze.

"What are you doing here?" I repeated.

"Oh, you know... I had a date with this gorgeous
woman, and she backed out at the last minute. I mean,
she fled so fast that there was no time to defuse the
situation happening around us, no damn time to talk
her out of it. Her actions caught me so off guard I
failed to respond quickly enough to stop her. The only
thing left to do was to get her, but that got fucked up,
too, because the little minx took her sweet time
driving home. I sat and waited in the only place I
knew she'd go, and guess what? She did exactly

what I expected."

He must have made up this speech while he sat around because I couldn't get a word in to defend myself while he recited a play-by-play of the situation.

"Yeah, about that..." I tried to pull away, but Wix wasn't having it. His warm hands came behind my neck and tugged me to him in a blazing kiss, smashing his lips hard against mine, consuming all my resistance to him. My body leaned into him as I wrapped my arms around his upper torso until there was no defining where he stopped and I started.

His back muscles contracted while I ran my hands up and down the hard surface. God, I wanted him, and I wanted this. Why had I run away from the situation? Why didn't I stay and let Duke and the others take care of it? Somewhere in my mind, I had to know they would have prevented the scene I ran from where I could not.

We parted, breathless, and looked at each other.

His face carried a look of guilt that made me want to apologize for him.

"Look, Bardot, I understand running. It probably seemed like the best damn thing to do. If you'd have only let me take care of it. That driver no longer works with the band or has anything to do with us. She should have called on the way to the hotel and let security arrange for you to be escorted to our suite."

I reached up and played with the cord running around his neck that lay above the first button on his shirt. "Wix, you don't understand how awful those people were to me. First, it was the guy in Houston who showed up to take me to the plane. He glared at me in the mirror when I told him I was going to see you..." I sighed. "He thought his job was to provide your next easy fuck. That I was the groupie being delivered for the band's enjoyment. I had to defend myself, and he changed his tune quickly, but the damage had already been done."

"That fucker's gone too."

"That's not necessary. You can't fire everyone who makes me feel bad or like trash. Besides, the driver in Austin was great. She gave me her card, talked kindly to me, and I never felt judged by her comments."

"I can, and I will. Those dumbasses aren't hired to make assumptions about why people are traveling for the band. The job description says drive our guests, not fucking judge them." His labored breathing told me his anger was becoming stronger.

"But she didn't. If anything, she went out of her way to be helpful."

"She failed to do the most important thing, babe. She let you out to the wolves without notifying anyone you were here. One phone call or message would have prevented the entire situation. She's gone."

I leaned in and quickly kissed his lips. Wow, did I love his lips. I didn't want to fight and argue. Our time together had a fast expiration date, but I couldn't let go of what the hotel people did.

"We'll see about her being fired." I kissed him again. "There's just one more thing I want to tell you, and that bitch can get whatever you decide on."

"Are we talking about the front desk clerk?" He eyed me carefully.

"Ye-yes. She and that dickhead who works security for the hotel."

"What else did the stupid bastard do?"

"He… well… he manhandled me. Like almost lifted me off the ground to stop me from getting to you." I pulled up my sleeve, and sure enough, dark bruises resembling a hand were forming around my upper arm."

"Son of a bitch. I'll kill the fucker for leaving a mark on you." Wix rubbed his thumb lightly over the marks. "He had no damn right to touch you, let alone cause bruises. Just wait until I inform the hotel manager of his dumbass employees. Okay, I'm done with that. I don't want to ruin the little time we have going over security, but you can bet the team Jones depends on for it *will* make this right."

I wasn't familiar enough with Jones to know what Wix was talking about. All I had been told is his manager, Jones, had some ties to a motorcycle club. The first time I heard about that, I wanted to ask if anyone like Jax Teller would be showing up. He was the only reference I had for an MC. I figured the guys would laugh at me for asking about a fictional television character, so I kept my secret crush to myself.

Strong arms tightened around me, pressing me against his body again. I knew I wanted him, and his actions said he wanted me to.

We needed to talk, but that could wait for now.

CHAPTER 24

WIX

As badly as I wanted to rip off her damn clothes and take her here on the deck, not caring who saw us, I knew she wasn't into exhibitionism. Me, I couldn't care less at one point but not with this woman. Then I remembered a bed, or berth, Bardot called it, was part of the hold past the kitchen area.

Somehow, in the short time we'd spent together, she did something to me. I felt possessive and not in a sharing mood. Our limited time together needed to be cherished just as Bardot should be.

Where the fuck did that come from? Cherished? Never in my whole damn life have I described any female as cherished. I mean, I loved the few guitars I've owned over the years, and my Fender P bass is treated better than the monarchy treats the crown jewels, but a woman? No fucking way.

Between hot kisses and roaming hands, I asked, "If you don't have a key to that damn lock, we're fucked."

"Yeah…" she managed to reply. "It's on my keyring attached to my purse." I felt her hand sneak out from under my shirt, making sure she traced the creases defining my abs. Her movements forced them to contract, causing her to notice.

"Ohh… I need to see more of these." Her fingertip rubbed downward through the dips and valleys. The zings of need barreled straight to my straining dick that took up all the extra room inside my jeans.

"You're killing me, babe." I bit down on her exposed neck while she searched in her bag. "Open the damn door." The words growled were at her. "Unless you want me to take you on the floor down there."

She pulled my head back by my hair to look into the gold-streaked green. "No, that's not going to happen. Too many onlookers, and the last thing you want is to end up in one of the tabloids having a rocking sailboat with this ass in the air." Her hand reached and pinched my butt cheek.

We quickly jumped down to the doorway, where my little sailor hastily unlocked the offending piece of metal, throwing the lock in the footwell. As Bardot slid the door open, her hand found a switch and flipped on a light inside before descending down the steep stairs with me close on her heels. I refused to let her go and break the electricity that flowed between us.

Making our way through the galley and into a

hallway where the head was located, she opened the door to a huge bed covered in navy and crisp white linens and colored accent pillows. It was difficult not to take notice of the richness of the teak wood that finished out all the walls inside the entire hold. Even a landlubber like me appreciated the amount of time spent caring for this boat. As an inheritance from her father, I believe she wanted to keep it looking grand with the pride he had instilled in her.

I grabbed her by the waist and pitched her into it with her laughing and squealing. As I climbed into the berth, she sat up. "You might want to lock the door behind you."

I felt my eyebrow raise. "Who the fuck would want to come on your boat?"

"Uh... let's see. Maybe some hot rock star or a pirate. There's always a pirate." Her index finger stopped at her cheek like she was thinking too hard with only a small smile to give her away. "And then there's Gilley coming to store supplies for the morning sail." Beautiful, mischievous green eyes captured me.

"Right. We wouldn't want those pesky pirates or the big guy showing up unannounced while I'm having my way with you," I replied with a smile before I kicked my foot out behind me, closed the door, then jumped off the bed to lock it. When I turned, she lay back on the high bed on stark, white bed pillows. The steep contrast to the dark-as-night hair on the bright white took my breath away, a rare beauty poised and waiting.

Earlier, when I saw her approach the boat, her soft, dark waves cascaded off her shoulders, making her look even sexier than I thought possible. Watching her come down the docks without her realizing had allowed me a minute to dream of every way I wanted to take her while we had time alone on the boat.

The soft movement of her hips swayed with each step, loose tendrils floating around her shoulders on the easy breeze from the water. God, she made my blood flow hot, and my desire reached a higher level with every step she took. I couldn't wait to have her beneath me.

I stepped closer to the bed and hoisted myself up and over her in one movement. As I rested on my elbows, her hands worked their way up my body, an inch at a time, until they looped around my neck. She pulled me down, meeting me halfway to have my lips. She nipped at first, and then with a harder tug, she assaulted me with a kiss that told me her need went as deeply as mine.

Damn, this woman.

I knew I was doomed.

"Before you leave, we need to have a long talk, but I don't want to spoil our time together," she uttered between bites and kisses to my neck. Some of them would leave marks, but hell if I cared. When I saw them tomorrow and probably a few days later, I'd remember this time even more.

I flipped her over, allowing her to continue to take the lead as she did with the kiss of fire she began her assault with. "Good, because talking wasn't on my list."

Her eyebrow lifted, questioning me.

"The only talking I want to do and hear are all dirty things we plan to do to each other tonight. Like right now... I need your mouth on me everywhere, or you'll be back under me so mine can explore all of you, making you dirty for me."

The lifted brow came down to form a smirk with her lips before she started inching down my body, making sure to rub hers suggestively against me along the way. When she finally reached low enough to find the hem of my T-shirt, her hands slipped under and gingerly touched my abs to drive me wild. Finally, her palm flattened out and crept upward, taking my shirt with it. I thought this sadistic torture was going to make me blow my load any second, so I took over and pulled my shirt off with one hand.

She giggled. "What's the matter, Wix? Impatient?"

"Like I said before, I think you're trying to kill me."

"And what if I do this?" Leaning down, she ran her tongue around my pierced nipple before giving it a slight tug that caused me to arch off the bed.

"Yes, dammit, Bardot. That works the same for me as it does for you." I watched her eyebrows lift as I almost tore off her shirt and snapped open her bra, letting it fall from her frame.

I pulled up on one elbow to guide her perfect tits to me, all while plumping one and using my index finger and thumb to tease the stiff peak. "Now, let's see what you think," I said as I began to mimic her torture of me. The tip of my tongue worked its way around the peak by the slowest increments my body allowed because every movement I made on her pushed me to jump ahead to sink inside her. But the look on her face made the slowness so worth it. Her head thrust back, causing the soft globe to push further to fill out and become firmer in my hand.

"On my God, Wix. That feels fucking amazing," she whispered as though it pained her to find words.

"Talk dirty to me and see what I'll do to you." I sucked the nipple in my mouth while tonguing and biting it lightly. I loved her full, round tits and knew I needed to revisit them later.

She sucked in a breath as though it was difficult to find enough air. "I think I could come just from the nipple play you're doing to me."

"Then, by all means, let me continue." I grinned at her with my teeth still attached to the hardened tip.

"No, I don't want to come yet," she answered with a loud inhale.

"Oh, babe. It'll only be the first time because I plan to make you come more times than you ever have in one night."

"I'm rarely ever good for more than one, so let's

save it for the best possible moment."

As I popped off the swollen pink pebble, I looked up at her beautiful face. "Bardot, that must be when you're with your vibrator because your body is so responsive when we touch that I know there will be multiple orgasms for you tonight."

Yes, tonight she'd discover a whole other side of herself. At least, I hoped she would. She alluded to problems in her past, during her teen years, that made me think there was a time when she experienced sex in a different light, but our time together would be different. Fumbling sex with horny teenage boys held no comparison to what I'd give her.

At some point, I hoped she trusted me enough to divulge those secrets that appeared to haunt her, but that was for another time. I only wanted her to think of me tonight.

My need took over, and I rolled us back on the bed. As badly as I wanted her to have control, my patience with her was spent.

Swollen nipples, plump breasts, and a heated look on her face were all I saw as I kissed, licked, and nipped at her taut skin, inching my way down her luscious body in search of the holy land. Her tight jeans blocked my descent, so I made quick work of relieving her of them and took the strings of her panties with them.

Lying before me with her skin blushed from desire, Bardot's perfection sent a new hot streak of deep lust through me. This look would stay with me for years.

"God, you make me want to do bad things, babe. Really bad things to you."

"Oh yeah, like what?" she teased by spreading her legs just enough to give me a peek of what lay ahead for me to indulge in every way.

I started with her slender ankle lavishing hot wet kisses and easy bites to capture her attention when she closed her eyes, enjoying the pleasure. Tiny goose bumps dotted her flesh from the sensation I caused as I moved up to her knee. I bent her leg to get at the soft skin on the backside of it which made her arch off the bed. As I continued my ascent up her leg, I smelled the desire telling me her body readied itself to have me. Smooth, shiny, needy lips waited for me at the apex of her thighs as she writhed on the comforter.

Part of me wanted to jump ahead and sink into her silky entrance while the other said no, wait it out, and you'll be rewarded with anticipation. What a dilemma to have. Everyman's dream with a partner they cared for.

I knew I was in deep, and now my brain said I cared. This was new territory for me, but I wasn't worried. Instead, I felt reassured this was what I wanted and prayed Bardot would develop the same feelings from our time together.

"Wix, please."

"Oh, babe, we're only getting started. By the time I finally give in to my need, you'll be begging me to fuck you."

"I'm ready to beg now." She moaned as her head whished back and forth on the pillow. Watching her dark hair scatter across the white background in striking poses gave me more drive to continue to worship her hot body.

"Tell me what feels good."

"Everything, Wix... it all feels great."

My tongue flattened and crossed over the smooth skin, bumping her swollen clit slightly. "Like this?"

"Oh my fucking God, Wix," she screamed out.

I snickered to myself at her words. "How about this?" I spread her legs wider and licked from bottom to top, ending at the engorged nub waiting for me.

"Fuck, fuck, fuck, Wix, *now*, please." My divine little sailor gasped. Her begging wouldn't keep me from getting her there. Her twisting and turning before told me she was close, but the trembles in her legs made me see it even more.

Rubbing my index finger around her opening, I slid in one and then two as far I could reach before turning them upward, seeking the spot to send her over the edge for sure. It only took a couple of sideways rubs across the roughened area. Bardot's body bowed up, her legs stiffened, and her inner walls clamped down on my fingers, convulsing and squeezing tightly to keep them seated inside her.

No fucking way would I remove them before she rode out the perfect orgasm on my fingers, except maybe me blowing my wad from watching her from the position I lie in. Her face glowed, as did the emerald eyes observing me, glancing down at her body. She looked stunned for a minute or two.

As she came down, totally spent from the ecstasy she felt, I wanted to stand up and strut around the small hold. I held back, though, not wanting to embarrass her in any way. Instead, I climbed up her body across the sheen of sweat left from what I had just made her feel. The glow she wore said all I needed to know.

"Babe, you okay?" I asked.

Without saying a word, she nodded. Maybe I stunned her speechless. Had no one ever given her the pleasure her gorgeous body deserved? What a shame with the way she responded to it. The dumbshits didn't know what they were missing.

As badly as I wanted to be inside her warm, wet sheath, I rolled beside Bardot to give some time for her to recuperate. Finally, she reached over and ran the back of her hand across my chest.

"That was... I don't even have words for it. Maybe... *sooo fucking good*?"

"Just good? Then, I didn't do my job well enough."

Her mouth gapped open. "Oh, you did your job well enough, all right. I saw the moon, stars, and maybe a galaxy or two in the space of a minute or less."

I rolled onto my side, resting my head on my hand. "Now, that's what I wanted to hear."

"So you need me to stroke that ego of yours. I'm sure you've heard a lot better compliments."

"Not from anyone who mattered, babe. Not one." I leaned down and kissed her pink lips.

CHAPTER 25

BARDOT

My body and mind were spent by the time Wix was finished with me. I felt like jelly from head to toe, including my mind. He held to his word and gave me two more fierce orgasms before he finally allowed himself the pleasure. This lust-filled night would never be forgotten, even if I never saw him again after today.

I slid out of the berth from the foot of the bed and padded quietly to the head, knowing flushing on the boat was bound to wake him up. After quickly brushing my teeth, I dug around below and found a toothbrush packet we kept for our occasional overnight guests. Leaving it on the counter for him, I wrapped myself in the luxury robe we also stashed away. To take advantage of the amenities we offered today was a first for me.

The K-cup coffee pot I kept on the counter waited to be filled with bottled water, so I took care to fill it to the top. Did Wix even drink real coffee every morning, or did he like the froufrou stuff with foam and delicate flavors? I dug around and found a few flavored creamers for him, just in case.

Before I moved to the upper deck, fat drops of rain played havoc on the skylight above the galley. With it still being early and not having guests until after lunch, I wondered if they would show.

Gilley's message came across as I waited for the cup to finish filling.

> **Gilley:** *you heard from them yet?*
> **Me:** *No, not yet. It's early though. Probably not awake.*
> **Gilley:** *you looked at the weather?*
> **Me:** *No, just got up. Why?*
> **Gilley:** *rain all day. I don't want to buy fresh groceries if they aren't coming.*
> **Me:** *I'll let you know asap.*
> **Gilley:** *I'll be waiting.*

Wix's feet hit the floor from the tall berth causing the boat to rock against the ropes that moored her. The door to the head shut next. I left out one of the plush robes in case he didn't want to don his jeans this early. After using everything in there for him, he strolled out in his boxer briefs. Now that was a look I didn't see every day. Yum. *No, Bardot.*

He leaned in and kissed my cheek. "Morning, babe."

"Good morning to you too." My lips lifted to a bright smile as I spoke, and a flash of last night's fun crossed my mind.

"I reached across the bed, and you were gone, making me unhappy until I smelled coffee."

"I didn't know if you drank regular or what?"

"Hmm... that's not what I had first on my mind when I found you gone, but I can wait." His eyes opened wide like his smile. He grabbed my hand and cupped it to his morning wood. "Hate wasting a good boner."

"You sound like Arch." No way could I resist that comeback. Not too much about those two was the same, but yeah, they both enjoyed joking around like fourteen-year-olds.

"No fucking way. That horn dog would have dragged you back to bed, coffee in hand." Both of us laughed at the comment, knowing it was probably true.

Simultaneously, we looked up at the ceiling when the rain started again, this time with a vengeance. He finally looked down at me with a raised brow.

"Think you'll be taking a charter out today?"

I huffed out and shook my head. While I was happy Wix might not have to leave so soon, canceling meant a loss of revenue. Gilley and I had bills to pay, and no clients meant no funds.

"Are you mad?" Wix asked.

Immediately, I felt bad for my attitude. "Damn, I'm sorry, not at you. No charters make it harder on Gilley and me." I looked up at him smiling, knowing my face betrayed me. I could afford to miss some charters, but not too many before it cut into my monthly budget. Upkeep on the boat, the slip fees, and my apartment all required quite a bit of cash flow per month.

"Then take me out on a charter today," Wix offered with that huge smile he gave audiences, which made me wonder if he felt pity for my position or was simply trying to be nice to me. Pity and handouts were not my style.

I depended on my boat and myself to take care of me. His offer made me believe he cared, which was a switch from most men who came around. Some expected me to take them on a free excursion because they showed interest in me. Telling them no resulted in never hearing from them again, but that was fine with me. If they only wanted me for their gain, good riddance to them. Users weren't welcome aboard.

"No, we can't. You heard the rain, and storms mean it could be dangerous on the water." I glanced back at the skylight.

"I didn't say anything about going somewhere. We can stay right here all day, no need to even get dressed." His smoldering look caught my attention as he reached for the belt tying my robe closed. Skin was all he'd find under the soft, warm fabric since I planned to shower after coffee.

"As a matter of fact, I'm thinking you've got too many clothes on as it is."

Dropping the ties and reaching for my coffee, he took it from me, then pulled the robe's belt open and gently pushed it off my shoulders so I stood bare-assed naked for him. I followed as his gaze roamed from top to bottom and back up ever so slowly. My skin flushed from his view, causing my heart rate to escalate.

"You're so damn beautiful, Bardot. To be here with you makes me willing to take risks." His voice grew thick with need.

Without a second thought, I turned and pulled him back into the bedroom, this time shutting the door with my foot and locking it behind me.

***

When coming up for air, I looked at Wix, who stared at me with a big grin plastered across his face. "It's still raining," he informed me. "Looks like I get to be your charter today, whether you like it or not."

"Yes, I need to check my phone to see if the guests checked in." I jumped off the bed and went in search of my cell. Just as I thought, they messaged saying they would have to postpone to a later date. Hence, no fees are collected for the day. My face reflected disappointment, even if deep down, I was ecstatic that

Wix and I had the day together.

"What's the matter, sweets?" He walked up, taking my phone out of my hands. "Is there a problem?"

"No, not really. I need to message Gilley to make sure he knows no charter today."

"Hey, is it about the money?" He turned and sat on the sofa, pulling me down to sit on his right leg. "I told you I'm happy to pay for the day to have you to myself."

"No, you're not paying for the day. It's not like you're getting the real experience. And me doing Gilley's job is a big *hell no*." My eyes found his. "You know, since it involves cooking and stuff."

His laughter echoed through the harbor, maybe even as far as the next club over.

"Oh, babe. Remind me never to eat your cooking if it's that much of a chore for you to do. I mean, I'm not the greatest cook, but hell, even I can whip up a few things." His choked words from laughing so hard made me want to grind my teeth.

"That was just mean, you know. True, but mean." My glare held no malice behind it because he wasn't trying to be cruel about it. "Good thing there's always Uber Eats and pizza. There's *always* pizza."

"This area seems fairly populated with food options, so we won't starve." He wiggled his eyebrows at me. "Of course, there are always other things we could do to forget we're hungry."

"Right, but if you expect me to do those things for

long, you'll have to feed me real food. You take a lot of energy to keep up with." I wrapped my hands around his neck and moved my legs across his lap. "What can I say... you wear me out."

"Fuck yeah, I do." He kissed me hard and quickly. "Let's order something."

***

Once the delivery guy dropped off our Chinese food and we sat on the cabin's floor to eat, I leaned back against the kitchen cabinet behind me and patted my stomach. "God, I'm so full now. What a way to fill me up."

A smirk rose across Wix's face. "That's what they all say, babe."

I grabbed the throw pillow from the sofa and threw it at him. "Yeah, yeah. The last shit I want to hear you say is what you do to all the 'babes.' " I air quoted for emphasis.

"Oh no, you don't. I haven't even thought about another woman since we've been together. Whatever fucking lives we led before this is of no concern. I can't even remember anyone before you."

"Right, right... I bet you say that to all the girls," I teased, but I had to keep my mind from going there with all the women I'm sure he'd slept with. What came before we met was on both of us, not something to worry about. That didn't mean I wouldn't give him shit, though, especially after his bandmates flaunted the stories in front of me. From watching them all together, they enjoyed making him squirm when other women were around us.

Wix came up on his hands and knees as he stalked toward me, rounding the picnic spread between us. Big warm hands came around the back of my neck and pulled me forward to meet his lips. The kiss might have been meant to shut me up, or maybe it was to set me on fire for him. Either way, it accomplished both goals.

His body swung around so he was beside me while his luscious lips continued to attack mine. Taking the opportunity to wrap his tongue around mine, I did the same with the deep kiss that set me on fire for him again. As he ended the kiss, strong arms picked me up and turned me to straddle him. Now, we looked eye to eye, and he captured my full attention. But the truth was, there was no place I'd rather be. At that moment, I realized my heart happily leaped into this situation but was it ready to be pummeled when he left?

"Bardot, look at me." His index finger raised my chin. "We both had lives before this. There's nothing we can do about it. Damn, it's probably good that I had lots of time to sow the proverbial fucking wild oats. What happened before we met is of no consequence to us now. All that matters is from the moment we met... from the moment we met is all that counts. Nothing we did with others will ever influence what we have going on now."

The midnight gray of his eyes pointedly told me his words came from honesty. No way could I tear mine from his with the sincerity he spoke. I loved that when he was serious about something, he said what he was thinking. But this time, we were on different pages. He thought my thoughts were on finances when they hovered over the coming heartbreak if I allowed myself to go all in with this.

Our time together would be short-lived. It was the type of relationship he had—love-'em-and- leave-'em, see-ya-on-down-the-road type of fun. I needed to decide if I was okay with that. I, in my heart, knew I wasn't. At that moment, though, my head said to run with it, take all he allowed, and deal with the fallout later.

God, it would hurt when he drove away on the bus to the next town.

I pulled in a deep breath and picked up where he left off. "Right, I know, and I'm sorry I brought it up. You and the guys like to harass each other about all your and their past conquests. It's funny to listen to y'all go at it with stories. Sometimes, I hate that I never had friends who shared stories with me. Not that mine are anywhere as outrageous as the band's, but still, it would be fun to have a friend who knew me so well."

His strong arms wrapped around me to hold me in a hug, pulling our bodies together as close as possible.

Whispering in my ear, "I want to be that someone for you, babe. Someone you create new stories with." Warm lips kissed my ear, causing goose bumps to shoot straight down my arm and side. I held onto him for dear life, knowing words like this wrapped around my heart as he was wrapped around me.

Wix's arms held me close, resting his head on top of mine.

The two of us didn't move, and when I felt his arms relax, I knew he was sleeping, so I closed my eyes and joined him.

***

Not knowing how long we stayed there, something caused my eyes to pop open. The rain picked that moment to stop, making the cabin too quiet. Before, it was the backdrop to everything. Now, it made the cabin seem to close in around us.

"It's not raining anymore," I offered softly, not wanting to wake him.

"Uh-huh," he barely whispered.

"We could go outside and look around. I mean, just to get out of here for a while. If you want to, that is."

"Sure, babe. Whatever you want to do as long as I'm there too."

Damn, could this guy get any sweeter? I felt another squeeze on my heart. As I stood, I offered him a hand to help him up from the hard floor he cushioned me from to nap. His eyes met mine, and he gave a small laugh.

"*Little you* is going to lift *big me* from here?"

"Hey, dude. I'm a helluva lot stronger than I look." I pulled with all my might trying to show him I could do it. Of course, he helped and popped up.

"Dude? Okay, that sounds fucking funny coming from you."

I let go and opened the hatch that kept us safe from the storms. The moon glowed from overhead now, and it treated us to its light cast across the smooth brackish lake.

"The clouds parted just for us to see," I uttered as Wix's arms wrapped around me from behind, and we looked out. Soft lights glowed across the harbor from other sailboats moored for the night.

"I can see why you like this place. Quiet, peaceful, but doesn't it get lonely here when you're on your own?"

"Guess I'm used to it." This time my words were lies. I hated being lonely on the boat at night. During the day and weekends, the boatowners and their friends kept the harbor exciting, but on the weeknights, when they all had homes in Houston to go to, I had my little apartment. One room. *Alone.*

We climbed off the boat and walked around the docks looking at the other boats. He asked questions, and I explained the different types of sailing vessels docked. The nautical world was an area Wix was completely unaware of, so it made talking about it more fun for me. Seeing sailing through a new set of eyes had me appreciating all I knew.

"Babe, I'm tired, and I know you are with driving back. Let's get back in that perfect bed of yours and get some sleep."

His face said it all. If mine looked half that tired, we both needed sleep. "Is this some kind of code for more sex?" I asked, lightening the mood.

"No, for once in my life, it means I want to sleep." Then he snickered. "At least some to rejuvenate me for fun and games in a little while."

Walking back and climbing aboard the boat, I locked the hatch, and we stripped down to underwear and my bra before jumping up on the bed. "Damn, I fucking love this. All the skin I want, just waiting for me. You know what would be even better?" Wix gave me the smile that stopped hearts while he was on stage.

"What's that?" I bit naively, guessing his answer.

"You naked. Yes, I think in the interest of time later, you should just go ahead and strip off the rest. I mean, look at those sexy-as-fuck panties... they're barely there anyway." He popped the side strip of elastic on me.

"Hey, what if we have to make a quick exit? I don't want to be naked." This drew a laugh from him.

"Fucking hell, Bardot. If you run out of here in that piece of fabric, the firemen couldn't do their job for looking at you. Maybe you should put on a shirt."

"Nope. Going to sleep just like this." I heard him grumbling as he slid under the covers and pulled me to him. "Go to sleep, dude." I felt him snickering.

This cocoon we spent the day and night in would soon morph into the real world.

But I refused to let that idea take hold of me before I slept.

CHAPTER 26

WIX

When I awoke with Bardot in bed beside me, it gave me an almost instant painful morning wood, which led to all kinds of interesting ideas. We had made love sometime in the middle of the night when another brief rain woke us both.

Made love? What the fuck? That wasn't something I did.

I rolled over and pulled her under my arm as close as I could get her while she continued to sleep. Her soft palm roamed across my pecs, and she snuggled in closer to me, all without waking up. Our bodies fit together like we were made as one.

Well, damn, look at me being all romantic and shit. But honestly, how did this happen?

Having different women all the time was something I told myself I was done with, yet here I am in bed with another woman. But Bardot wasn't just another woman. This woman possessed unusual power over my thoughts. Every time something happened since we'd met, my first thought was of her. How would she feel about it? Would this have any effect on her or us?

Us? Fucking hell. *Us?* When did this happen?

My time away in Austin might change things. Would I see her soon, not again like I thought about girls I enjoyed, but when? What would happen when the band resumed the tour?

So many damn questions were tossed and turned in my head while she slept peacefully. I kissed the top of her head, causing a soft moan, reminding me of the sounds she made while I pounded into her. My stone-hard dick twitched. Even asleep, I wanted her, but time didn't stand still long enough to commit these days.

Hell, the band only bargained to postpone a few shows while getting this damn documentary made. I hated this shit. Making up shows was a pain in the ass for everyone, especially fans. Our excuse didn't hold weight to me, but Jones thought it would all be okay.

Then there was the big guy at Paradise Productions, Mr. Knox. Who was this dickhead, and what kind of bullshit were his ideas going to lead to? All I understood was he had some deep pockets or a fuckton of pull to halt our tour. Tour dates were usually etched in stone, at least until the pandemic happened. Now tour life took on all new rules, like this detour.

"I can hear your brain from here, Wix. What's going on inside there?" my sweet bed partner said in a sexy, rough voice. "That type of sleeping never leads to something good."

Her fingers lightly drifted over my chest. Watching the tips and feeling the sensation as they drew patterns on me made my heart lurch and my chest squeeze tight. *Damn, I'm in too deep already.*

"Just thinking about the tour." I didn't want to sugarcoat it.

"Yes, you'll be leaving soon, won't you?"

So I could look down into those emerald orbs that had a way of capturing my attention, I flipped her over and covered her with my body. "Yeah, when I left, they agreed I could stay until the shoot was ready to take off. Mr. Knox wants his daughters to run the show. Who knows what they'll want to do, but they better get with the program because our time is limited."

My nose slid down her neck, inhaling her scent. Yesterday's perfume lingered, and the fragrance took up a special place in my heart. I knew every time I came across the scent in the future, she'd dominate my thoughts.

"Let's not waste another minute in bed then." She pushed me aside and stood searching for clothes. "I'm hopping in the shower. You can go next."

"If I joined you, it would be faster. Remind me again why we're in a hurry." My eyebrows wiggled.

She gave me an incredulous look. "Dude, have you looked in that shower? I have to stand sideways to use it. I want to go first so I can watch you take yours. Your big body inside that small space will be a laugh a minute to watch," she said, walking around the corner and out of sight.

"Are you saying I'm too big to use it? Guess I could take a swim with soap." I stared up at the ceiling, not liking that idea.

Her face peeked around the corner. "In that water? Are you shitting me? It's brackish at best. You know it flows off into the gulf, right? Why would you want to bathe in salty water?"

I glared at her for concealing what I'm assuming was a naked body. "Come back in here, and I'll explain it to you." My best panty-dropping smile spread across my face, knowing what it did for her.

"Yeah, right. We'll never get cleaned up if I do that. Be helpful and go make us some coffee."

What? Rebuffed by a female when I turned on the charm.

She truly loved her coffee.

***

We walked down the Kemah Boardwalk taking in the sights, watching the water, and dodging rainstorms. It could have been a dreary day, but with Bardot, she always made it fun. Having lived here all her life, she knew all the fun places to go. We ended up at a waffle factory across the bridge from the wharf area.

An older home, it had weathered many hurricanes and came back looking none too worse for wear. They served international coffees, which got Bardot all excited. The best thing, though, was the savory dessert waffles.

Sitting by a window at a tiny table, we watched the rain pound the small house across the street—so much for a cruise today.

"What do you want to do?" she asked, looking over her steaming drink.

My eyes met hers. "Be with you."

"Aw… aren't you just the best charmer."

"Really, I came here to spend time with you. I want to know more about you, so hit me with your best untold story. Some deep dark secret only a few know."

The longer I spoke, the more intense her beautiful eyes grew. Never did I realize she might actually have some bad shit to share. I wanted to know her. All of her. The good and the bad. God knew I hadn't been an angel while growing up. I gave my parents pure living hell for years.

She finally put the hot drink down and replaced the plastic lid before leveling me with those eyes that now looked sad, then a deep breath escaped her. "There are so many things I did wrong growing up, Wix. None of it I'm not proud of." With her shoulders hunched, she moved to the edge of the metal chair, primed to bolt if necessary.

Grabbing her now-empty hands, I replied, "Babe, we all did dumbass things when we were growing up. Some more than others, some worse than others. I'm okay with it and a great listener, so let's have it. Break some arms? Kill someone? How bad can it be?" I tried to keep my tone light, making what she told me not seem as awful as she thought.

The moment my words left me, I knew what she kept to herself fell in the tragedy category. The look on her face said it all. Maybe I needed to choose my words more carefully because the tortured look she wore spoke of heartbreak and not from some first-love situation.

I reached around and pulled her chair across the worn vinyl so our knees touched without letting her hands go. Instead, I twined our fingers together, trying to offer comfort and understanding, feeling like she needed it to begin.

"I told you that my mom died when I was young. My dad trusted me with everything. Remember me telling you the neighbors even tried to step in and offer some advice, but he shut them down?"

I nodded, not wanting to interrupt her confession. These days she recalled were in high school. Arch and I fucked up so much in high school, so I felt like I understood where this was going. But nothing prepared me for the type of pain she lived through.

"My new so-called friends took me to parties with people I should have never learned about, much less become new friends with. This all happened during the time I went to school. It only lasted my freshman year. I did it to please Dad, but nothing I did during that year came close to pleasing even the worst parents."

"I don't know. We did some things even Arch isn't proud of." She needed to hear that we all fuck up.

"Yeah, I learned the hard way that poor decisions have consequences, and some of them have life-long consequences." Her eyes drifted over to the window behind me, where she seemed to lose herself in a vision I couldn't see. I untwined one hand and ran my thumb back and forth across the backside of hers, trying to keep her in the moment. But she had drifted away in thought. I leaned forward and pulled her to me. Our foreheads touched, and she sucked in a breath.

"Thought I'd lost you there for a sec," I whispered softly.

"Maybe I lost myself."

Somehow, I felt like her comment went much deeper than I ever imagined this would go. In my mind, she'd tell me about skinny dipping in the lake or taking her dad's boat out without permission. If only her memories were that innocent.

"You're back now, but please don't feel like you

have to share. I'm more than willing to share any burden you carry, though." *Oh shit, was I the right person for this?* It didn't matter because I didn't want her to feel like she was alone any longer in life. She felt the urge to pour this out, and I wanted to be the one who soaked it up. Someone to take it away from her or at least hold a portion of her heavy weight. This might give her a way to breathe a lighter breath.

"No, it's okay to talk about." Her eyes met mine again with some renewed resilience. A small smile crossed my face, and she returned it. "It was a long time ago, anyway. I should be over it all by now."

"Some things have a way of haunting us when we least expect it."

"So true. This ghost visits my dreams, even after a great night, like the ones we've had together." She pulled in a deep, cleansing breath and began again.

"My friends took me to a group of warehouses further south from where we lived. The shady area wasn't somewhere we'd gone before because, hello... shady... like trashy and, in some places, destroyed. Old equipment, trailers, and cars littered the outside of the metal buildings that sat behind a tall fence with razor wire on top.

"I remember saying something about that wire, and the others laughed, saying the owners didn't like people sticking their nose where it didn't belong. I asked myself if I was that nosey person that night, but we went through a chained gate that wasn't locked.

The guy driving commented that someone had left the lock through the chain but not set when he climbed back in from opening the gate wide enough to get through.

"When we all got out, two of my girlfriends went laughing and skipping ahead, leaving me behind with two of the guys."

"Are you sure this was you doing this shit? You're so cautious all the time," I had to ask.

"Yes, sadly, I've not always been this way. I think what happened to me that night probably scared it into me. Too bad it wasn't something else."

I squeezed her hand, trying to help her feel comfortable talking to me, but I wondered what else I might do. The action gained me a little smile which was more than I had hoped for.

"Anyway, we went inside, and a lot of kids our age had a wild party going... dancing, drinking, and playing stupid drinking games. You know what I'm talking about." Again, I nodded.

"Our group joined them, and at first, I stuck close to my friends until this hot guy came over and asked me to dance with him. The current slow song caused me to think for a second, but I'd had a few beers and some shots, so I didn't think it through.

"After the dance, he didn't let me go. We walked back to where I'd seen him sitting, and he pulled out a chair, sat down, and pulled me into his lap."

"Uh-oh. The old lap trick." I wanted to lighten her

burden with the comment, but it didn't last.

"Yeah, something like that. I mean, this guy was seriously hot, and he never even looked at another girl that night once I arrived. We danced a few more times, and he went to get me a drink from the keg. I watched him walk over there and back with it."

Fuck, I knew where this was going. Seen this happen too many times. My stomach felt like it would give the waffle factory back its awesome breakfast. It churned with fear for Bardot.

"We sat around drinking for a bit. I noticed my two girlfriends weren't in the building with me, but one of the guys I came with stood across the room playing beer pong. I remember him looking at me and shaking his head like he wanted me to understand a message, but I was fifteen. I didn't know silent messages. I knew how to captain a boat but not how to tell when someone was trying to help me." Her voice moved up an octave with that statement.

"It's okay. You don't have to continue, Bardot."

"Yes, I do... I have to. These are things you need to know before we get any deeper into whatever this is."

I leaned in and kissed her softly. "I'm here, babe."

"So... the others at the table drifted off shortly after that, and I told Tyler I had enough to drink because I was feeling really tired. He offered to take me home, so I let him. I mean, we didn't live but like twenty minutes away, and he was at this party with my friends. He had to be okay, right? He left me for a second and went over to the guy playing, and by the time he returned, I could hardly hold my eyes open.

"Tyler helped me to his car and put me in the passenger seat. I remember him buckling me in because I told him I could do it myself."

"Yeah, I can see you saying that. Always taking care of yourself."

"Except not that night," Bardot barely said loud enough to hear. "God only knows how I gave him my address, but I did. I'm not sure where he took me first, but we got into the back seat of his truck or rather, he put me in the back seat. That's really the last thing I actually remember. The rest of that night is a blur.

"When I woke up, I was propped up against the door to our apartment sans bra and jean shorts. Never did find those things."

Other than the silent tears running down her face, no other emotions showed. She wiped them away with her hand while I watched her, then turned the watery green up to meet mine. My heart ripped further apart with each word she uttered, and her tears made the final jagged rip.

I slid forward and wrapped her in my arms. What I wanted to do was wrap her in my love, but I felt like my words came so late to the party. It was ten or more years ago when this happened. Bardot would never forget the horror of the night, and she hadn't let it define her life, but she needed to know it didn't change my mind about her in any way.

"Babe, none of this was on you. Peg it on the sorry son of a bitch who brought you home and the friend who allowed him to do it. What the fuck was that friend thinking? That something only might happen to you with this dickwad? Did the friend know it had happened before? This is on them. Not you."

A hard look met mine. "You're right, and I know it now. It took me a long-ass time to finally see that, though. Lots of therapy, some formal, some on the water, just living. Sailing saved me, Wix. I can't leave it behind. I need the freedom the water gives me."

With each word, my arms held her tighter, closer. Maybe I needed it more than she did, but that was selfish of me. She bared her soul with these words, and now that I know, I think I love her even more than I did. *Love?* I needed to save that thought for later. Bardot needed my full attention with these admissions.

Pulling back from me, she wiped away the final tears. "Okay, enough of that for today. Now you tell me something funny, so we can move on from this. *Please.*"

The way she formed the word 'please' begged for something, not simply a request, so I regaled her with several on-the-bus stories that could make a prostitute blush. It lightened the mood, but in my heart, I knew she suffered from the memories.

A need inside me wanted to know what more she saved from telling. 'Enough of that' said there was more to this story, and I damn sure had questions, but now wasn't the time. She wanted a reprieve from the heavy shit then I was just the person to give it.

I wanted to take her sadness and make it my own instead. If I could find the dick who raped her, I'd find a way to make sure he never did it again.

Later, a call was going to reach out to Duke to locate someone local who could do the research and solve the problem.

CHAPTER 27

BARDOT

"Let's say we go do something fun." He whipped out his trusty phone and googled fun things to do on a rainy day. Watching the device over his arm, it took him to several places close to us from golfing off a platform to a Main Event indoor amusement center.

"How good are you at golf?" He grinned and asked me as we walked to her car in the wet parking lot. The laughter I returned with, complete with a sarcastic undertone, left him wondering how bad or good I really was.

"Let's go, rock star. I'll show you my lack of skills off the water." I showed him a brighter face but knew it covered the sadness I kept deep inside. Nothing he could do would make what happened right, especially after all this time, so I had to let it go like I did back then.

Even with the rain sprinkling down, the concierge at the huge golfing facility allowed us to have a cubicle. When Wix said he had maybe hit a golf ball a few dozen times in his life, I had to be all in on this. It turned out he was equally as bad as me hitting that dimpled hardball.

I chose an aqua ball to his hot pink one. Our tastes were complete opposites when it came to colors. While mine fell in the calming category and the colors of the ocean, he wanted more stimulating ones. But that was okay. Opposites attract.

My first swing sent the ball flying sideways to the platform, causing him to almost land on his ass with laughter. I knew mine would be bad because he had to be covering for his skills from all the fake laughter he carried on with.

"Okay, Mr. Rock Star. Let's see you do better."

"Hey, not one to fucking brag here, but even I can do better than that." He stepped close to the teed ball and first did a few practice swings, mimicking his best Tiger Woods impression. Inside, he knew he better come through after his wallowing-laughter show and dumbass bragging.

Concentrating on that hot pink ball, he swung the club back and let go with force, seeming to surprise himself. He looked out over the artificial fairway, knowing it went a long way but couldn't spot the damn thing. I looked out at first and then back down to the tee.

"You might want to look down, Mr. Rock Star." He had to feel the smirk on my lips without looking back at me. He grazed the ball enough for it to roll forward six or so inches.

"And what exactly were you saying about being better than me? Something like, 'even I can do better' or some nonsensical shit as that, right?"

The entire play followed the same route. We both got a touch better after watching a YouTube video on how to make contact with that damn ball.

Turning in our clubs, we returned to the car with a ringtone blaring from his back pocket.

"Yeah? Yes, I heard you. No, I'll be there. Later." Jones' words harshly boomed through the electronic leash. "Why didn't I turn the fucking device off this morning?" His head turned to see me staring at him. "You have to go, right?" I knew disappointment covered my face, and that wasn't fair on him.

"Yeah, but it's been great being here with you, though. I feel like we really connected this time as just two people without all the stupid shit to deal with. You feel that too? Tell me you do."

I let out a quiet huff. Some other female doing this would probably be dismissed, but this was me, and I knew he took it to heart.

"I'm sorry, babe. I hate leaving, too, but this is my band that needs me. I can't let them down by not showing. The label would have my ass for it too."

Belying the truth, I looked at him with soft eyes

while my hand came to rest on his thigh. "I know you're right, but it doesn't mean I have to like it. Honestly, I'm shocked they allowed you this much time away, so I can't be angry."

"I'd say you look disappointed, and dammit, I hate disappointing you." His hand wrapped around my neck as he pulled my lips to his. The lingering kiss said everything I wanted it to. *Damn, I knew I was going to miss having him around.* We finally started connecting on a deeper level and bang, he had to leave. *Again.* One of us was always leaving and I fucking hated it.

"So, back to Austin, huh?" I asked as I pulled out of the parking lot. "We need to go by the boat before heading to the airport."

"No, we can't. I don't have time. The plane will be here in less than thirty minutes. I didn't leave much there, so keep it safe while I'm away." His hand rested behind my neck as I drove.

"Yeah, I can do that." So many other words came to mind, but I kept them to myself, not wanting to sound clingy or needy. Guys didn't like those traits. That was a girl I never wanted to be. Making it on my own was how I rolled, and with or without him didn't change that in me.

The trip to Hobby Airport took less time from the golfing venue, so we made it right before the plane arrived. Since it came in where private jets landed, Wix could walk straight to the steps that popped out, this plane being smaller than the others he flew on. Guess the 13 Recordings label had several to choose from.

We said goodbye with a quick kiss because a lingering one was too hard for us. Letting him get inside my head and heart killed me, especially right then. I hated saying goodbye to anyone I was close to since I never knew them to return.

On the drive back to the boat, Wix sent me a quick text.

> **Wix:** *Dammit Bardot, why didn't I get a long, slow kiss?*
> **Me:** *It's too hard to say goodbye that way.*
> **Wix:** *Fair enough*
> **Me***: Glad you see it my way. ;)*

As the sun decided to peak through the overcast sky, I pulled up to the boat. At least I found a reason to be happy. Jumping into the cockpit, I opened the locked cabin door and walked down. With each step, my senses picked up on Wix's presence. He'd left behind something to torture me, a scent uniquely his. His T-shirt lay in the middle of the floor at the opening of the bedroom.

"Typical man." I reached for it and held it to my nose, breathing in his presence. Maybe I'd sleep in it until he returned or I heard otherwise from him. He made no promises of what was to come for him or us.

Hell, for all I knew, that could have been a forever goodbye without me realizing it.

"Damn, damn, damn!" I screamed inside the small area, creating an echo around me. Why did I let him in? Why did I give him my secrets, ones he had no business knowing? Those words were never meant to be shared. Not to anyone. I locked them away long ago in a tidy compartment in my head and threw the key overboard.

With a brave face, I went to my school counselor after it all went down, and she suggested I seek further help than what she could offer. Her face told me she pitied me, which was something I hated. As hard as she tried, I refused to give up the piece of shit who hurt me.

Yes, I'd been raped, but thankfully, he must have wanted someone who would lay still and be quiet. I knew I didn't respond or put up a fight because there were no bruises or many marks other than some tiny bite marks in strange places. My butt cheeks were covered in them. Thank God he didn't force anal on me. That I definitely would have known the next day.

As far as I could tell, I had only been fucked and had his semen shot across my back. My shirt was stuck to me, and the odor was easy to identify. I threw the clothes away and showered with extra hot water and an entire bottle of liquid soap. Then I soaked in the tub to make sure nothing was still on my back that I missed. My skin glowed a bright pink tone for a good hour after.

Now, I knew all the evidence I needed to catch this monster washed down the drain with all my cleaning. Back then, shame, anger, and terror blocked out reasoning.

All I wanted to do was forget it had ever happened, which was easy since Dad was on the boat all night. I opened the door and let myself in, took care of me first, and then disposed of the clothes.

One piece at a time, I dropped the stained clothes on the gas grill sitting idle on our patio. I watched the shirt flare up in the small orange flame, trying hard not to think about who redressed me. My panties hit the fire next. The spandex didn't burn as easily as the cotton but instead coiled in on itself before finally melting away. Green flimsy material resembled me inside, shriveling in on myself to justify the pain I carried, knowing what had happened.

I'd made a rookie mistake every female should know. Despite the soft words Wix used with me, and ultimately, I knew this was my fault. My dad had preached safety to me and never put myself in a position for someone to hurt me, which is exactly what I did. Taking a drink from a virtual stranger allowed him to take control of me.

"You're a dumbass, Bardot."

My words fell on deaf ears.

Hadn't I said them a thousand times?

Screamed them to the heavens while out on the

water alone?

Cried them out when I woke from the nightmares I suffered from?

They were what caused me to seek counseling—no sleep, guilt, shame—and all the emotions I buried in that box long ago now floated around again.

This was all water under the bridge. So I put it back in the box and locked it away. No one needed to hear the words or know what I went through.

Grabbing my laptop, I logged into the schedulers to find we had a charter in the morning. Gilley probably had the grocery list already lined out from his meal preparation. With my pity party over, I began cleaning away the evidence of the best time of my life from the inside of my baby. Rumpled sheets and damp towels evoked memories of our time together for me to envision while I polished teak and shined stainless.

The guests deserved a sparkling clean vessel to enjoy for the day. Cleaning allowed me time to think as well as use it as a form of therapy. I considered all sorts of outcomes for Wix and me while I remade the berth. If he could walk away, so could I, but I refused to discard the precious time we had together. Some of those moments in time overwhelmed me while they happened, but now I stored them all away for when I was lonely, and I knew he would chase my deserted feeling away.

Up top, I heard Gilley's giant feet making their way down the docks. Glancing back into the hold, nothing revealed the time Wix and I spent there, so it was all good. My world floated on water and felt level again.

"Figured if your company was gone, you'd be here." Gilley greeted me with a smile.

"How'd you know I had company?"

"Stopped by yesterday to see what we needed to replace and saw the mess. You never leave stuff like that lying around knowing a client would be aboard in the next few days."

The red heat started at my chest and worked its way up through my cheeks. He'd seen clothes, panties, and rumpled bedsheets and knew what had gone on down there. How did I even reply to that?

Gilley's full-sized laughter began as quickly as my embarrassment. "Looked like y'all had quite the time. Maybe I should bring a female down to the docks sometime."

I stuck my palm up in the air. "Shut it. I don't need anything else to make me cringe." My hands covered my face.

"Girl, you're a grown-ass woman. You can do what you want on your own boat. No need to get all in a damn tizzy over it. I'm just saying if you'd let me borrow it sometime, I might have the same luck as you." He wiggled his eyebrows at me.

"Uh... sure. Just let me know when you have an, uh... date and want to bring them here."

He made it sound like I picked up some guy for a one-night stand here on the boat. Eww. Never would I bring some random down to my boat. This was my private place when charters weren't scheduled. Spoiling the mystique the boat held for me by doing something that stupid would not happen.

Wix fell into a different category. What we had hadn't been random to me. Granted, we had only been together a handful of times, but when we were, they meant something. At least they did to me. He told me they meant something to him too. We weren't in love or anything because that idea seemed crazy. His days were taken by his first love, music, and mine, water, so we didn't stand a chance.

Gilley and I scrubbed, polished, and shined, readying the boat for the following day. Three couples booked the boat for the entire day, so we needed everything in tip-top condition. Several luscious meals would be served and sailing down to the mouth of the channel before looping out into the gulf and back, making it a full day.

I hoped the weather held out because this time of year, it always played havoc on planning.

***

"Great day, skipper," Mark offered his hand as he spoke. "I never realized how long it would be getting to the gulf, but you handled it like a pro."

I stared up at the guy as his wife slid in beside him. "Yes, you have the best skills at handling this big boat."

"Thank you, both. I appreciate the comments. I'd really appreciate it if you'd put that on the comment cards or the website. Reviews are important for the business."

"Not a problem at all. We have lots of friends who love to sail but don't want the hassle of owning a boat such as this gorgeous one," Mark continued. "I'd be happy to recommend you to them."

My smile stretched across my face. Word-of-mouth from a client proved to be our best advertisement.

"Gilley and I would be happy to have them aboard."

"Until next time,' Drew said and waved, stepping over onto the dock. "Adina and I'll be back soon."

The group made their way up the parking lot while Gilley and I started the cleanup all over again.

This was my life.

Sail, clean, sleep.

Sail, clean, sleep.

Repeat, repeat, repeat.

As I washed down the front deck, I looked across Clear Lake. Boats scooted back to their hiding places for the night. A loud party boat made its way into our harbor, the revelers having fun. They danced, sang off-key, and then laughed at themselves. Friends having fun.

Laying the water hose down, I dropped to the wet deck.

This was my life.

CHAPTER 28

WIX

Bang. Bang. Bang.

"Get the fuck up, guys. We have places to be," Jones' annoying voice muddled through my hungover head.

"Go away, asshole," Arch bellowed in return to the obnoxious noise.

"No can do, guys. Roll out and get dressed. We need to be at the studio in fifteen. I'll get coffee now, so meet me at the car." He hit the door a few more times to bring home his point.

"Motherfucker had to show up at the ass crack of dawn." Arch's feet hit the floor in the bed across from mine.

Back in our suite in Austin, the band drank ourselves into oblivion the night before. We jammed and wrote a new song before the drunken behavior got the best of us. The lyrics I formed in my head on the plane ride back wouldn't leave me alone, so working with my mates, we wrote the music for them.

This often happened when one of us found something or someone who affected us. Inspiration. Bardot definitely affected me in a good way, so the music's upbeat melody made it all the sweeter to play.

No doubt this woman dug in deep under my skin. She held a place no one had been in a long time. My head still tried to wrap around the idea, but my heart was all in already.

"Some dope lyrics you laid down last night," Arch commented as he slammed the bathroom door. I rolled off the side of my bed, hoping my jeans from yesterday lay close. Opening my eyes, even with the blackout drapes shut, caused the pounding to worsen.

I slid them on as far as I could, leaning back against the bed. Finishing the job required me to stand. Damn, if I wanted to try.

The bathroom door popped open, and it became clear Arch was ready for the day. I never understood how he did it. Drink and smoked himself stupid the night before and rebounded like an NBA superstar the next morning. My body wasn't made that way. Maybe it was a sign I shouldn't do those two things so heavily.

Arch eyed me half on and half off the bed. "Bruh, look gnarly this morning."

"It's your fault. Where'd you get that shit we smoked? Are you sure it wasn't laced with something extra?" I felt more than hungover.

"It's all good. You're just turning into a pussy. Ever since you returned from seeing your sweet cheeks, you've been acting full-blown cunt caught."

My brain might have been working in slow motion, but no one would refer to my girl as a cunt. I rounded on him. "Do not refer to Bardot as a cunt... *ever.*"

Arch's hands came up, showing him backing down. "Sorry, bro, but really... we've all noticed it. Don't get me wrong, that babe is probably worth it, but dude, find your balls, or did she hang onto them for you?"

I glared at him before pulling out a clean vintage black Ramones T-shirt. "I don't know what you're talking about because my balls are firmly in place." I grabbed my crotch for emphasis.

"Uh-huh... could've sworn you came back without them from the way you've been acting." He sat and leaned back on his rumpled bed. "What happened down there? You've been keeping that shit locked down tighter than virgin panoche."

He wanted details I kept to myself about our time on the boat. Those days together meant everything to me. *Was I pussy-whipped?* Yeah, maybe, but fuck it, I didn't care. I wanted her with me as much as possible, but Bardot had a hard time with this life, especially after the last visit to Austin.

"I want her, Arch. Bad. I want her with me all the time," I finally admitted as we closed the door to the empty suite. We heard the door slamming before we left our room, so we knew Trotter and Kenzo had gone ahead without us.

"Bruh, are you sure about this? I mean, look at the shit that happened last time she was here. It didn't work for her. We're a hot band right now. It's going to be like this for a long fucking time, hopefully." He eyed me carefully on the ride down, where we caught up with the others and climbed into a van.

Jones started talking as soon as the door closed, ending our conversation, which was fine by me. Not ready to share my realization with everyone yet, I gave Arch a pointed look, and he nodded in return, knowing what I meant.

"Okay, so today we're going to have a meeting with everyone involved. I've set up all the preliminary bullshit needed to make this happen as quickly as possible. They already know the band is ready to get back on tour, so it should be a painless meeting."

We all grumbled our thoughts about postponing, and Jones took it all in. "Look, guys, I want you to understand this is something 13 Recordings wants done. The PR Department believes this will propel Copper Crowns to the next level."

"Is it going to make us better musicians?" Kenzo asked.

"Nope, not one damn bit," Trotter offered.

"You're right. It won't do that, but it will get you in the media on other platforms than simply playing music can do." He took a deep breath. "Just think how much your fans will love being able to watch you over and over on Netflix and YouTube." He pointed his finger at Trotter. "That won't make you better, but it will make you a household sensation as well as a great musician."

Trotter turned back and eyed Arch and me in the back seat. He didn't need to say anything because we knew what he was thinking. He turned back to Jones. "Guess we'll see then."

After the short drive and walking into the building, we all stepped into a boardroom where five chairs were waiting for us. I looked over the group sitting around. Two gorgeous blondes, an older woman with a laptop at the ready, and a few executive types waited for us to make our appearance. Nothing about this looked promising to me.

"Good morning," Jones offered, breaking the tension.

A middle-aged man in an expensive suit stood and offered Jones his hand. "I'm Daniel Knox." He turned to the two beauties. "These are my daughters, Tracy and Tessa."

I looked at the twins and saw nothing but trouble. Spoiled princesses here to allow Daddy to please their whim. That whim being us. *Ugh.*

The two gave a slight wave of their hands before Knox introduced the rest of the people at the table, who stopped looking at the papers long enough to say hello.

"The team here is having a first look at the agenda for the shoot. Jones approved it all yesterday, so this meeting is just a formality to let you get acquainted with the team. The girls will be running point on the entire project, but please know I've covered this plan with a fine-tooth comb so there's nothing on here I rejected. That's been removed before today."

Kenzo spoke up immediately, "What about us having a chance to do the same? Shouldn't we get to add our input?"

Knox blinked rapidly as though shocked we had an opinion. "Well, I... uh..." He turned to Jones. "Jones here went over the plan and assured us it was all good."

"Well, damn, if Jones said it, it must be perfect." No one around the table mistook Kenzo's meaning nor his sarcasm. "How about we take a beat here and allow the four of us, with Jones, to skim over it so we know what's what?"

It made me happy to see the suits' eyebrows go up into their hairlines. They thought this was going to be a quick sign-off on their little pet project to please Knox's daughters. Kenzo always took the lead on important matters, and this time, I was happy to see him doing just that.

Kenzo stood, and the rest of the band followed him through the door with Jones on our heels.

"Let's find a place to talk, guys," Jones hastily spoke. He opened a few doors before coming across an empty conference room. "Please understand I took out all the items I knew you would never agree to. I looked at it from the band's perspective, trying to keep the professionalism and integrity I know Copper Crowns stands for."

We took seats around the table with Kenzo at the helm. "Thank God for that. Right, guys?" The three of us nodded. "Tell us what we're not going to like, Jones."

Jones thumbed through the pages looking at certain places he had marked in green. "There are a few scenes with the girls that you might enjoy, but like? That's a different story."

"The girls?" Arch wondered aloud. "Knox's twins?" Leave it to Arch to bring up the women.

"Yes." Jones didn't expand on it. He deliberately kept something from us that he knew we might balk at.

"So, how many fucking scenes are we talking about here? I thought this was a documentary. Nothing about those two chicks is part of our past." Kenzo continued with questions we all wanted the answers to.

His wife would never be happy. She barely tolerated the women at concerts and in our music videos. We rarely had women in them because we wanted it to be about the music, not the extras.

My thoughts drifted to Bardot. How would she feel about the two women, given their looks? And would the scenes be suggestive? One more thing to talk about.

Jones spoke up, "It is a documentary, and while they will assist the director they hired, who has worked with some huge names in the industry, the girls will also be in a few scenes. Most of the video will be montages from past shows edited in and from press junkets, interviews, and music videos the band's done. We only need to film some intros, some made-up videos from the music, etcetera."

"How long are we talking?" Trotter went straight to the point. Our responsibility was to our fans, not Knox's pet project to promote his daughters.

"With the tight timeline we've given them, they're going to try to get filming done in three days. Later, we might have to fly back here to add some extra footage they feel necessary for cohesion." It became obvious quickly that Jones had all the answers planned. He knew the band well enough to see how this would play out.

We trusted Jones. The guy came from a questionable background with him and his brother, Grey or Grit—he went by both names. The dude joined the Defiance Motorcycle Club in NOLA to escape the life his dad set out for him and to search for some chick. Jones, being the firstborn, followed Daddy's orders to get a business degree but drew the line with joining his dad's enterprises. Jones was made for the job. His smooth talking and business sense helped make Copper Crowns the band we were today.

Taking a brief time off, Jones told the band he had to go to NOLA for his dad's funeral. The old man got caught up in an awful cult ritual costing him his life. Jones shared a little of how his father died, and the story made us all recoil, telling him no more information, please.

When Jones came to us months later to do him a huge favor, we were all happy to help. The guy became part of our band of brothers in the beginning. Sometimes we had to put up with dumb shit he came up with, like this documentary.

We flew to NOLA and played at a wedding for some of the Defiance MC's club members. The rough group of men and their 'old ladies' greeted and treated us like family. Our ideas of what a motorcycle gang and club were supposed to be changed that night. We made good friends until one of the ranked officials in the club's old lady went into labor. What a scene that was. They left in the newlyweds' limousine, but that was another story.

Motorcycle clubs get a bad reputation for the so-called bad things they do, but from what I saw, they're a tight-knit group of people who band together to be a family of their own choosing, like Copper Crowns. We came together for a common cause, and even though our personalities ranged from moderately conservative to off-the-charts crazy, we formed our own family.

Bardot needed a family, and I wanted to give that to her. I needed her to see she wasn't alone in life. Right now, she walked a lonely path. Sure, she had Gilley, but after him, what kept her grounded? The boat? The water?

Not too much comes from those ties in the way she needed. Yeah, I see why she felt a connection to them. Her family raised her to find peace and confidence with them, to use the water as a place to connect, but that's not a life for someone as vibrant and energetic as Bardot. She needed a force to drive her, keep her safe, and above all, to love her.

Dammit, there's that word again. Could I be that person for her? Would I ever be enough for her to attach a lifeline around?

I want to be her rock, her home, even, but my band had to play a huge role in our relationship like her sailing did. Is that even possible to have them both, given our schedules?

Her past holds complications, and the way she ended her story, I'm not sure I've heard them all, but I'll get to the bottom of it because before she can move forward, she needs to deal with the memories that haunt her.

I'm not saying I eased through childhood or my teen years, but compared to losing her parents and then the date-rape trauma, it was a walk in the park. My parents might disagree to some extent, but they love me unconditionally. I knew they would love Bardot too.

The fuck? Now I'm introducing her to my parents?

These ideas kept getting deeper.

Trying to be honest with myself, I do want her to meet them. My parents have always played an important role in my life, and when she becomes attached to me, she becomes attached to them. I hoped the idea wouldn't scare her off.

"Wix? Wix?" My arm took a hit from a fist, bringing me back to the situation before me. Rubbing away the pain, I looked around at the faces staring at me. "What?"

"While you were taking a tour through that head of yours, the rest of us decided we could do three days and no more. Are you on board with this?" Kenzo asked me.

"Sure. Three days. We can do that, right?"

I had no fucking idea if we could or not.

Three days of filming would prevent me from seeing Bardot, but at least the guys understood.

CHAPTER 29

BARDOT

"Babe, good news. We're going to be in Austin for three days." The excitement in Wix's voice carried through the phone. "I know last time was shit, but can we have a do-over on you coming here, please? This place is awesome, with so much live music everywhere. It's my kind of city."

Bursting his bubble of enthusiasm, I replied, "No can do, rock star. I have a charter tomorrow morning." I needed to change the wild ringtone he woke me with to something softer. He had programmed it in my phone when he set up his contact information, and it was a little too rowdy for me first thing in the morning.

"That's okay. There are still two days left. I'll fly you both ways, and you'll never miss a minute of charters." He sounded like a kid convincing his mom to buy Captain Crunch.

"But another could come up before the day is out."

"That's easily solved. I'll be your charter. See, no loss of income. I'll call the company right now."

"Wix, you can't do that. It's loss of income for you."

"No worries, I have plenty of disposable income. Just say you'll come. I'll make sure it all goes smoothly. You'll come directly to me, not the hotel."

Someone in the room called Wix. "I gotta run. Think hard and fast, babe. I need you here with me. I miss the hell outta you."

"Right." My answer came with a note of sarcasm to it, but how could he miss me when he had the other three stooges around?

My phone dropped on the sofa as I looked out over my apartment's balcony. For a change, I stayed here last night. I had slept on the boat since Wix left, so I could snuggle into the pillow he used. It helped me feel closer to him, and smelling his scent calmed me. I hated waking up to an empty bed but not enough to go home.

But, not staying in the apartment for several nights always created some anxiety. The last thing I needed was a break-in, so I came back yesterday.

The door opened to exactly the way I left it—cold and sterile. This place never felt like a home to me, but I needed a place to keep my things and in case the clients wanted to stay on the boat. It happened more than I liked, so we kept her stocked. The added payment helped me in the end.

So little of my apartment looked like home. I added a few pictures of my mom and dad around and even had some of me as a child. The rest looked exactly the same as the day I moved into my sparse collection of furniture. I didn't need much flying solo.

Maybe I should try the roommate thing again. The first time ended in a nightmare, but I was older and wiser now and knew what to look for.

"Nope, Bardot. You vowed not to do that again," I spouted off to the empty living area. The walls echoed my words back. "Damn, this place could make the Pope lonely."

A few chores needed doing, so I opened Spotify on my phone and looked up Copper Crowns. Naturally, they had a huge collection of their music on it, so I started listening, especially to the bass solos that played occasionally.

Wix told me he didn't sing, but I swore I heard his voice in the background on a few songs. Maybe he didn't feel as though his contribution to the sound made any difference. I found myself listening harder for him to shine through.

A slower tune started with a bass introduction, causing me to stop changing my sheets. The low sound carried through my apartment. The melancholy notes caused my heart to hurt. Did playing this make him feel the same way?

As I fell back on the bed, I listened as Kenzo

crooned the words into the mic. Each line of lyrics pulled at my heart to the point tears fell and rolled down my temples to the clean sheet. Rarely did songs evoke emotions from me, but with the despondent notes, words, and the haunting melody Trotter played, my tears kept coming.

The tune ended on the same quiet riff it began on. I sat up straight, wiping away my tears with the back of my hands. If Wix were here, would he wipe them away for me, or would I even cry?

"Stupid, Bardot, really stupid," I whispered. I didn't need someone to wipe away my tears since I'd been doing it for years on my own. When was the last time I cried alone, anyway? Not that I had wanted to, but that was a luxury I tried not to indulge in because it started a spiral that took me down some bad roads.

I cried with Wix because, dammit, he made me feel things I thought were long gone, but sitting in my bedroom crying over a song, nope. Not doing it.

As I finished the bedroom cleaning, my phone started with his ringtone again.

"Are you ready to give me a time now? I had a little break in the action, so I wanted to set this up for you now if possible. If you only knew how badly I wanted you here, right now. I mean, you'd be waiting at the airport already."

"Stop. Stop. Stop." His word vomit sent my brain into overdrive.

"Oh, shit. Sorry. I've been on set pretending to play

my bass, and that gets my blood flowing."

My eyebrows shot up. "Why are you pretending to play?"

"That's the way they shoot it. We go back and add the sound in the studio. Need it sounding fucking great for the final product." He laughed as he said the words. I loved him being in a great mood—it tended to spill over onto me.

"Back to my question, babe. You coming?"

My fourteen-year-old inner self wanted to make a crude remark, so I let it fly. "That's what he said."

"Why, Bardot, are you making a joke?" Even though I couldn't see his face, I knew his smile increased from his voice.

"Sorta?" My sound went higher with each letter. I used to be this fun person, someone who made jokes and teased, but that left me long ago—the night of the incident. *I could be that person again, couldn't I?*

Before the thought left me, I heard him howling with laughter. "You made a joke. That's a first." He worked the words out between his fits.

"Okay, okay. I can be funny, too, so stop laughing."

"But it was funny as hell coming from you." His breathing almost returned to normal. "So what's it going to be?"

When Wix got a plan in his head, changing the subject appeared out of the question. This idea was one of them.

"I guess I can come for a couple of days. At least

until y'all leave Austin. I can ride back to Houston with you and then take an uber home from there."

"Great plan. I love it since it means I get you all alone on the bus."

"Alone? You mean with the band, don't you?"

"Yeah, but those fucknuggets don't count."

My mind drifted to all the trouble we could get into in the back of that bus, making me miss him in a completely different way. I didn't just miss him. I wanted him. Badly.

"When can you leave?" Mr. Insistent continued.

"I need to go to the boat and make sure she's good for me to be gone a few days. Pack a few clothes—"

"The less, the better." I knew where his mind went or did it stay there?

"Then go to the airport," I continued.

"Okay. The plane will be there in two hours. That should be enough, right?"

"Yes, that's perfect."

"No, babe, you're perfect. And I'm going to worship you when you're here to show you how much I believe that."

"Sweet talking will get you everywhere, *babe*." I used his term of endearment with as much sarcasm as I could muster.

"Ohh... I like it. But if you're gonna call me babe, I'll have to find another word."

"Right. You do that. You have all afternoon to think about it."

"Just thinking about you getting here is making me hard already."

"Hmm... guess we'll see what I can do about that when I arrive."

I pushed the red button ending the call. Needing thirty minutes to the airport, I had to get busy, starting with the boat. Some of my 'going-out' clothes were stored there.

With the few things I had at the apartment in a duffle bag, I headed to the boat to tie it down better. The hatches were closed already, but I unlocked the cabin and went in to finish up. Being gone for only a few days, I didn't need much, so it didn't take long.

Little room in the cabin allowed for decorating, but I did. Old pictures of my dad and I stayed in the cabinets because clients didn't want to see that. I pulled one of the last ones out before he died and ran my finger over it, clearing the dust off the glass.

We were happy then. Mom had passed, but we found some happiness being together on the boat. It was our tie to each other. No matter what else happened around us, the boat kept us anchored.

The knot in my throat threatened tears, so I returned it to its resting place. I'd cried already today. "Once is enough," I remarked, closing the door and latching it.

As I climbed out and began locking up, I saw the security guard drive by. My hands went up immediately to stop him.

"Hey, Bardot. What's up?" Gene, the security guard who had worked here as long as I could remember, asked.

"Hi, Gene." I waved at him standing on the dock by the boat. As I stepped off the boat and headed toward him, he smiled his easy smile. "I wanted to let you know I'll be gone for a few days. Keep an eye on her for me, will ya? Gilley would be the only other person who might show up, but other than that, no one steps on the boat."

"Sure thing. I'll pass it along to the temporary man we hired. I'm going on vacation myself. The wife and I are headed to Alaska on one of those cruises. Be our first real vacation in ten years, and I'm ready."

"Gene, that's a long time between vacations."

"Shesh, don't I know it, but I needed to get my two kids through college."

"Yes, I can imagine that took all the extra funds and then some."

He stepped back to leave. "I'll be sure and tell him to keep an eye out."

"Please do, and Gene, y'all have fun but stay away from the bears," I called out as he walked down the rest of the pier, waving over his shoulder.

Heading up to the airport took the exact amount of time I had. Interstate 45 was always a crapshoot on traffic. A fender-bender caused a slight delay, but I slid in just in time to see the small plane Wix took off in last time taxiing down the landing strip.

I wondered what all this private flying cost him. What he made being in a popular band never really crossed my mind, but it obviously meant lots of money.

After climbing aboard, we took off with ease, and the gentle hum of the motors put me to sleep almost instantly. I had flown only a few times before Wix, but I felt like this mode of transportation was sweet. Probably shouldn't get too used to it.

The plane descended into the Austin airport, landing with a hard bump. "Sorry, ma'am. We've got some crosswinds here today," the pilot spoke through the headset he'd given me before takeoff. He must have seen me sleeping because he never spoke to me during the flight.

A loud wind noise occurred as the door opened and the steps unfolded. I picked up my bag and started down them to see Wix waiting for me. He twirled me around several times before kissing me senselessly.

"This is a wonderful surprise. I never dreamed you'd be waiting for me this time." I returned his kiss with equal fervor, realizing how much I missed him. His tongue slid across my lips seeking entrance, and I opened for him.

"Mr. Stoker?" the pilot interrupted, breaking us apart. "Sorry to interrupt, but I need to take the plane to the hangar."

Wix saluted the guy, causing him to laugh, and we walked the short distance to the limousine with me plastered against his side and him holding my bag.

"Babe, you just don't know how much I've missed you. I know it's not been that many days, but it seems like months. You're too far away from me."

"Wix, you know what my job means to me. It's everything I need to survive." I realized he had no idea, nothing to compare it to living life on the run, but I missed him too. Our time together made me see how much I needed a connection with people, specifically him.

He made me feel things I had forgotten long ago. I operated in a holding pattern at this point. Just being close to Wix drove the point home like nothing else.

He pulled me closer and kissed me hard before resting his head on mine. "I know we're on different paths, but that doesn't mean I can't wish for it to be different. Let me ask you this…" He took a deep breath before continuing, "What lifestyle suits you other than sailing? Could you see yourself working off the boat or water? Have you ever wished to do something else?"

"You asked a lot more than one question. Your enthusiasm is cute, Wix." My lips formed a slight smile.

Never really considering it, I took a breath and rolled the idea over in my head. Doing something not related to the ocean or sailing seemed outrageous. Obviously, he had seriously thought about it if the reflection in his eyes indicated his feelings.

A slight tremor flowed down my back from his

words and gaze. They sounded like he wanted something more than the brief moments we shared.

This was *my boat* we were talking about. Yes, when a charter pissed me off, selling out sounded good, but I never truly gave it any more headspace than necessary to calm down before dismissing it. Water was my life.

I took a beat before answering him, "I have no idea. What would I be good at besides sailing? Great question." A dreidel during Hanukah spun slower than my mind at the moment.

"Don't sell yourself short. You have mad skills, Bardot. People-pleasing skills. Hospitality skills. Companies always have room for those."

Roger Rabbit eyes popped at him. Had he lost his mind? The last thing I wanted to do involved a company. While we both worked with one, neither of us worked for one.

"Are you fucking serious? A company? You want me to work for someone? No, never, not happening."

He ran his hand down my hair. "Calm down, babe."

"Don't tell me to calm down. Would that work for you or any of the band members to work at a nine-to-five job? Hell no, it wouldn't." Talk about being pissed off and him telling me to calm down. What the hell was he even thinking with that comment?

He grabbed me and pulled me in close, but I pushed against him. He rocked me back and forth. "I'm sorry, babe. Really. I didn't mean it like that. I was just throwing it out there. That was the first thing I thought of. You do have tons of skills that you could use in several industries." Finally relaxing his hold, he kissed across my forehead and then down to my lips, where he left a quick peck.

"Don't change the subject with kisses, Wix. The idea of working for a company makes me physically ill... like I could vomit right now."

"No. No. No. We don't want that. I'm sorry. I knew you had strong feelings about what you do. I just don't want you to think you aren't capable of so many other things."

"That's the point, though. I don't want to do *other things*. I'm happy."

"Okay. Let's forget about it and be happy to be together."

But his words brought up the exact feelings I had asked myself earlier.

Was I truly happy? If I wasn't, what would it take to make me happy? *A new location? Friends?*

I turned and looked at him. God, he was beautiful. The storms raged in his gray eyes, and I knew he wanted to say more.

Was falling in love the answer?

CHAPTER 30

WIX

By pulling up to the side door directly at the elevators, we escaped any fans or disgruntled hotel employees. The two who caused problems before had taken jobs elsewhere. Bardot glanced around, and I knew what she was looking for.

"They're gone, babe. Took other positions elsewhere."

"Good. I mean, not that I wanted them to be fired, but some sensitivity training might have helped."

Her kind heart for people backed up what I already knew. She treated others fairly and probably even looked out for the little guy.

As soon as the elevator door closed, I turned to her with hooded eyes, telling her exactly what I wanted. She slowly backed into the corner of the metal box that sped to our destination mirroring my look. Dark, long eyelashes covered her shimmering green circles, giving them a mysterious vibe as though she kept a secret from me.

After the days ahead of us, I hoped there would never be another secret between us. If I doubted the desire I held for her, it vanished when she stepped off the plane. Now, my heart beat like it could leap out of me and run up the stairs to beat us to the top.

With my hand over her heart, it mimicked mine in every way. She felt it. We both knew what this was, even if we weren't ready to exchange feelings for words. Hell, maybe I was ready with the words hanging off the tip of my tongue. The idea scared me, but I was ready to deal with them.

But Bardot? It could send her running. She ran before. She sought her safe place when presented with something that pushed her. When confronted with difficult circumstances, she retreated, and her self-preservation kicked in. Living alone for so long had caused her reactions.

I was done with her bolting. No more being alone for my girl. Yes, she's *my girl*. I wanted to give her what she needed, a place to belong. No more solitary life for this woman. I planned to take that away, be the one she ran to and the place of refuge she sought— someone to hold her, love her, keep her safe, and be the one to call home.

The solid door whisked open to an empty suite. Before I left the studio, I asked the guys for a few hours of privacy. Readily agreeing, they knew how bad I had it for Bardot. With the bad attitude I exhibited during our time apart, my brothers wanted to see me happy.

She made me much more than happy. I felt like my other half reconnected when she was around. It took me a bit to understand how this happened, but now that I had, something had to change. I'd give her our days ahead before approaching the subject again.

As the door shut, we came together hard and fast. Time for slow and easy would come later. Right now, I had to have all of her.

We attacked each other in the most delicious of ways. Rolling from the door to the long bar separating the kitchen from the living area, we pulled and ripped clothes in a frenzy. The dark jeans she wore proved impossible to get off with her shoes still on, so I stopped at her ankles. *Fuck it.*

I flipped her around and pushed her head onto the cold stone before us. Her breath sucked in when her perfect tits touched the chill of the quartz.

"Oh God, this makes my nipples harder than they already were, Wix. I want you even more."

"You'll have me, but it's going to be rough, babe. I can't wait any longer."

My finger ran from her perfect ass down her slit to find soaked panties. "You're ready. I feel your need waiting for me." Part of me wanted to stop this insanity and taste her first, but my dick begged to be inside her.

In our effort to get together, she had managed to get my jeans unbuttoned and unzipped, so I pushed them down enough to release my rock-hard cock. "Babe, are you on the pill because I can't wait to find a condom? I need inside you, right fucking now."

"Yes, yes," she screamed with need as I continued to move between her swollen bud and her opening. "Just fuck me already."

"Demanding... I like it." I smirked. "Just looking out for you, babe. Always."

"Great, but I'm still waiting, rock star." She turned her head, killing me with her needy look.

The precum glistened waiting to see if I put it out of its misery or not. I rotated it around her opening only to see more of her cum, anticipating my next move.

"Wait no more, babe. It's on." I slammed in with more force than needed, but there was no way I could stop myself. Amazing. Her warm walls caressed my length and created a tingle that ran up my spine.

No, boy. You've got a long time before I'm coming.

The first move I made to pull out, she rocked back with me. "Fucking like it inside you?"

"Yes. Now do it again. Harder. I need it hard and fast. *Please.*"

Giving her what she needed was exactly why I was put on this earth. I pumped into her over and over with everything I had in me. The screams and moans she gave me with each push told me I complied with her wishes.

"Fuck, Wix. I'm gonna come already."

"Then do it. I'll give you all the orgasms you want." I reached around and connected with her bulging clit, circling it over and over before giving it a slap that sent her over the edge immediately. My girl liked all kinds of kinky stuff to set her off.

God, she undid me. The quivering of her tight muscles inside made that tremor from before return. My balls pulled up with only a few more hard pushes, which propelled ropes of cum inside her warmth, where her pulsing sheath milked me of every drop.

"Fucking hell, Bardot. That was the best. When can we do it again?"

A slight snicker drifted over her lips. "As soon as you recover, I'm ready."

"How did I get so damn lucky to find you?" I asked as I stood up and helped her off the counter. If her muscles were tight like mine, I knew she hurt.

Wrapping my arms around her, I kissed her softly. "You okay, babe? That was pretty rough."

She laid her head against my chest as her toned arms wrapped around my waist. "I'm perfect now."

Sometimes her words wrecked me. She thought she was perfect after I took her hard on a countertop? This woman had to be made for me—we were made to be together. Didn't she see it now? Didn't she understand my needs and hers were the same?

I looked up and silently prayed, something I rarely

ever did. *Please make me the man she needs and make her see we are meant to be together.*

"Let's go clean up and order some room service." I tugged her down the hallway to my room and en suite. The inner caveman in me said to throw her over my shoulder and carry her off to parts unknown, but she'd never be down for that.

After climbing in the shower, the warm water sluiced over us as we made love until the water cooled. Hot lovemaking became my favorite while we washed each other in the aftermath.

Dressing in sweats, she retraced her steps, stealing my worn T-shirt off the floor in the kitchen area. A knock at the door meant the food waited for us. We moved to the buttery soft leather couches but chose to dine on the floor around the live-edge coffee table.

A river of blue ran through the middle of it which sparked an idea. "Babe, have you ever thought about doing charters elsewhere besides Kemah?"

After taking a huge bite of her cheeseburger—*yes, we ate gourmet food*—she looked at me while she chewed, wrapping her head around the question. "No, I guess I haven't. When Dad was heading up the charters, he'd go up and down the Texas coast to various ports for weekend or weeklong adventures, but I never ventured that far."

"But you could if you wanted to, right?" So many ideas came at me all at once.

"Sure. I hold several kinds of licenses for boating."

"Do lakes and rivers count?" Nothing about boating ever crossed my path, so I knew incredibly little about the industry.

"Yes, I guess. Sailing is sailing but a river?" One eyebrow cocked up as she looked at me. "I'm not sure a river is cut out for sailing unless it's super wide, but would it be deep enough? I'd have to look into that."

"Just something to consider." Purely selfish motives came with this line of questioning since the California coast had tons of boating opportunities. With the band being signed with 13 Recordings in LA, she could have her boat brought or sailed over. Who knew?

"Marbles or rocks keep rolling around inside your head, Wix." She giggled softly. "I can see it happening. What are you thinking about with this line of questioning?"

I wasn't ready to show my hand yet, but her quick thinking picked up on my thoughts. "You don't actually think I'd want to relocate across the country, do you?"

Not being able to lie to her, I nodded. "Why not, babe?" I linked our fingers together across the tabletop. "Nothing is holding you here in Texas. I'm not going to lie, Bardot, I want you with me. If you won't come to me, then it might be hard, but I'll come to you."

"You'd move to Texas? For me? Are you crazy?" Her voice climbed an octave higher with each word.

"That's insane, Wix. Your life is with the band, and the band is in LA."

Making a move to her side of the table, I pulled her into my lap. "You're right, but Bardot, I'm serious. Listen to me... I. Want. You. With. Me." Every word came out staccato-sounding. "I realize you probably think it's too fast, and I don't want to scare you, but I feel like our connection is too strong to let it go. We belong together. You and me. I'm willing to do whatever it takes to make it happen."

Her face turned all kinds of colors.

Yeah, too soon to let that all go on her.

She straddled my lap, wrapped her legs around me, and squeezed me tight. Her hands ran up my arms before she caught them together behind my neck. Pulling me in for a long, lingering kiss, she then leaned back and looked at me.

"I feel like that's the most beautiful words anyone has ever said to me. I mean, not that I've ever had an offer like it before, but it's still wonderful."

I cocked my head slightly to the side, wondering what she was trying to say. "Does that mean you'd be down for me moving here to be with you?"

A commuting relationship sounded next to impossible, but I wanted this more than anything I've ever wanted in my life, next to seeing Copper Crowns be successful.

"Wix, there's no way I'm asking you to do something so ridiculous. Your life is in Cali."

"But you're here, babe."

She laid her head on my shoulder, connecting her warm lips to my collarbone. Sitting here, connected to her, we stopped talking. I wanted her to decide without too much coaxing.

While it seemed spur of the moment, I was willing to wait for an answer.

Before we found the answers, the door swung wide, and the other three walked in making noise.

Arch stopped. "Hey, we caught them between doing the deed bunny style." He made a fucking motion with his entire body. "All that must have worked up a hunger for real food instead of—" He stopped before saying something totally wrong for Bardot's ears.

I stood and pulled Bardot up with me, happy we were dressed. "Hey." I nodded at them. "You remember Bardot."

"Who else would it be, dude? You've talked about her nonstop since returning from Houston." Trotter came over and kissed her on the cheek. "Good to see you again."

I wanted to kiss him myself for saying that. Bardot needed to know I always had her on my mind.

"Yeah, his whiney ass about missing you was getting real fucking old," Arch added. He pulled her in for a big hug. "You gotta put this dumbshit out of his misery. He's fucking killing the vibe around here."

Leave it to Arch to express himself in a way that endeared him more to my sweet babe.

Kenzo walked in last and gave her a quick one-sided hug. "Good to see you taking care of our boy here. In case you weren't aware, he's got it bad for you, girl."

Like I knew they would, my brothers came through for me. Asking them to be nice to her when we talked about them leaving for a few hours, I didn't expect them to take it this far, but these guys always had my back when I needed them. They understood how much I wanted this to work from all the sulking I'd done when I returned alone.

"What's the plan, my sweet Bardot?" Arch probed for more information about our evening. He loved getting in on all the action when the chance arose. "You two fueling up for another round of fuckfest or what?"

My hand came up, and I pointed in Arch's direction. "First, she's not your sweet Bardot or anything else that fucking sounds like it. And second, please keep your douchebag comments about our sex life to yourself. It's not even on a need-to-know basis for you. So fuck off."

"Dude, I was simply inquiring about your plans for the rest of the day." He sounded like I hurt his girly feeling. "We were thinking about hitting up some of the smaller venues here in Austin. Stay in and... do whatever. Or... you wanna come with. Makes no diff to me." The pout on his face told me he was teasing.

"Aw... Wix. I think you hurt his feelings," Bardot

commented as she moved to stand in front of him. She bear-hugged his big body. "We'll go out with y'all. I don't want to see you moping around all evening."

This will be the best fucking night in forever.

With caps pulled low over our hair, glasses, and other disguises to fend off recognition from fans, we headed off on an evening of adventure. Jones contacted several places with bands playing, asking for VIP seating, making things easier for us to enjoy the night.

When we arrived at the studio the next day with Bardot, she looked around, mesmerized by the equipment waiting for the crew to work their magic. Jones arranged a special chair for her to watch the fun from, which was where she sat most of the day, laughing and enjoying the different shows we put on for the cameras.

Tracy and Tessa started the morning acting all butt hurt that another woman sat in on the day but got over it when Bardot introduced herself, gushing about how awesome the actual documentary was sure to turn out. Who knew my babe had it in her to suck up to others until I remembered she did this all the time on charters. I swore this awesome woman had customer relations built in her. Pleasing clients came as naturally as sailing her boat.

Before any of us realized the time, the band finished up and climbed back on our bus to head to NOLA. Jones finagled tour stops and managed to make everyone happy this time out.

Saying goodbye to the twins, Knox, and the crew, we took off for Houston to deposit Bardot in the waiting car Jones had scheduled.

CHAPTER 31

BARDOT

I refused to cry.

That was until I sat in the back of the hired car, then I let it all go. Tears flowed down my face from the overwhelming sadness I bottled up from the time I stepped on the tour bus until it stopped in Houston to let me off.

Our time together rushed by with all the fun and games. From hanging with the band to the sexy moments we shared, it all played havoc on my emotions as I watched downtown fly by on our way south to Kemah.

"Ma'am, I'm Travis. Sorry, I forgot to tell you. I was instructed to either take you to an apartment or a yacht club. Which do you prefer?"

My rough, sandpaper eyes hurt when I rubbed the tissue across my face. I glanced at the young guy, who sat quietly while I fell apart, sitting directly behind him. "Take me to the yacht club, please. I need to check on my boat."

"Sure thing. I can wait there and take you to the apartment if you need me to."

"No need... I can uber over to it."

"Mr. Stoker and Duke asked me to wait until you were settled in one place or the other, so if it's okay with you, I'll stick around until you decide where you're staying."

His easy-going voice coaxed a grin from me as he watched in the reflection. "Leave it to Wix to see to everything and to Duke to make sure I'm safe." Duke followed the band all over Austin when we were out bar hopping. Jones made a few contacts with another band he felt had promise, so our evenings became a win-win for everyone. Getting to be with Wix in his element topped the wins for me.

Travis returned the smile and said, "Yes, ma'am."

We stopped in the parking lot, gathered my bags from the trunk, and headed down the docks. Our light conversation continued as we made our way to where the boat waited.

Only, what the fuck? No boat. No *Miss Midnight*. I blinked a few times, looked around, and dropped my packages. "What? Where is she?"

Running up and down the cement docks, my boat was gone. "*No, no, no!* This can't be happening. Where is she?" I screamed at the top of my lungs, spinning around before collapsing. "Not my boat. Who would take my boat? It's all I have left. It's all I have." Hysteria took over, and the ability to think vanished. I screamed, and my cries were out of control, not caring who heard me.

This was my life missing.

It was everything.

It was all I had left of my dad and everything I lived for.

"Why? Why would you do this to me?" I shrieked. "When will every damn power in the universe stop trying to kill me?" My sobs caused me to randomly suck in breaths and sheer panic took over.

I couldn't breathe.

I couldn't think.

I couldn't live without my boat.

A phone came to my ear. "Babe. I'm coming. I'll be there in a hot minute. Don't move." Wix's words drifted through the speaker, but my mind didn't comprehend them. Travis sat down next to me on the dirty cement.

"I'm so sorry, ma'am." I glanced at him and sat up, leaning into him as he dialed 9-1-1 next. I listened to him rattle off all the information he had, not being any help to him. My staccato breaths continued.

"Listen, Bardot," Travis spoke. "You need to breathe. You're having a panic attack."

I felt him move around until all I saw was his face in front of me. "Breathe with me, Bardot. In, one two three four. Out, one two three four. In, one two three four. Out, one two three four. Come on now, you're doing it. Let's go again." This virtual stranger got my brain under control.

The tears continued to fall, but at least I had a flow of oxygen getting into me. Loud sirens sounded in the distance. Before they arrived, even louder footsteps thundered toward us.

Gene, the security guard, squatted down beside me. "What's the matter, Bardot?" His words were softer than the footsteps he used.

On a stuttering breath, I spoke, "Gene, she's gone. *Miss Midnight* is gone." A fresh round of tears began with intermittent sobs and gasps.

"No way. It's here somewhere."

"This is my slip, Gene, and I know where I left her. She's been here for years."

Gene had also been here for years. He knew my dad as well as he knew this was my slip in the club. I never docked it elsewhere.

The portly guard stood and walked quickly down the rest of the dock before returning, counting and looking over moored boats and empty slips.

"God, Bardot. I'm so sorry. I tried to go on a short vacation, leaving someone we hired in my place. The guy seemed like he knew boats pretty well, and he was vetted by the company before he started working. We always run them through several databases before they're hired."

"Where is he now?"

Gene stopped and looked around before squatting next to me again. "The truth is, he got in trouble for climbing on other boats. One of the owners came down to find him sitting on the back of his vessel, drinking a beer. We let him go the next day. That's why I'm back so soon. Our cruise got rescheduled when our plane to Miami got canceled. We couldn't get there in time to make the ship, so we put it off until later this year. The security company called me back to work when they fired the idiot."

The color drained from Gene's face as he spoke, "I'll call the company right now and get all the information we have on him. Ten to one, he's who did this."

Gene made his way up the dock to his cart and took off, throwing rocks up as he accelerated.

A chuckle came out of Travis, causing me to look at him. "Sorry, I just didn't know golf carts could burn rubber."

I looked over where the cart had been sitting. "Yeah, me neither." My words were dry and lifeless.

A police car abruptly stopped in the lot. Two officers made their way down, and I stood to meet them.

"Evening, ma'am. You report a boat theft?"

As my head bobbed in answer, my heart shattered because the last words I ever thought I'd say poured out like one long word. "Someone stole my boat."

Calmly, he introduced himself and his partner to

the two of us. Maybe he thought if he remained unruffled, I might also. Was he ever dead wrong? Nothing he said would influence my emotions right then.

"I left her docked here..." my finger pointed to the water, "... where she's always waiting, a few nights ago while I went to Austin. I came back to an empty slip. Who knows how long it's been gone." My voice felt foreign as my words now slowly drifted from me. The anger I felt initially seemed to have given way now to shock. I could not wrap my head or my heart around the idea that my only lifeline to my dad sailed away with a stranger to an unknown location.

After taking down all the information from us, the kind man closed his tablet and looked at me while scratching his head. "Honestly, we don't get many calls from this marina, especially stolen vessels. The information will be sent to the missing boat database. The other authorities have access to it and will be on the lookout for your boat, Miss."

"Does this mean no one's going to be actively looking for it? Like the Coast Guard or the game wardens or anyone?" I stared between the two policemen.

"No, we usually put out a bulletin that the boat is missing, and while neither of those will be looking for it specifically, they'll keep an eye out while they're in the water."

My glazed-over eyes met the man's speaking, but

my body remained still. "That's not acceptable," I replied, barely above a whisper.

"Sorry, ma'am, but that's how boat theft is currently handled."

The slow beating of my heart suddenly accelerated. Adrenaline pumped through me, causing my demeanor to change from lethargic to hyperactive in no time, as though a drug had suddenly kicked in.

"That's a line of shit if I've ever heard one. We need to be proactive about this. You don't understand... that boat is my life. It's my job, my home, and my connection to my family. It has to be found."

A snicker sounded away from the circle of people standing together. "I should have known you'd be jumping in this with both fucking feet, babe." I knew Wix said the words before turning to look. Moving around the others blocking my view, I leaped into his arms with a fresh new round of tears.

My arms and legs wrapped around his body. "They took my boat, Wix." He held me close, speaking into my ear.

"I know, babe. We'll find it." He pulled back and looked at me before dropping a soft kiss on my lips. The familiar touch helped calm me. I buried my face in his neck while he continued to squeeze me tight. We finally pulled apart when someone made a noise behind me. He stood me on my feet, looking over at them.

"I'll hire a team to immediately start looking." His

words were for me, but he said them loud enough for all to hear.

The shorter of the two officers approached us. "We advise not doing this on your own. Anyone who steals a boat of this size and value is not someone to mess with. Best leave it to the authorities."

"Yeah, that sounded like a helluva plan until you said no one would be looking." Wix heard more than I realized, and now he refused to back down from the man. Looking at me, he continued, "A team will be here any minute. Duke got on that shit as soon as I told him what happened."

"Not sure who this Duke person is, but he won't be allowed to interfere with the game wardens or the Coast Guard. If this dream team he's gathered shows up, they need to know they'll be arrested as fast as the thieves can." The officer clarified how they felt about the situation, but Wix and I knew the likelihood of them finding the boat rated slim to none.

"The private security team will not interfere with something you said yourself wasn't going to be happening, so I don't see a problem here," Wix informed the two.

"We never said anyone would be looking for the boat. We said there would be no one actively looking. The Texas game wardens and Coast Guard patrol the channels, the bay, and the gulf. They will all know as soon as it's added to the database, and both groups will be on the lookout for it."

"And so will my guys," Wix added. "Only more effectively since it'll be their only job."

The two officers exchanged glances realizing nothing they said would change Wix's mind and let it drop. "We'll be in touch, ma'am," the first officer said. He turned to Gene, who waited off to the side while Wix and I spoke to the police. "We need to have a list of the employees who worked the days the owner was gone."

"No problem. We keep it in the office here on the property. If you'll follow me, I'll turn it over to you." Gene wanted nothing more than to see the thieves caught, making me feel like he cared about what happened. He knew what *Miss Midnight* meant to me.

Wix, Travis, and I watched them drive off before Wix spoke, "Travis, you up for some nighttime boating?"

"Hell yeah. I love the water."

Looking at Wix, I felt my eyebrows scrunch downward. "You aren't going on the water to look tonight. That's why you have Duke coming in."

He put his arms on my shoulders, linking them behind my head. "Sure do. I hoped you were coming too since you know these waters better than we do."

Like a lighthouse beam, my face lit up. "Your damn right I am. Let's go."

He grinned at my enthusiasm. "Sounds great, babe, but uh... we need a boat."

"Not a problem. I know all the people in this

harbor. Let me make one call. Travis, you might want to change clothes, and I need to call Gilley to tell him what happened." Before I finished, he moved toward the limousine.

Fifteen minutes later, a twenty-five-foot bay fishing boat pulled into the harbor from the lake. My friend, Patrick, came into the slip where my boat should be moored, throwing me a line to tie off. "Here she is, Bardot. Just bring her back in one piece."

And just like that, the three of us had a great boat for doing some detective work. With my anger tamped down some, my thoughts turned to places someone might try to hide a boat the size of *Miss Midnight*.

Sure, the harbor had hundreds of boats the size of mine, but if the thieves were the dumbasses I figured they were, they didn't bother to remove the burgee flags I flew. My dad started flying the swallow-tailed shapes when I was a kid, and I was careful to replace them when they became tattered.

They helped me to know our boat anywhere on the water. As a child, they all looked the same to me, so we picked out brightly colored flags to help me identify ours. Never having to use them in years, my heart swelled with the idea that Dad would be with me every step of the way to find our baby.

With Wix aboard, I felt my confidence returning. He believed in me and knew how important finding the boat was to my well-being and peace of mind. I realized at that moment he got me. He understood my needs in this world and was willing to do whatever it took to make sure of my happiness.

"You ready?" he asked, looking at me standing behind the wheel of the boat. "Travis, look at my babe being all 'captainish' for us. She's a badass behind that wheel." They laughed at the face I made. If they only knew how long it had been since I had driven a bay boat like this one, they wouldn't be joking about it.

"Y'all might want to sit down before I take off," I informed them as I made my way out of the harbor and into the marked channel of Clear Lake. With all the different yacht clubs around the lake, I knew we had a long night ahead.

The first boat docking area across the lake proved useless to us, so I made my way out into the bay and down the coastline to the next harbor area.

I felt Wix move in beside me on the double bench and wrap his arm around my waist, pulling me closer to his body. He hit me with that smile of his, which made me wish we were anywhere but here or anywhere without a third party on the boat.

"You realize the boat might be in Mexico by now, right?" he said in my ear, making it possible to hear his words as we sped along.

"Nope. Don't think that way. Think positive. It's going to be here."

Sadly, we wasted hours late into that night with nothing to show for it but an empty gas tank.

CHAPTER 32

WIX

As I watched Bardot navigate through the harbors and private inlets during the night, I realized more than ever how tied she was to this life. I wanted her with me, but she wanted something completely different. Granted, it was all she knew, but how could I ask her to give up this life for mine? How long would it take her to grow to resent me for asking it of her?

The other side of this coin was that I could show her the world. Our lives together came with a price, but opening her eyes to so much more excited me. If she traveled with the band, she could sail around the world with the boat. Opportunities to sail existed everywhere, but she loved her life the way it was. *Could she possibly be open to trying something new?*

I knew we had to take a beat and have a serious conversation about this soon. I left the band high and dry to be with her, and I needed to get back to the only thing I loved doing, playing with Copper Crowns. But I realized at that moment, I needed her to make my life more complete. Sure, the band was important, but Bardot, well, she now took up equal space in my heart.

After docking back in her slip, we went to her apartment for some sleep. My head spun with my thoughts of us being together. My girl's exhaustion became apparent as she moved restlessly around her queen-size bed that felt like a twin with us both in it. My feet hung off the end, so I took up most of it with her spooned against my front in the small space I left, sleeping diagonally. This would work for the short time we had here.

Her warm body felt amazing tucked in next to mine when I woke. This was how I wanted to wake every morning, but asking this of her seemed like wishful thinking. The other guys would have some say about having her on our bus constantly. Kenzo's wife might also have something to say about this as well.

Jacqui never wanted to travel with the band. Her busy life as an ER doctor kept her constantly on the go, but somehow, they made it work. They agreed to an open marriage because of their schedules, but he had not been with a woman other than Jacqui since their marriage.

The idea of having sex with another woman or her another man made me sick. *I don't share*. Period. At all. She would be mine, or this between us would *not* work.

Her phone blasted on the tiny nightstand beside her. I grabbed it to allow her to sleep longer, but she rolled over and swiped it up before I reached for it.

"Yeah?" Her sleepy, rough morning voice made my dick stand at attention. Just having her next to me did this anyway, only now she was awake. I propped up on an elbow and listened as she turned on the speaker.

"Good morning. I'm game warden, Dallas Philley. I need to speak to Bardot Bohen."

I saw wild green eyes open wide. "This is she." Her voice was now strong and in charge.

"Ma'am, I need you to come to this address to look at a boat for identification. We feel sure it's yours but want you to identify it for us."

"We'll be there in twenty minutes," she rattled off as she jumped out of bed, removing the soft camisole and tiny shorts she slept in. Damn, there went a perfectly good opportunity to have my way with that hot body of hers, but finding her boat was far more important.

We raced out of the parking lot for the short drive to an address near her apartment. Driving up, we spotted a green truck with the Texas Parks and Wildlife emblem on the side.

"This is it," she muttered so softly I almost missed it. I grabbed her hand, stopping her from getting out.

"Babe, whatever we find, it'll be okay. We'll make it right." She nodded back, her face unreadable. I knew her anxiety level topped the charts, yet her appearance was calm and cool. Was this an auto-response from all the bad shit she had suffered in her life? No wonder, though, with all the problems she faced alone.

"You're not alone this time, Bardot. Never again." She nodded once and pulled from my grasp. I felt her uncertainty about my words. I got it—people left her when she needed them the most, both physically and mentally. Her dad abandoned her when her mother died. Left to her own devices, she coped as best she could, and it didn't turn out well.

We made our way to the uniformed man and woman standing in a shell-lined driveway that dropped over an edge where it sloped down to the water. The shambles of a shack stood in the middle of a yard of disaster. Boat and motor parts lay in disarray among weeds and grass, some tall enough to hide whatever lay abandoned. Tall swing-like structures holding pieces of machinery on pulleys took up another space. *What kind of place was this?*

"Hello, I'm Bardot Bohen." She offered her small hand to the two officials. "This is my—"

"Boyfriend, Wix Stoker," I offered my hand as I spoke.

"Dallas Philley, we spoke on the phone. This is Casey Gann, who is the one who spotted the boat while out on the water early this morning."

Casey spoke up, "I ran the boat numbers on the missing boat database, and it came back to your name but not this address. We always get suspicious and want to check."

"I'm glad you did. I can't believe you found her." Bardot's demeanor lightened with each word.

The two game wardens looked at each other before the woman continued, "Well, I don't know how happy this is going to make you, and it might not be yours."

Even though the perceptive woman said words to lighten the blow, I knew she wouldn't have alerted us if it was only a hunch on her part, and so did Bardot. A look of horror and white took control of my girl's features.

I reached for her, but she pulled out of my embrace. Accustomed to facing problems alone, she acted like she didn't need me. *What would it take for me to show her differently?* I made a mental note to work on this as much as possible.

"What do you mean?" she asked.

"Let's walk around back, ma'am. We need you to identify the vessel."

We followed them down the shell drive, passing the parked trucks. Two men sat in the back of one of the trucks, but neither of us paid them any attention as we made our way to the back of the house and down a hill toward the muddy water lapping against a homemade dock. The weathered structure rested haphazardly, leaning to one side with what was left of a boat tied to it.

A sudden deafening scream stopped me in my tracks.

Bardot fell, but I caught her before she hit, going down with her in a heap as I wrapped her in my arms. She stopped breathing in an instant, then gasped for air. Another panic attack was coming. The sounds she made hurt me on a level I never knew existed.

She sat more erect after she took in some air. "Holy fucking shit. Who? How?" eked out of her in between the shallow breaths she allowed herself. "Why? Why would they do this to her?"

Before us sat pieces of a burned-out hull with the leaning mast held up by the boat's wires or maybe mud. It swayed like the wild growing swish cane around both sides of the dock. Nothing needed to hold what was left. The destroyed boat and Bardot's soul rested on the bottom, sunk to murky despair.

How did she recover from this? Nothing I said or did stood a chance to change this. "I'm so damn sorry, babe." *What else could be said?* "This is so fucked up. So unfair to you."

Giving Bardot and me a minute to take it in and her to get her breathing under control again, Philley and Gann walked up closer to the structure. "We are sorry to find what was left of this boat. I'm sure it was a fine watercraft before those two got ahold of it," Philly offered as they passed us.

Bardot's face came up to face him. "What did you say?"

"We have the two people from the house in the truck. Caught them moving the parts from here to the barn in the front of the house. Looks like they've been running a boat chop shop. Police are on their way. They've had their suspicions about this place but never could catch the people involved. Sneaky, these two. Police suspect they're just the boat thieves, meaning someone above them takes the parts. That's who they want more than the two in the truck."

"Who are they?" Bardot asked. "I've lived here all my life. I know a lot of people on and around the water."

"Sorry, we can't give out that kind of information," Gann spoke up. She looked hard at Bardot. "The police will be here shortly to take them from us to lock them up for now." The woman looked at her partner and then at Bardot. "Nothing's to say you two can't stick around to see the transfer."

Gann gave them an out on identifying the two and still allowed Bardot to lay eyes on the sorry bastards. We looked at her without commenting, knowing what she'd offered.

Sirens grew loud as the two police cars slid in behind Bardot's car. The same police who showed up when we called about the boat missing, not making me happy. They didn't give two shits about helping the situation yesterday. I hoped they changed their tunes this morning.

After making introductions to the game wardens, the police walked down to see the boat's remains stuck in the mud but came back quickly. "You say you have the two detained?"

Gann spoke up, "Yes, they're handcuffed in my truck." Bardot made her way to the doorway with the police on her heels. Before opening the door, Gann turned to find Bardot standing directly behind her. Watching her move with cat-like skills amazed me. Ready to leap on the men with claws bared, my girl waited.

The fuckwad thieves didn't stand a chance where she was concerned. Given the chance, she would face them down before ripping into them. Philley caught Bardot by the shoulders and pulled her back before releasing her to allow the officers to do their job. I knew she wanted to get to the pair but forced herself to stand still with Philley so close.

I stood by, afraid for her when maybe I should have been scared for the criminals. My feisty girl didn't have a killer instinct, but at that moment, I had my doubts.

The first man climbed out with the game warden's assistance, which seemed too kind to me. Let the dickhead fall on his face. Average height, but there was nothing that made him stand out but a few poorly done tattoos bleeding out of his short sleeves. The second man towered over Gann, but she held him like the professional she was. His long hair and scruffy beard, combined with his height, created a different type of man than the first.

Turning, I looked at Bardot to see if any recognition crossed her face. Her hard stare at the tall one made me turn back to look him over better. *Was he someone she knew or knew of?*

"What the fuck!" I heard her words but couldn't stop her before she rushed and climbed him, all while beating and pounding the man before Philley or Gann stood a chance of removing her from the guy. She punched the guy's face, screaming like a banshee. Philley finally removed Bardot from the guy with her still kicking and screaming and handed her to me, where I grasped her around the waist with both arms as she struggled to get free.

I held her while Philley stood between her and him, never taking his eyes off Bardot. "It's you," she shouted around the game warden. "You sorry piece of fucking bottom-sucking scum. I should have known I'd run into you sooner or later here in Kemah. You couldn't stop ruining girls, you had to turn to thievery too? You stole from me once before, but never again." Her body twisted and turned as she tried to wrench herself from my hold around her, kicking and screaming the words. The strength in her small body amazed me, but I held fast not wanting to hurt her.

"I take it you know this man, Miss Bohen?" Gann asked.

"Do I know him? Hell yes, I know this piece of shit. He raped me when I was fifteen years old. He drugged and raped me before depositing me back on my doorstep alone. How could you do this? Wasn't stealing my body and sanity enough for you? You had to take the only thing I have left from me?"

Bardot shocked me with her words. I knew them, but now she shared them with the world. Those memories she kept locked away from everyone until that night when she broke down and told me. Repeating them to me cost her, but now to let them go for everyone who stood there shocked me. The surprised authorities heard it all in the shouts and screeches coming from her. Tears ran down her beautiful face, but now her pain no longer hid under the surface.

It took another tragedy for Bardot to admit what happened, another moment of chaos for her to face before she divulged something she felt was so heinous that she kept it hidden in her heart.

A few minutes of yelling and crying continued before she collapsed against me, her body and mind spent from the confession she had kept hidden for so long.

I turned her in my arms and wrapped her tightly against me. She enveloped me and buried her head under my neck, incessantly crying, so I scooped her up with my arm under her knees and carried her back to the car.

Placing her in the back seat, I climbed in beside her, pulling her onto my lap. I needed to hold her, to let her know I was here, and the demons she had held onto for so long could finally be let go.

"It's going to be okay now, babe. He'll be put away," I offered with a soft kiss to her temple.

She shook her head. "Don't you see, it's my word against his. There's no evidence..." Her words were spoken brokenly between sobs. "I should have gone to the police or told someone back then."

"Even if it's not for your rape, it'll be for the boat. Either way, he's going to jail." I felt her nod against my chest. Getting this out in the open was what she needed to do so long ago, but with no one to understand and offer comfort, how could she?

That was about to change.

Now, she had my brothers and me.

We would have her back.

We would be her family.

***

Once we finished up at the police station, we made our way back to the apartment where I put an exhausted Bardot in bed. What a bad fucking day. It was like the worst anyone could ask for. With nothing for me to say that would change the outcome, our ride sped by silently. Her adrenaline was completely spent, and she passed out before we were halfway there.

Thinking about my own life, I realized it had been a piece of cake compared to the tragedies she faced. And all alone too. I knew it had to change, and right then, I made up my mind.

My phone vibrated, so I moved to the front steps to not wake her in the small space her apartment offered. "Yeah?"

"Yeah yourself, fucking trader, taking off like that to be with your girl," Arch barked into the phone. "Where the hell are you?"

"We're at Bardot's apartment. Shit just got real here, bro."

"Oh, hell. Sorry, bro. I'm putting you on speaker." His reply was the opposite of his light-hearted first comment. "Okay, we're all here, including Jones. What's happened?"

I repeated the story to them, including the rape from her teen years. Dead silence. I knew the shock worked through them as it had me when she first recited the horrid story.

Finally, Jones spoke up for the group, "Dude, I can't tell you how sorry we are for all that's gone down. I feel like Bardot needs to come with us for a while. She needs to be with people who can take care of her for a change since it sounds like she's been doing that on her own for so long."

I scratched my head before my palm rubbed down the back and across my neck. "Yeah, about that..."

Kenzo spoke up, "Whatever you both need, we'll

figure it out. Just bring her." All the guys expressed similar comments over the speaker. "Hell, I'll get Jacqui here to make her feel better having another female."

"Thanks, guys. A lot. I appreciate what you're saying, and that's what I wanted to hear. I'll call back as soon as she wakes. She was in bad shape when we left the police station, so I'm going to let her sleep, then we'll fly over to NOLA."

Jones replied again, "Right. Let me know, and I'll see about getting the plane there for you both."

"Thanks, man. Hey, can you take me off speaker for a quick minute? I want to discuss something with you."

Seeing as Jones had ties through his brother with a motorcycle club I wanted to address something with him. I knew they weren't close or anything, but there were some things I wanted to see happen outside the realm of the police. A club held leeway to events that happened off the radar. Taking care of my babe's problems became my priority.

"Yeah, what can I do?" Jones asked.

"This might be too much to ask, but I need something to happen that's not exactly police friendly," I explained and offered my thoughts on what needed to happen to this motherfucking Tyler. Jones readily agreed with me on both accounts, the police's hands tied with the piece of shit sitting in jail for robbery. Unless they could find witnesses to corroborate Bardot's story, Tyler would go free from the rape charges.

With her only fifteen at the time, no limits prevented the charges from being filed, but no one knew about the fucked-up incident. Bardot thought she did the right thing at that time because she believed she had no one to turn to. Circumstances had changed now, but the law still needed the damn evidence.

The MC's system of justice held different rules. I wanted them to carry out the justice this fucking bastard deserved. They didn't have to kill him, but castration would work as well.

"I'll see what I can do, but I can't promise anything, Wix. We don't have a tight relationship, but I'll take it to my brother and let him decide what he wants to do with the information. Who knows how many other girls this dickhead date-raped and walked away from. His brothers don't put up with that kind of fucked-up shit." Jones spoke truthfully, so I knew to be happy with whatever happened in that situation.

"My thought exactly, and I doubt the police are going to go looking with it happening several years ago."

"You're right. Let me make some calls."

"Thank, Jones. I'll owe you big fucking time for this. It's not exactly in a manager's job description."

He briefly laughed and added, "When are half the damn things I do in my job description? But this, well... it's a different situation, and I'm more than willing to try to get justice for your woman."

"That she is, dude. She's it for me."

"You're sure?" He sounded surprised.

"Hell yeah, I'm sure. This time we've spent together has sealed the deal for me."

"Okay, Wix. Just know, we are all on board with this."

"Thanks, bro. I needed to hear that."

CHAPTER 33

BARDOT

The silence around me caused my heart to race as I woke. It only took a moment before I realized the covers on me were my own which helped to calm me. The warmth beside me held me close. Wix's body heat brought me back to reality in just a few blinks.

My arm draped over his abdomen, and our legs tangled around each other. A massive hand held me close to his side as I was tucked under his arm, and my head used his pecs for a pillow. Having him beside me felt like the best thing I had felt in forever.

When my eyes shot around the room, I saw clothing scattered here and there from both of us. Being naked next to him felt right until the memories of yesterday flooded my head.

I sucked in a deep breath and sat straight up in bed.

"Babe, it's still early. Let's sleep a while longer." His

warm hand wrapped around my upper arm and tugged on it to get me back next to him, but I resisted the temptation.

"You need to wake up, Wix. There's too much to do to spend the day in bed. I've got insurance people to call. And I probably need to go back to the police station to see what they're doing with Tyler. Then I need to go to the marina and look at what needs to be replaced."

Wix didn't understand all the shit I had to take care of. Lots of items would have to be replaced or cleaned before I could start back to chartering. *How did he possibly think I could leave?*

He joined me, sitting in the middle of the bed. "Bardot, stop for a second. Let's get up and make a plan before we go running off anywhere. I spoke to Jones last night while you slept, and he wants you to come with me on the road for a while, at least."

My forehead scrunched up as I turned to look at him. "What? No. I can't go anywhere."

"Why the hell not?" His nostrils flared in frustration.

Untangling myself from the covers, I stood beside the bed, looking for my clothes. Having an important conversation while naked equaled a bad idea. I needed to make some serious decisions. *Me... naked... decisions... Wix...* those things combined were not good.

With my panties and his T-shirt on, I threw his

jeans at him. "Get up. We've got to go and do things here, not on the road."

"Babe, I'm telling you there's nothing left for you to do." He followed me into the kitchen, watching me turn on the coffee maker with a new pod inserted.

"Yes, my life's upside down. There's so much to do."

He grabbed my arms and spun me around. "Bardot. Listen to me. Your boat is gone. Your things inside it... gone. While your insurance will cover most of it, the only thing you can do is make a list of those items. Where do you think you're going to go for that?"

"To the boat," I shot back at him. He stared directly into my eyes. I watched as the gray turned the stormy color it did when he was angry or frustrated. "What?"

He moved me to my small couch and sat down, pulling me into his lap. "Babe. Do you remember what happened yesterday?"

"Sure. We did a lot of things." He returned with a puzzled look and nodded at me.

"Do you remember going to the dock where your boat used to be moored?"

As soon as 'used to be moored' came out of his mouth, reality hit me square in the face. My head played tricks on me. While part of me knew something happened, the rest of my mind said carry on. There was no boat waiting to be restored. The pieces left at the dilapidated dock behind the house were not worth restoring. The remains might as well be buried at sea or disposed of in a heap somewhere.

A trickle of the warm tears started down my cheeks, and I caught them with the back of my hand. Wix's words finally made sense to me. The truth of having no boat set in, leaving me once again feeling abandoned.

I had nothing.

I had no one.

Starting over this time, I was on my own to drift through the world with no ties to hold me.

How would I do life?

Wix's lips kissed my cheek, tasting the saltiness my tears left behind. "Tell me what you're thinking, babe. I'm right here and going nowhere, at least not without you beside me."

I saw his hand holding mine on my lap. I raised my eyes to finally meet his. "What?"

He pulled me closer to him, and I laid my head on his shoulder. "What am I going to do with my life? Everything I knew went down with my boat. The most important piece of me sunk with it. I'm alone again, Wix. Only this time, I'm left with nothing. No way to start over."

Wix tugged at me to look at him before repositioning me to straddle his lap. "Look, Bardot... I'm here. I'm not going anywhere without you. You do have a home... with me... with us. I talked to the guys this morning, and we all want you to join us until you're ready to make decisions about your life. You don't have to decide today or even next week or in the months to come. Come with us. See some of the world. Think about what you want to do, then we'll talk about it and decide what we're going to do... *together*."

I stared at him, trying to understand what he was saying to me.

"Did you listen to what I said, babe?" His soft words penetrated the fog in my head, and I nodded.

His forehead met mine, and he whispered, "Tell me what I told you, please."

"You said the guys wanted me to go with the band for a while." I pulled back and looked hard at him. "But how, Wix? How can I just up and leave?"

"Easy. We pack what you want to take from this apartment, or even better, I'll hire someone to pack it up to send to storage. Just take the clothes you want for now because you'll be spending all your time with a bunch of horny degenerates in close quarters, and I don't share well with others." His beautiful smile ended his words. I loved his smile. It made me feel special and wanted.

"But—"

"No buts, babe. Just come with me, and we'll see some shit, go some places, and play some great music. When we're done, most of the insurance should be taken care of, and we can meet with whoever we need to get it finalized."

"You make it sound so simple. Just... up and leave."

"What's keeping you here?"

I knew deep down he was right. Nothing kept me from going with them but me. No one was around to tell me I couldn't go on the road. There was so much of the U.S. I hadn't seen. My life revolved around this port."

"Babe, you know I'm right. The world is full of places you've never seen. Hell, I've only seen a few. We can explore all the boating areas together. My home sits close to one, and I'd give everything to show it to you."

"You live on the water?"

"No, not technically, but I live close to it. You'll have plenty of money to buy another boat. Hey, wait, we can buy a boat together and live on it. That would be fucking awesome." He pretended to put on a cap and stuck up his hand like he had a sword in it. "Just call me Captain Wix."

"Ha, I'll be the captain, sir."

"Mmm... sir. I like it. You can always call me sir." He leaned forward and kissed me with his lips sliding easily across mine, but it quickly became more intense when his tongue sought entrance into my mouth.

I wrapped my hands around his neck and pressed myself against his bare chest. What started as a morning discussion turned into something hot in a flash when he stripped his T-shirt off me, leaving me only in my tiny panties.

His lips kissed down my jaw, where he nipped at

the skin on my neck and licked and kissed away the twinges of pain he made. Our hands explored the naked, warm skin of each other while he pushed me back enough to trail kisses down to my breast. Running his warm tongue around the nipple only made it pebble hard as he took it between his lips and sucked it into his mouth.

The sensation shot straight to my clit, forcing it to swell and need attention as badly as my other breast. Wix gladly plucked it between his thumb and index fingers before squeezing and twisting, driving me wild on his lap.

"I need you," I whispered to him. "Please."

"Whatever you want, babe. Just tell me." He pushed me back further, holding me off the floor with one arm around my back while his other hand's fingers left light but rough touches. His guitar strings caused calloused pads on his fingertips, and one touch from them drove me insane with need. "I need you to tell me, Bardot. What do you want?"

His voice, strong and clear, penetrated my head as his finger slid over the top of my panties, creasing the material as he played across my lower lips. My swollen clit loved the attention but needed so much more.

"Please."

"Please, what?" he asked.

"Please, just touch me. I need it."

"Oh... like this?" His finger dipped under the silky

material and strummed over the engorged bud, waiting for attention. The light touches only teased me into a frenzy.

"Wix. Oh my God, do something."

"You mean this?" The assaulting digit circled my clit before slipping down to my opening. "Whoa, babe, all of this liquid tells me you're needy, aren't you?" His finger dipped in and pulled some of the molten wetness up to torture the swollen bud again.

"*Fuuuccckkk*, Wix."

"Yeah, babe? Need something?"

"You, I need you." I sat up and wrapped my hand around his hard cock on the outside of his boxer briefs. "You're not playing fair by torturing me." I pulled him free of his underwear and pumped up and down a few times before running my thumb over the precum waiting for its turn. Smearing it down and around the smooth head's edge, I circled it just below it, where I knew he was more sensitive.

"*Fuuuccckkk* me." He imitated my words before flipping us over so my back was now on the couch. He pulled my panties down so quickly, I heard them rip at one of the seams. I didn't care as long as it got him inside me faster.

Taking my left leg, he hiked one over the back of the couch and the other off toward the floor, spreading me open to him. He wrapped his palms around my thighs and pushed down as he plunged inside until we were skin to skin.

"Ohh... that feels amazing, Bardot. Are you okay?"

"Yeah, but don't stop there. Move."

"Yes, ma'am." He pulled back and pushed in hard again, and I loved it.

"Again," I screamed at him. My wish was his command. "It's what I need right now." He pounded into me, pushing me until my head was at the side, and I loved every move he made.

Before the position became uncomfortable, he lifted and flipped me over, pushing me on the arm. Lining back up with me, my ass up in the air, he pushed in hard and fast.

"Babe, this is perfect," he screamed before leaning over me. "But it's gonna make me come faster." With one hand still wrapped around my thigh, the other made a beeline for my clit. The orgasm built faster, and I felt the tingles starting at my toes.

"I'm gonna come, Wix."

"I know, babe, your toes are curling up." He continued pushing and pulling inside me, and I felt his bare cock swelling.

"Yes, yes, right there. Wix, Wix." My orgasm hit hard, and my inner muscles tightened around him, sucking him deeper inside.

"Babe," he yelled once before the warmth of his load coated my walls.

"Whoa, that was something else," I whispered as best I could through the heavy breaths I took, trying to get some oxygen in my lungs.

"You bet it was," he said softly as he wrapped both arms around my waist, locking me tighter against him. After making a few easy pumps into my slick channel, he pulled out and lifted me with him as he stood.

"That was the best, Bardot. Hot, hard, fast."

I spun around in his arms to look at him. "Was that to make me want to follow you anywhere?"

"Damn right it was. Did it work?" He hit me with that rock-star smile he saves for his audience.

"Yes, I suppose it did."

***

"Well, look who decided to rejoin the fucking band," Arch greeted us as we walked on the bus.

"Yeah, yeah. I know you bunch of dickwads missed us," I replied with a grin and flipped him off.

"Damn right, we did. We got music to make," Trotter added.

Bardot stepped around me and smiled at Arch, Kenzo, Trotter, and Jones sitting behind the banquette playing poker.

"He brought a tagalong, though," she offered with a soft smile.

"Wouldn't want it any other way," Arch said as he passed me up and lifted Bardot in his arms with her kicking and screaming his name. The laughter sounded like the best music I had heard in a long time.

"We ready to rock and roll?" Jones asked us all.

"You're fucking right we are," the band answered at once together.

"Then sit your asses down and let the driver go," Jones commented as he discarded a playing card on the small table in front of him. "We've got places to be, and as usual, we're running late."
o the family.

THE END

Find out more about Kenzo and Jacqui
in their book which is next,
along with more Wix and Bardot as they figure out life
on the tour bus and in Malibu, CA.
Our Broken Tune

If you want to read more:
My Favorite Tune crosses over with
Incinerate by K E Osborn.
NOLA Defiance MC by K E Osborn

Would you like to read more about Bardot finally getting her payback?
You will find all the answers in:
Fixate by K E Osborn

MORE BOOKS FROM THIA FINN

Before the Second Show

Kiss Me Before Flight

Be Understanding

Becks Part One and Two

Fall Boys (Two book series)

Assured Distraction (Four book series)

Hayden's Timbre (An Assured Distraction Novel)

ACKNOWLEDGMENTS

First, I want to say a big thanks to all my readers who stuck by me during this dry spell I call, Covid Catastrophe. I appreciate those of you who continued to tout my books so that others might find them. I lost my way for a bit from family tragedies during this time. Stephanie Seay, Kay and Kim Osborn, my sister Mary LeFebvre, and my longtime friends, Rene Heard and Debbie Orlowski kept me sane. I cannot say thank you enough to you all.

Second, my family means everything to me. My husband, Steve, of forty-six years continues to encourage me to do what makes me happy. While he likes to interrupt my train of thought when I'm writing, I know he's there to back me up. My daughters and sons-in law, along with my three grandchildren, complete my world, although any additions they want to add to our brood is fine with me.

Finally, I couldn't make it without my PA, Julie Lafrance. We are on the same continent but in different countries causing our face-to-face time to be a rarity. She not only checks on me but she keeps me going with this wild business of publishing. She also takes the time to make sure I'm okay. She has my back in all things, and I love her for it. That, and she keeps Steve from driving me crazy on a daily basis. All I can say is Julie knows a lot about a lot of things making her his BFF on some days!

On a more serious note:

This book is a work of fiction, but some situations discussed are of a sensitive nature.

If you or anyone you know is in emotional distress, suffers from any sort of abuse, including violence please seek help or assist them in obtaining help.

Crisis hotlines exist everywhere, so please don't hesitate.

If you live in:
USA call RAINN - 1-800-656-HOPE
Canada call 1.888.407.4747 for help
UK call The Samaritans 116 123
Australia call Lifeline Australia 13 11 14

Check these links for more books from Thia Finn.

AMAZON
http://amzn.to/2mgw5oq

WEBSITE
http://www.thiafinn.com/

TWITTER
http://twitter.com/ThiaFinnCGrif

INSTAGRAM
@cegriffin.thiafinn

BOOKBUB
http://www.bookbub.com/authors/thia-finn

FACEBOOK
https://www.facebook.com/cindy.griffin.752

About THE AUTHOR

Growing up in small-town Texas, Thia Finn discovered life outside of it by attending The University of Texas, only to return home and marry her high school sweetheart. They raised two successful and beautiful daughters while she taught middle school Language Arts and eventually became a middle school librarian. After thirty-four years, she retired to do her favorite things, like travel, spending time off-roading with family and friends, hanging out at one of the Texas Hill Country's beautiful rivers, reading, and writing.

She currently lives in the same small town where she grew up, with her husband and Chihuahua, Josie. She can often be found stalking on social media, watching Netflix or Hulu. They will be moving to another small town shortly to be closer to the family.